The

HAPPINESS
THIEF

The

HAPPINESS
THIEF

A Novel

NICOLE BOKAT

Published 2021
Printed in the United States of America
Print ISBN: 978-1-64742-057-4
E-ISBN: 978-1-64742-058-1
Library of Congress Control Number: 2020917549

For information, address:
She Writes Press
1569 Solano Ave #546
Berkeley, CA 94707

She Writes Press is a division of SparkPoint Studio, LLC.

Book design by Stacey Aaronson

THE
HAPPINESS
THIEF

prologue

—

Winter

I THINK I KILLED MY MOTHER.

Jeremy had asked Natalie what made her unique. That was the most straightforward answer. She didn't dare say it aloud, certainly not on a first date with someone she was beginning to like, someone she wasn't sure she deserved.

Instead, she told Jeremy about how she'd been in a car crash when she was young, and how it left her with a brain injury, which wiped out much of her memory of that time. When she admitted she felt guilty, he asked if she'd been driving and they laughed because, of course, she'd been thirteen, much too young. *He has no idea what I'm capable of,* she'd thought.

Hours after their date had ended, and Natalie was alone, unable to sleep, she felt the air in her room thin out. She switched on the lamp on her side of the bed, the comforter tangled in her feet. Panic was like a fistful of knuckles to the chest. She heard her breaths coming fast: *huh, huh, huh.* She rubbed the skin under the rim of her pajama pants where a rash was certain to flare. When she opened the drawer of her nightstand, she shuffled through the ear plugs and coins. She touched the small, silver flashlight she'd shoved to the back, a taunt, a reminder of who she was.

This wasn't the plastic purple flashlight that had been confiscated by the police, slipped into a plastic bag. Or maybe they hadn't even bothered holding onto it as evidence. They'd noted it in their report but wouldn't have used something that looked like a toy against her, a girl who'd been reading in the passenger seat on a dark night. Supposedly, she'd confessed to her stepfamily that it was her fault, that she'd shone the light into her mother's eyes. She could only remember that she didn't want to go where they were headed. She'd sobbed in her hospital bed, concussed and in shock, willing herself to forget; and even now, so many years later, the details were out of reach long after the physical damage had healed. Had there been another vehicle behind them on the road? She couldn't be certain.

What she did recall was that flash piercing the bone black sky and her mother's scream, "The light's blinding me. For Christ's sake, what's going on?" She could smell the vinyl seats, the coffee with Sweet & Low, her mom's scent—lemon and flowers and mint. The Dunkin' Donuts mug shook in the holder.

Their station wagon had careened, and Natalie tried to brace herself, arms hurled everywhere, nothing to hold onto. Her head was thrown backward, then forward, a snap as if her neck was torn from its socket. She felt an awful thrust, then the whirling stopped. Blankness. She struggled to wake, stuck at the murky bottom, lungs bursting, until her eyes popped open. The windshield on the passenger's side had cracked to form a web. Yet the glass had stayed firmly in place. The silence was profound. The last thing she'd seen before she passed out was her mother's head smashed against the steering wheel, blood seeping down her hair like a red waterfall.

Natalie's hand found the container of pills. She untwisted the top and popped one into her palm. Pretty in pink, friendly as a child's teacup. The water glass was lukewarm; she only needed a sip. The tablet winked at her, as if promising all problems would be washed away. Down the hatch.

What kind of monster are you?

2

one

——

The Previous Fall

THE ANNUAL HAPPINESS CONFERENCE WAS PACKED TO CAPACITY, with almost five hundred therapists, spiritual leaders, life coaches, and guests—including Natalie, who had no idea what happiness was anymore. The room was dotted with small, linen covered tables. Each held a slim silver vase with one white lily, the petals of the flowers draped around the pistils like elegant wrap dresses. The waitstaff zigzagged through the crowd with trays of hors d'oeuvres.

Natalie regarded her stepsister, Isabel, from across the room, *Oh, I wish I were you* competing with *I'm so proud* in her gut. Admirers swarmed around Isabel, touching her with wonder like children at a petting zoo. Even though Natalie was distracted, the woman next to her didn't seem to notice and crooned about the dharma of "self-actualization and intention," gesturing in her ankle-length cape, a giant bird with a sparkly purple wingspan. Not wanting to laugh, Natalie covered her mouth with a paper napkin.

One of the speakers approached her, emitting a strong patchouli and sandalwood aroma. "I'm a colleague of your sister's," she said, grasping Natalie's elbow so that multiple bracelets jangled together. "Danika Singh. Isabel pointed you out to me."

Natalie recognized the woman's tawny complexion with the beauty mark above her lip, the deep-set eyes, from posters at the conference. "Do you work with her?"

"I live in Sydney. I catch her at conferences a couple of times a year."

"Sorry I missed your talk. What was it, again?"

"I'm the founder of The Mindfulness Museum in Melbourne. It was about our mission."

What kind of exhibits you got: open spaces, nothing on the walls, very expensive air?

"Sounds intriguing," Natalie said.

"I heard about your father's death." Danika's grip on Natalie's elbow grew tighter. "I'm so sorry."

"Thanks. He wasn't technically my father; he was married to my mother."

Danika nodded. "I hadn't expected Isabel to show. She's a real trooper to honor her commitments."

"That's what she's like."

It was. Isabel was worried about finishing the second book on schedule and, now, with Garrick's death, she was grieving in her hidden heart. Yet, in the lexicon of their cobbled together family, Isabel was the powerhouse and bulwark, while Natalie was the sensitive one, sadness coating her like oil. Over the years, she'd tried talk and behavioral therapy, peach pills and baby blue ones. And the ever-handy pink ones. This time, after Natalie's husband deserted her, Isabel had insisted: *why don't you let me help you?*

Danika gazed above Natalie's head. "I'm sorry, I have to speak with someone before he leaves. I'll circle back."

She scurried away. The "self-actualizer" was gone, as well. Natalie listened to the air humming with whispers and coughs, murmurs and laughs, the scraping of chairs and clinking of glasses. Three days of being bombarded by positive thinkers, thrivers, meditators, and yogis, and this was the final event. When a server passed by, Natalie nabbed a coconut shrimp on a skewer and a glass of sparkling water.

A middle-aged man sidled up. "Are you a patient or practitioner?" He was bald, with a starfish-shaped rash on one cheek.

Natalie shook her head. "Neither."

"You're not wearing your name tag. Very mysterious."

"And you are?" She glimpsed at his label, then felt a cool hand on her bare skin and flinched.

"It's just me," Isabel said, rubbing the tight spot where Natalie's neck met her shoulder. "Didn't mean to scare you."

"Dr. Walker," the man exclaimed, thumping his hand to his chest. "I heard your lecture yesterday. You were wonderful, and *Get Happy Now*, I just devoured it in one sitting!"

"Thank you so much," Isabel said. Natalie could see the weariness in her smile.

"I'd love to discuss in more detail."

"Of course. I have a few minutes now and, if you'd like, we can exchange contact information."

While they chatted, Natalie eavesdropped on another conversation nearby.

"I was brainstorming." This was a female with an Irish accent. "Rolfing is okay, and acupuncture. But she's not keen on Crystal Reiki."

"Releasing energy blocks?" This accent was harder to place, maybe Dutch or German.

Natalie took out her phone and texted her teenage daughter, Hadley: *What is rolfing?*

"Ready to go?" Isabel whispered in her ear. "I'm tired."

"You must be exhausted."

"It's been good for me."

When they stepped out into the sapphire night, the lapping sound of the Caribbean Sea called out. Natalie asked, "A quick walk on the beach?"

"I'm too beat. Let's go back to the resort."

Natalie had offered to drive so that Isabel could celebrate with her flute of Blanc de Blanc, refilled more than once. But navigating on the left side in this British-ruled island was tricky, especially once she hit the more desolate streets, the night sky a swatch of chalky black. She followed the crooked arrow, the sign for curve.

"Did you have fun?" Isabel asked. "Pick up any good tips from the lectures?"

"I can feel myself blooming with optimism."

"C'mon, Nat! You have to give the ideas a chance."

"I am, I am."

In her rearview mirror, she saw another car, maybe thirty feet behind her. "I thought your talk was great, best one."

"Well, thanks."

Natalie had peered up while Isabel gave a lecture on the podium. Her beauty was a mixture of Nordic features and tiny bones, as if there were East Asian ancestors hiding in the corners of her European lineage. Her skin was so naturally light it was nearly translucent, the vein in her forehead slightly more prominent each year. Natalie had erased that imperfection in the book jacket photo, as well as the rosy tips of her ears. She'd been so pleased with herself: her one professional portrait. But, *Isabel!* Her words soared. Some attendees used their cameras or iPhones to record while she spoke. Others scribbled notes in the Moleskine journals sold in the wellness bookstore. Natalie caught it too, that frisson of excitement: *maybe this will work.*

Suddenly, her vision was filled with a blare of white light. As she slowed down, the car veered. There was a thunk against her bumper.

She slammed on the brakes causing the car to buck. "What the hell?"

"Shit!" Isabel cried out next to her.

Natalie fumbled with the seat belt cutting into her middle. Her hands felt big and clumsy as if they were swollen. Yet the door opened without resistance. "That idiot behind us was flashing his brights. I couldn't see where I was going."

"Of course not," Isabel said.

Standing on the pavement, Natalie's legs trembled. There was a slight breeze. The heat had relented after a day in which the sun had throbbed like an angry heart. She watched her stepsister reach over to switch on the high beams and then rush out, her tight blond ponytail swinging.

There was nothing, no one there. Just a long slash of street and the moon, a silver rowboat tipped on its side. In a palm tree a few feet ahead of them, Natalie saw a hooded iguana crouching. Behind them, the other car idled, the headlights turned off.

"I was being careful," Natalie said. "What was that driver doing?"

"I'll find out," Isabel said. "You stay here."

"Oh, God."

"Take deep breaths," Isabel said. She counted, slowly, until they were both inhaling and exhaling in even segments. "Go sit down. Let me deal with this."

Natalie slid into the passenger seat this time. She felt as if she were a teenager again, nearly three decades ago now, her mom shouting. *Stop it. This isn't Mom's car. You're safe.*

Her thumb pressed against her neck's pulse, charting its *rat-a-tat* like rainfall against the window. She placed one hand on her belly and the other on her breastbone, repeating a yoga technique to regulate her oxygen. She noted 11.00 p.m. on the dashboard and then shut her eyes.

VISUALIZE A SAFE PLACE! One of the speakers at a seminar she'd attended had given that command. Her mind offered up the lawn of her childhood home. She'd been four years old and Isabel seven when their parents married. After the ceremony, there'd been a small reception in the backyard. Natalie had watched Isabel cartwheeling between the rows of tables once the guests had left, her sleek body spinning through the air, backward, forward. Natalie had stared at this lithe creature, with hair like a cream-colored pony's, who'd coached her to try as well. "I'll spot you," Isabel had said. "Nothing bad will happen to you."

Natalie reached both hands out to ground herself in the present. The glove compartment was warm from the Caribbean weather, and she anchored her weight against it. She looked at the clock. 11:12 p.m.

Had she lost track of time again?

She opened the door and leaned out. A tall man stood next to her stepsister.

Natalie said sharply, "What's going on? You had your brights on."

"I'm so sorry about that," he said in an English accent. "It was only for a moment. I couldn't see anything out here."

Natalie rose slowly and walked to the front of their rental. The man was holding a flashlight, which illuminated a few streaks of blood on the bumper and dark stains on the road. Her nerves sparked. "Jesus!"

Isabel rushed to her side, "Don't worry, Nat."

"Whatever it was ran away." The man gestured to the patch of greenery, a few trees among it. "I think it was a dog."

"*Think?* Could it have been a person?" Natalie's voice quivered.

The man shook his head. "It was on four legs and small."

"We have to help."

When she nearly stumbled forward, Isabel grabbed her. "Whoa. You're not going after anything, sweetie."

"Let me try."

"It's dark as hell in those bushes."

"I'll do it," the man said, holding the flashlight vertically so it shone on his face and upper body. His eyes were a surprising Delft blue. "This was my fault; it's the least I can do."

"Thank you," Isabel said.

Once he walked into the thickets of shrubs and the slender thatch palms, Natalie said, "I'll be okay."

Isabel relinquished her grasp. "I didn't want you running off on some goose chase now."

"I wasn't going to."

Was I?

The man returned quickly. He shrugged. "Nothing there."

"We can't just leave," Natalie said. "We can't abandon it to suffer. We should keep searching."

"Whatever it was will be all right. It can't be too injured if it ran off," Isabel said. "Let's get back to the hotel."

He asked, "You're staying at the Grand Reef, aren't you?"

Isabel clicked her middle finger with her thumb and asked, "How did you know?"

"I've seen you. I'm staying there, as well."

"Ah, makes sense." To Natalie, she said, "Let's go, kiddo."

"Okay, but we have to call someone, animal rescue, or the police, when we get back to our room."

"Of course, I'll do it." Isabel sounded her usual self: composed, certain.

Suddenly, Natalie remembered that feeling of confidence, that assurance that the world would work in her favor. The hours in the darkroom with her mom, the time her mother gave her first camera and taught her how an image could lie—a wrinkle or blemish could be airbrushed away—but a good photographer captured the soul. The next day, Natalie had gazed at the ice rink after the Zamboni machine had smoothed it to a perfect gleam. It was like a camera, she thought, fixing the image. Every Saturday in winter she had glided onto that surface with her mother, steady on her feet. Not for a moment did she fear a fall.

two

NATALIE JOLTED AWAKE, UNSURE OF HER SURROUNDINGS. SHE blinked at the sight of the bright furniture, saffron yellow curtains and apple-green chair. This wasn't her bedroom.

She scurried to the window to push back the drapes. Outside the two-bedroom suite was the balcony and the first morning views of the Caribbean Sea that unfurled indefinitely. The sky was blanketed with pink and white clouds. The ocean glittered like rock candy.

The living space was a burst of colors: cobalt blue couch and gold and red rug. The curtains were open, as was Isabel's bedroom door. There wasn't a hush of noise; Natalie opened the door gently, so as not to wake her stepsister. Isabel had been going non-stop since arriving at the conference—a good distraction, everyone agreed, as her dad had died merely days before this long weekend. One heart attack had landed Garrick in the hospital, the second one had killed him as he lay in Intensive Care. *She must be exhausted.* Yet, inside, the sheets were turned down, and the puff of silk nightgown lay on the pillow. Isabel was gone.

A note on the kitchenette's counter read: "Work breakfast with Ole downstairs. He's staying at the Cove; has an early flight back to Denmark. Hope you're feeling better. XO, Belle."

The car key with its plastic THRIFTY tag lay next to the note, like a provocation. Natalie grabbed a mug out of the cabinet and opened the refrigerator door. Next to the half and half were a tub of butter, three water bottles, and a plastic container of sliced watermelons. She noticed now that the coffee pot was two-thirds full. Not a meal, but she was willing to wait. The digital clock above the microwave read 6:37; most likely there wouldn't be many people on the road, not at this more secluded end of the island so early in the day. No commuters here. She could check now if there were signs of an injured animal and be back before Isabel returned, sympathy in her eyes. *You were that worried? I shouldn't have gone with Ole.* Natalie would forgo a shower and rush down the back stairs with her camera.

Nerves humming, she was vigilant but not afraid, not yet. When she got to the car, the bumper was clean. She peered closer, as if the drops of blood were hiding from view. Nothing. She touched the plastic, already warm from the dawning sun.

She drove slowly, as she had no street name, no GPS to guide her. The trees stood steady and strong, like warriors in fancy headgear. The agaves' green tentacles waved above their trunks, shredded wood that resembled skirts. She made a turn, then another, noticing the curve sign, certain she'd found the correct place. She stopped near the shrubs on the right side and got out.

Natalie walked up and down the road, studying the ground, the dirt and pebbles, the grass leading into the bushes. She knew from experience behind the lens that what the naked eye saw wasn't always all that was there. She stopped when she discovered a patch of dried blood no bigger than a quarter. Then she lifted her Nikon and took a burst of shots. She imagined more proof elsewhere, a splattering, a trail through the bushes. She scoped out the foliage. In the leaves nearby, there were specks of reddish brown; Natalie tore off a leaf and held it to her nose, not sure what she expected to smell. She stumbled among the twigs and white flowers, looking for paw prints but found none.

After twenty minutes, she decided to buy a local paper, with a bag of nuts and raisins, at a grocery store on the way back to the hotel. She felt a whoosh of relief. Maybe she'd overreacted—which made sense given her history. There was no news of car accidents, much less injuries, in the *Cayman Tribune*.

~

ISABEL WAS STILL not back in their suite. Natalie decided to head for the beach, Nikon around her neck. She bypassed the empty pastel lounge chairs under the canopies, billowing lazily like sails. The warm water lapped over her toes as she snapped shot after shot. By midday, the sun would press down on her shoulders with an incessant grip that would leave a mark. But at this hour it was a balm.

Hand up in a salute to block the light, she turned to see a man a few feet down the beach. There was something so glossy and richly colored about his appearance, as if he were shot through a gold filter. She had to lift her head up to recognize that he was the man they'd encountered on the road the previous night.

Natalie walked towards him. Up close, his face was slightly lined around the eyes and mouth, his sandy hair streaked with blond. He was dressed in cotton slacks that fanned up at his calves, a starched shirt with the sleeves rolled to the elbows. He was holding polished loafers in one hand.

"Hi," she said. "Remember me, the animal lover?"

He smiled. "Of course. I'm Simon Drouin. Feeling better?"

"Yes, thanks."

"Good. You look lovely this morning."

"Thanks," she said, glancing down at the white sand. She knew the compliment was a lie, that she had thumbprint smudges under her eyes, that the angles of her cheeks and collarbones were sharpened to a point from weight loss. "Funny meeting you here, I mean . . . the same beach."

"I'm staying at the hotel."

"Right," she nodded. "You mentioned that."

"And your charming companion, sleeping in?"

It was like a line out of a Victorian novel. Natalie wanted to blurt out, "She's married to a wonderful guy. Don't bother."

"Having breakfast with a colleague," she said, "about a TED Talk on Flourishing."

"Oh, dear. That last bit eludes me."

"I thought you were here for the conference."

"Lord, no. Are you part of this whole . . . production?"

"Along for the ride. I'm here with my stepsister, Isabel. The 'charming companion.'" He laughed. "She's a speaker."

Simon pointed to the camera. "You're not the official photographer?"

She shook her head. *If only.* . . . But she'd long ago given up on the flow and movement, the animation of human life.

When he bent towards her, Natalie felt a flush of excitement. The last time she and her almost-ex-husband, Marc, had made love was a year ago in April, the magnolias in full bloom. Her entire adult life she'd been yoked to one man. She'd been married for seventeen years, had just turned forty-one.

Natalie said, "I *am* a professional photographer, actually. But not for this event."

"The Happiness industry seems to be booming. And for good reason, the world being what it is. I confess, I did sneak a peak of a brochure at the front desk. The hotel has a pile of them. Your sister is prominently featured."

Of course, he'd noticed *that.*

"She's a leader in the field."

"Impressive, I suppose. Just can't imagine this whole business works on Brits. We're lacking in your natural optimism."

"Don't be fooled by our reputation. Anyway, there are people from all over the world for this. What about you? Do you live in London?"

"New York now."

"So, you must have picked up our 'can-do spirit,'" she said. "I'm from Boston. Natalie, by the way."

"Nice to meet you, Natalie. I travel up to Boston sometimes for work. I wonder where I might have seen your pictures."

"There's a platter of truffles in October's *Boston Magazine*."

His eyebrows rose. "Mushrooms?"

"Chocolate. But I've shot those too. I specialize in food."

"Really?" He patted his stomach. "If it were me, I'd put on twenty pounds."

She nodded. "Common misconception. I'm more like a food mortician. I know what it takes to get my subject looking good. It's not pretty."

The spray bottle filled with water and corn syrup, the browning agents to enhance color, the glycerin to make the food shimmer, the brushes to create an artificial luster: the presentation of nourishment rendered inedible.

Simon laughed. "I like that: *mortician*. It's rather perverse."

"That's me," she said.

Not the way you mean.

"Good to know," he grinned. "Do you sell to private clients?"

"I have a nice mutton you might like to hang over your bed."

"Ah, dear, no. Do you ever take other things, landscapes or portraits?"

She had a few of Marc and Hadley. That was all. When she was first learning, she loved shooting people, but after her mother died, she stopped, as if she couldn't really see them anymore.

"Not professionally. You can check my website if you're interested. It's my name, Natalie Greene with an 'e,' then dot com."

"I *am* interested. A little perversion never hurt anyone. Would you like to have dinner tonight? Alas, I don't think we'll find any mutton here."

"I would," she said.

It had been a year, two months, and three days since Marc had moved in with Elizabeth, a colleague he'd met in a team building event. When Isabel nudged her to start dating, Natalie had found the suggestion ludicrous. "How can I trust anyone again?" she'd asked. But one meal with sexy Simon, with his rakish boasts—so different from her Holier-Than-Thou turned cheater ex—might lift her mood. "Only we're leaving later this afternoon."

"Ah, that's right. My loss."

They exchanged a look, his eyes holding hers.

"It was nice meeting you, Simon."

He extended his hand. "Until we meet again."

Meet again? Was that a line or a promise?

"In case, you're ever in New York, my personal email is easy to remember," he said. "SDrouin@hotmail.com."

Hotmail indeed.

Natalie climbed the steep back steps, raising her camera to her eye. From the palm tree craning towards the second floor, the bearded, bejeweled Iguana stared out at her. Its skin was wrinkled and ill-fitting, like the wrong-sized coat. As she zoomed in on the creature in the tree, she felt a shot of pleasure as if it was she who was being observed.

Her suite was the first one on the right, and she imagined Simon watching her enter it. It was cool, and the central room was alight with color. Natalie placed her Nikon and sunglasses on the dining table, then stepped onto the balcony. The day was a quilt of blues, the patchwork of ocean stitched to the sky.

She felt alive, the world before her.

Natalie surveyed the guests on the patio below. A young mother walked behind her toddling child to the shallow end of the pool. She observed another whose cadence—the lightness of her walk, the swing of her sarong at the back of her calves—reminded her of someone. The woman's hair was long and whispery. Thin but curvy, she had a small waist and long legs.

Natalie could smell her mom's citrus and mint perfume. She saw the woman turn towards her and mouth the words: *What did you do to me?*

Natalie grasped the balcony's railing, bending her knees to ground her. Once she reached the glass doors, she squatted on the carpet, waiting for the spell to pass. Her throat wasn't working correctly, wasn't swallowing. She crept to the kitchen where her pocketbook lay on the counter and spilled the contents of her bag: wallet, small tub of concealer, and bottle of Xanax. With the tranquilizer floating on her tongue, she slunk to the fridge for a water bottle. It took several gulps for the pill to slide down. Once on the couch, she charted the neon numbers on the hotel clock. Five minutes passed. Then ten. She heard her first psychiatrist say:

"Survivor's guilt."

She'd seen Dr. Davidson for a year after the symptoms from her concussion had abated. He'd begun each session with, "Anything new to report?" He had a lazy eye that made him appear to be both asleep and awake at the same time.

Only once did he ask her to elaborate on what she recalled about the accident.

"My mom got spooked, and she shouted at me. I did something wrong. Not sure what . . . but I know it's true."

He'd leaned forward in his chair, his one good eye, under a crepey lid, focused on her. "You survived."

Natalie had stared at her yellow sneakers. She was just a kid in a batik blouse and ripped jeans, but she'd felt that wasn't the right explanation. Something was amiss, literally missing, a gap in time in which answers were trapped.

Natalie unclenched her jaw, unlocked the muscles in her shoulders. The tranquilizer had kicked in. A few minutes later, she pulled out her cell phone from her canvas pocketbook and texted Isabel: *Lunch? The Wild Orchid.*

Her sister's words glowed green: *Yep! See you at noon!*

FRESHLY SHOWERED AND in a sundress, she met Isabel on the patio of the hotel's restaurant. They sat on wicker chairs, each with a beach view, sipping their mineral water and waiting for their meals to be served.

Isabel bent towards her. "You look glazed over, sweetie."

"Damn." Natalie squeaked a laugh. "It must be the heroin."

"You'd be blushing, and your pupils dilated. Xanax?"

"Minor attack."

"I was afraid that might happen."

"This is going to sound crazy." Natalie's throat hurt, as if a fish bone had grazed it. "From the balcony, I thought I saw my mom."

"Oh, god," Isabel said. "Last night must have triggered this."

"I keep thinking of Marc, how he insisted I brought these episodes on, indulged myself."

Marc, who found it increasingly hard to tolerate her inability to break free of her broken childhood, who hated her periods of rumination, the obsessive inward gaze. "Distract yourself," he'd say. "Your life is good."

"Fuck him." Isabel squeezed the lime wedge into her glass until it was depleted of juice, the rind curled. "Telling you to grin and bear your pain, then screws someone else."

Natalie scratched a dry patch on her arm. "The thing about my mom . . . in the vision, I mean. She asked what I'd done to her."

Isabel made a clucking sound. "I'm sorry it's back, the misery of many names."

Natalie's moniker for her shape-shifting ailment, labeled at various times, by various specialists, as PTSD, Postpartum Depression, panic disorder, and generalized anxiety.

"Me too. What you said in your lecture about set points and how 40 percent of our happiness is within our control. I don't think that's true for me. Probably genetic."

Natalie had no idea if this were the case. Her mother had been shy, quiet, with a flute-y lightness to her. Only with her Leica hanging like a grand jewel on her chest did she acquire a quiet confidence, a sense of inclusion in the larger world. Natalie had no memories of her father, who'd died a few weeks before her second birthday.

Isabel asked, "Can I make a suggestion that you'll immediately rebuff?"

"Sure. I love a good rebuff-able suggestion."

Isabel laughed. "Come to my workshop. I have one starting up when we get home."

"We've been over this. I'm not a group person."

"You can try it once, and if you hate it, not come back. No charge."

The waiter arrived with Isabel's fish tacos, Natalie's duck salad, and two seltzers. Isabel popped a piece of grilled Mahi-Mahi covered with cheese into her mouth.

"So, a man tried to pick me up on the beach."

"Of course, he did!" Isabel whooped. "You're a catch."

"Somehow I keep forgetting that. The guy lives in New York."

"Still, it's good. Baby steps. Was he palatable?"

"Better. He was the man from the road last night."

"Definitely eye candy—from what I could see." Isabel took a sip of her bubbly water. "Maybe not the best choice, though. Association with a car accident, your mom."

"I hadn't planned to run off with him. Anyway, he seemed more interested in you."

"Don't do that thing you do."

"What thing?"

Isabel shot her a wry smile. "Devaluing yourself. He asked *you* out."

"He did."

"Promise me you'll come to just *one* meeting of my group. I swear, it will help you conquer 'the beast.'"

"Okay, Doc."

Natalie watched as a small green lizard crawled under a neighboring table. She felt a hint of cold, even as the sun branded her where her shoulder and calf missed the umbrella's protection.

three

—

OUTSIDE LOGAN, THE AIR WAS AN INSULT OF COLD. "THANK YOU so much," Natalie said, embracing her stepsister.

"My pleasure." Isabel hugged her back. "See you Tuesday?"

The workshop.

"Yep," Natalie said and slid into the backseat of the Uber.

Her mind was already on her daughter whom she longed to call. But what if Elizabeth was in earshot? Once she'd overheard Marc and his girlfriend in the background while she was speaking to Hadley. Elizabeth had laughed loudly. There was a sense of entitlement in that laugh.

In the morning, Marc would drop their teenager back home and Natalie would get to spend the day with her. She texted Hadley: *I'm back. Can't wait to see you. Love and miss you.*

While dragging her suitcase up the stairs to her brownstone, Natalie heard the hum deep in her backpack. She stood at the front door, reading the words on the screen: *At the movies with Dad and E. Can Dad drop me at Sophie's tomorrow? Love you, too.*

She glanced down at the stone pot on the first step, which was empty of flowers. The dirt looked dry, a cigarette butt sticking out. She reached for it and tossed it in the bushes. Which tenant in the building would wish to make their shared home ugly?

Sorrow tickled the back of Natalie's throat. There were moments like this when everything seemed to be falling away. Once, she'd asked Marc if their teenage daughter's desire to spend more time with her friends than with them ever left him bereft. He'd shaken his head. "It's natural, better than her clinging to us." She'd felt chastised.

In the warm vestibule, she typed: *Of course. Have fun at Sophie's. Call me when you want to be picked up.*

On the second floor, Natalie turned the key and blinked in the dull light of her hallway. An empty nest—and she was still three years away from that—was a bittersweet swerve compared to the tragedy of her mother's death. She just needed to remind herself that not all loss was catastrophic. But loss was right in front of her: a year ago her place had been punctuated with wires, the connective tissue between one gadget and another. The abundance of cables, earphones, extenders, switches, and adapters, some coiled up with snake-like heads and mean little teeth, were Marc's only mess. They could be found on the coffee table, the kitchen counter, her bedroom dresser. All these were gone now.

Still in coat and boots, she headed for her office to listen to the messages on her landline. She would arrange her work schedule for the upcoming week and do her laundry. By the time her vacation clothes were dry, the night would be over.

The first was a robocall about her electrical bill from that morning, which she erased. The second was from the day before, a woman's scratchy voice. "Hello? Natalie? This is Ellen Arden, Garrick, uh, Professor Walker's assistant from the university. We didn't get a chance to speak at the funeral. I didn't feel up to attending the reception."

Ellen at the service: oyster-gray hair and an oxblood scarf wrapped around her neck. The older woman's eyes had glinted like silvery fish, and her mouth was a knot of grief.

"Poor thing. She has no life outside of her job and my dad. I won't be surprised if she dies of a broken heart," Isabel whispered to Natalie when they'd first taken their places in the front pew of the eighteenth-century church, with its Ionic pillars and ballooning chandeliers.

The reverend stood beside the coffin, in his white robe and black stole tucked under a roped belt. "Enlighten our Hopes, O God."

Isabel's eyes were on the King James Bible open in her lap.

The closed book was heavy in Natalie's hands. She envisioned her stepfather—his slender frame, his thicket of straw-colored hair, his long, thin face—laid out in the chestnut box. There had not been a viewing, but Natalie knew that Isabel had chosen Garrick's blue blazer with gold buttons and his Oxford shoes that she'd polished until they shone like sugary caramel.

Ellen's voice gained volume. "Garrick asked me a favor, that last night, when I visited him at the hospital. To pick up a manila envelope for you at the office, in case something happened to him." Her voice caught. "To FedEx it to you. There was some uncertainty, well, *I* wasn't certain. Never mind that. I'm sending it in the morning. You should get it in a few days. Please accept my apology for the delay."

There was a pause, so that Natalie thought the message was over.

But then, "The package, it's private. Let's keep this between ourselves."

Natalie laughed at this suggestion, the stoking of melodrama.

Once, a few months after her mother had died, the live-in housekeeper asked Natalie to summon Garrick to the dinner table. She moved gingerly, the carpet cool under her feet. Her stepfather was ensconced in his leather chair, behind the desk with the gleaming veneer, head bowed over the pad and pen on which he wrote his papers to be published in renowned legal journals. Garrick squinted and asked, "Yes? What is it?" as if he were trying to place how he knew her. That look of bewilderment captured their relationship, Garrick's and hers, housemates with only the people they loved in common.

What mysterious parcel would he send to her, a stepdaughter he barely recognized?

ISABEL WAS PERCHED atop her walnut desk, legs crossed under a pencil skirt. Her eyes were focused, her hair obedient in its ponytail, her nails manicured in a shimmery white. Natalie noticed how her face looked tighter than usual, like a garment short on material. "Welcome to the first session of 'Changing our Brains for Happiness.'"

Natalie sat on a cushioned chair among the fifteen arranged in a semi-circle in Isabel's loft, her new office. Thirteen women and two men. It was a luxurious space, painted in a stark white: high ceilings from which hung three modern light fixtures, nearly floor-length windows, and several columns a richer almond shade.

"To begin today's session, I'm introducing a tool to help facilitate that change: my new iPhone app, *Wired Happy*. I developed these techniques with my husband, a Harvard-trained neurologist. He's more accomplished than I am." She swung one leg over the other. "But you're stuck with me, I'm afraid."

The other participants laughed. One called out, "It's you we want!"

Isabel touched her chest lightly with her fingers. "Thank you. So, without getting too technical, I'm going to talk this evening about how our minds have a negativity bias. This may sound like New Age nonsense, but it makes sense that human beings are more sensitive to negative events. Primitive men and women needed to be attuned to threats in order to survive. We've evolved to respond more powerfully to adversity than to comfort and pleasure. While this was a helpful adaptation for our hunter-gatherer ancestors—and is still a necessary tool in times of crisis—it's not particularly useful to us when we are living our day-to-day lives."

Natalie had heard her stepsister speak on this subject at her lecture on Grand Cayman. Hunter-gatherers sounded like wolves, which were related to dogs. Once, when she was a kid, Natalie had seen a dead dog on the highway, its tongue lolling out of its mouth. "Oh, poor thing," her mom had cried, behind the wheel. "Don't look, girls."

Did I kill that dog? Did the animal drag his wounded body into the bushes to die alone?

Isabel said, "What scientists have discovered is that our brains have plasticity, which means they are capable of transformation. My app, *Wired Happy,* combines cognitive, behavioral, spiritual, and physical techniques. Along with what we learn here, my app will help you to alter your habits, or as I like to put it, to *grow* your own happiness."

A murmur of excitement rippled through the group. Natalie thought of the Chia Pet from her childhood, its slogan: "the pottery that grows." She'd soaked the terracotta turtle in a bowl of water, and an ugly green bush sprouted instead of the fur she'd expected. Thinking about it now, Natalie realized how she was like that figurine: a distortion, a disappointment—or something even worse.

"Our brains are stubborn organs that stick to their set patterns," Isabel continued. "It's like your body when it's out of shape. You need to train it to be active and fit, to heal itself."

"I try to heal myself through self-compassion," Prama, the yoga teacher on Natalie's left, whispered to her. She was a willowy thing with auburn hair down to her tailbone and a painfully earnest voice.

She'd explained to Natalie right before the meeting that her real name was Heather. She'd chosen her Sanskrit one for its meaning, "true knowledge free from error and above doubt." Natalie wondered why Prama was here if she were the repository of wisdom.

The yoga teacher closed her eyes and said, "I find as winter approaches, it's a natural time to turn inward. Don't you? That's why I signed up to do the workshop this cycle."

Natalie smiled and observed her more closely, her maroon tights, Uggs, and silky ankle-length wrap-around dress, some cross-pollination of a sari and a kimono. The dress looked light as butterfly wings. She must have frozen outside, unless self-compassion kept her warm. What would that feel like, being able to so readily forgive herself?

Isabel reached behind her and grabbed bound manuals with turquoise covers. "Let's start with my written program, your handbook. This package will reinforce the concepts we discuss here. There's additional information online at the web address listed on the first page. Some of the exercises might feel self-indulgent at first—all this taking one's own emotional temperature." She smiled at her audience. "But they work."

Natalie noticed the girl across from her gawking at Isabel, the way Hadley would at Beyoncé in concert. Her hand was raised, eagerly; she looked young enough to be in college. She was pixie-faced with a pert nose and short, spiky brown hair and multiple silver earrings in both lobes.

"How long till I stop obsessing about the bad shit all the time?" she asked when Isabel pointed in her direction. "I'm meditating. I cut out sugar—okay, except for a few Reese's Pieces a day. I'm eating organic, you know, other than the Reese's. I volunteer at Planned Parenthood. Okay, only once." She raised her first three fingers and slapped her thumb over her pinky. "Just trying to keep myself together after rehab. We have no twelve-steps here, right?"

Isabel looked at the girl and nodded. "Nope."

"Should I, like, work for the homeless or Planned Parenthood or immigration? With all the crap going on now in this country, you know, I'm wondering if helping people would make me feel better."

"Volunteering is wonderful and important," Isabel said. "But there are no rules or requirements here, Ms. Anshaw."

The man on Natalie's right side mumbled. "Wouldn't be the worst thing."

Natalie turned around to face one of the men in the group. His eye roll made her smile. He was attractive in a slapdash way: curly brown hair, the sides of which jutted out like twigs, tortoise shell glasses that magnified dark eyes with slight pouches under them, the five o'clock shadow of a man not yet committed to a beard. She guessed he was in his early forties; no wedding ring, she quickly noted.

"Why is it so hard *not* to be self-destructive?" the college girl asked.

Prama, collarbones sharp as ivory tusks under the skin, said, "In yogi, we call that 'misdirected prana.' Coming to this workshop is the first step towards readjustment."

"Yogi's a Jill Stein voter," Natalie's neighbor said quietly. "Trust fund baby who reads Goop religiously."

Natalie stared at the ceramic bowl of stones on Isabel's glass coffee table in order not to laugh.

"Changing habitual behavior is a tough challenge," Isabel said. "But I promise if you come every week and follow the program, you'll start seeing results before the twelve weeks are over."

Natalie flipped through her manual. Could someone like her, someone with damage so deep it might be encoded on her DNA, "cultivate mindfulness" and "find meaning in failure"?

When the two hours had passed, Isabel said, "Next meeting is a couple of days before Thanksgiving, so I anticipate a smaller turnout. For those who are traveling, have a safe and wonderful holiday."

An animated rumbling ensued as the other workshop members gathered their things and dispersed. A few flocked around their instructor. A peach pulp haired woman droned on about "staying present." As soon as she stopped talking, Prama/Heather cited "the heart Chakra."

"Excuse me," Natalie interjected. "Can I have a second?"

The others turned and peered at her like a cluster of cats, their eyes shining in the dark.

"Let's catch up next time. I'll address everyone's questions and concerns," Isabel reassured. She took Natalie's elbow and led her to the opposite side of the loft, behind a pillar. She waved to her students and waited for them to all clear out.

"I'm so glad you came," Isabel said. "Sorry about the constant interruptions from that girl with all the questions."

"Do you know her?"

Isabel shrugged. "She's been to my lectures, hung around to talk. She'll settle in."

"One of your super-fans." Natalie's thumb spun her bracelet around, over and over. "Listen, something kind of weird happened."

Isabel popped open her eyes the way she used to do when they were kids and Natalie was frightened of sleeping alone in the dark. "What?"

"I got a phone call. From Ellen."

"Ugh, sorry. She's insufferable. What did she want?"

Let's keep this between ourselves.

Natalie's allegiance was to her stepsister, not Garrick's assistant. Why should she abide by Ellen's instructions? "Seems Garrick left an envelope of something for me. She said she was FedEx-ing it right away. I should have it in a few days."

"What's in it?"

"She didn't say. I figured it's a copy of his will. If he left me part of his estate, it's yours." Having paid for her college, and put money into an investment fund for Hadley, Garrick had fulfilled his fiscal obligation to her. "Do you think that's what it is?"

Natalie noted her stepsister's stricken expression, the gleam lining her lids when she averted her eyes. "If not his will, what?"

Slowly, Isabel sat down next to Natalie, her breath a light breeze between them. "I have no idea."

"Yes, you do. What is it?"

"You'll see when you get the package."

"What do you know?" Natalie asked, desperate to tear the truth out of Isabel, whatever secrets or doubts she'd harbored all these years. "I'm not a kid anymore, I can handle it."

Isabel shook her head. "I would have called you to come, but I thought he was recovering. You hate hospitals, why make you come?"

"I would have if you'd called me."

"Cardiac arrest," Isabel had blurted out the first time. Her step-sister phoned while Natalie was reading her notes for her History final, sophomore year of college, and as soon as Isabel blurted, "My dad's at Mass General," the dates of the French Revolution sloshed across Natalie's mind like melting snowdrifts. She was seized with the black terror of transport, of waking up as she was being lifted into the ambulance and rushed down Washington Street.

"Of course. But how could I know he'd have another heart attack? Maybe Dad sensed he was dying and was trying to make things right. He asked me to give this letter to you, but I refused, and we argued. I'm only guessing . . . Ellen would do whatever he wanted."

"What was in the letter?"

"I never read it, but he was agitated, pumped up on drugs, Nat."

Natalie pressed her palm to her chest, felt the quick, insistent beat within. "Why did you refuse to give it to me, what was in it?"

"The accident." Isabel sighed. "You think Dad didn't know how it destroyed you? How you went from doctor to doctor?"

"Garrick never paid attention to me."

"He felt guilty, that's the reason he turned away." Isabel placed her hand on Natalie's knee. "You're shaking."

"Dr. Davidson called it survivor's guilt. But mine was more than that. I always sensed that."

"He wanted you to know that he blamed himself for that night, for everything that happened."

Her leg was bobbing, a buoy in choppy waters. "I still can't remember where we were going, what my mom and I were talking about. Everything, even the months before, are spotty."

"I know, Nat. I've tried to help fill in the blanks. But Dad and I weren't in the car with you."

Natalie stared at the wood panels on the floor through a blur. She needed to focus, to sharpen her vision. "So, what did Garrick want to tell me?"

When Isabel inhaled deeply, Natalie saw the strain in the hollows under her eyes. "It was Dad's *Come to Jesus Moment*. I can't be sure what he wrote in his morphine state."

Natalie's throat felt grainy and tight. "Did Garrick confess to *you* where we were going that night? Or did you know it all along?"

"Leave it alone. That's what I advised Dad, too. It's like picking at a wound, infecting it over and over, instead of letting it heal."

"But it never does."

There was a slight shift in the loft's ambience, as if the molecules in the air had quickened. The words came before Natalie's mind processed the question. "Did I talk to you about going away, being *sent* away? Was that why I shone the light in Mom's eyes, because she was sending me somewhere that night?"

Isabel reached for Natalie, smoothed the hair behind her ear. "You were just going to a therapist, that's all it was. That's not as scary as you're making it."

Natalie let that sink in. It felt true. "Why, Belle? What was wrong with me?"

"You were having issues with the stress in the house. Laura thought Dad was having an affair with Ellen. You were terrified they'd separate."

"Lake Grove. What is that?"

"The name of a boarding school."

She thought of the ones Hadley mentioned where the rich kids went to ensure they'd get into Ivy League schools. "I'm betting it wasn't like Andover, this place they were going to ship me off to. What kind of school was it?"

"It was for kids . . . who were struggling with emotional issues. But, Nat, it was *normal* what you felt. You'd lost one family, and now you were going to lose another."

Tears ran down Natalie's cheeks, a silent cry. "You and me. We didn't have blood binding us to each other."

"I used to say that, those words exactly. Nat . . ."

She squinted as if through a peephole into a dark room, "I remember it now. What I was. What I've done."

four

——

NATALIE'S CAR WAS PARKED ON THE NEXT BLOCK, AND SHE RACED through the damp cold to get there. She heard her cell phone ping. Engine on, heat turned up, she checked the message. It was a text from Hadley: *Mom, u almost here? Waiting.*

It was after nine, the time she'd told Hadley she'd be in Belmont. *Leaving in five minutes,* she texted back. She could picture Marc's scowl, the lines deepening between his brows. She would have to drive more quickly than she liked.

She was on I-90 W, raindrops landing on her windshield, when the highway seemed to wave and shimmer as if from tectonic shifts in the landscape. She reminded herself: the world was fine. *She* was off-kilter. Her mother had wanted to put her into a special school. What if her problems hadn't begun with the crash and her lost memories? What if she'd been born with something missing?

Her phone beeped again. Eyes on the road, Natalie scooped her cell out of the cup holder and pressed the Home button without reading the name on the screen. "Hi, Hads. I'm on my way."

"It's Marc. Hadley just called me. She's wondering where you are."

Her pulse quickened. "What do you mean she called you? She's at your place."

"No. You were supposed to get her at Sophie's."

"Oh, god, I got mixed up. Can you call her?" Natalie searched for the exit so she could turn around, head east. The rain was worse, streaking down the chalkboard sky. "Tell her I'm coming."

"Sophie's going out to a party. Hads doesn't want to be alone there."

"On a school night? That doesn't sound like the Slaters."

"I can't answer for them."

"Of course not." She was the one familiar with the quirks of Hadley's friends, the habits of their families—Sophie hated red licorice but loved black; her mom posted a chore wheel on the fridge every Sunday, and her Dad wore suspenders to work which he snapped loose as soon as he took off his coat. "Just call and tell her I'm on my way."

"I'll ask her what she wants to do," he said and hung up.

When her phone rang again, she anticipated the pressure of Marc's voice in her ear. "Did you reach her?"

"Hadley's tired. She wants to go home. I told her to borrow money from the Slaters and call a cab, that you'd pay them back."

"Okay. Does she have her key?"

"She said she always takes it with her."

Another reprimand: their fifteen-year-old daughter was more responsible than she. *Good.* Her head throbbing, she thanked the god of biology that her daughter had inherited Marc's sensible nature.

"I'll be home soon." A truck roared past, and Natalie grasped the wheel with both hands

"Did something happen to upset you?" he asked more gently, a vestige from their marriage when he still loved her.

For a moment she imagined them in their bed, facing each other in the dark. Puddles of shadows would dot the floor, while outside the night's crescent moon would glow. They'd be close enough that Natalie would smell the musk of his skin, the mint from the toothpaste. "You were a child," he'd reassure her. "The crap with your family, the accident, none of it was your fault." He'd cradle her head on his chest, and she would see from that angle that they'd soon be making love, followed by the sound of Marc's quiet snores, her body soothed.

But this new Marc would never console her again. Anything could be used as fodder against her now.

"Jesus, Marc," she said. "I was at Isabel's group and lost track of time, that's all. You don't get to check up on me anymore."

"You're right. What you do with your time isn't my concern. But Hadley is. She comes first."

"Seriously? You're the one who moved out."

"Not on Hadley."

Natalie looked at her arm, the one still steering. The veins to her wrists flowed like runnels below the thin slice of skin. She could twist the wheel sharply and justify Marc's reasons for bailing on her.

She said, "Ask your daughter how she felt after you left."

"Of course, she was angry. But we got through that. Hadley understands it wasn't about her; she's forgiven me."

"Really? Are you sure about that? 'Cause what you did was unforgivable."

Not as bad as what I've done.

She never saw her mother's face. Her hair was sprawled over her head, which was collapsed onto the wheel. But Natalie had smelled the sweet, slightly rusty smell of blood.

"Look, I know how you react when you're really stressed," Marc said. "Hads can stay with me more often, if you need time, just until you feel better."

She felt a muscle twist and tighten in her chest. She pictured Elizabeth's earnest face in the photo she'd tracked down on Facebook once Marc let slip his girlfriend's last name. She'd felt a thrill of triumph as she studied the plain face, the wide forehead with the hair swept back behind a headband and the practiced, thin-lipped smile: *I'm prettier than she is.*

"That's super generous of you, offering for my daughter to spend more time with you and your fucking girlfriend so I can recuperate from you dumping me."

HADLEY WAS SITTING in the lotus position on her bed, her laptop in front of her. Natalie glanced at the sapphire and marigold batik hangings of the Indian goddess on her daughter's wall. Druga—the mother of the universe—her large, slanted eyes lined with kohl, her eighteen weapon-carrying arms, seated upon a growling tiger. "I'm not, like, becoming a Hindu," she'd said when Natalie asked about her recent redecoration. "I just think she looks really powerful. I like the idea of a goddess to believe in."

Natalie sprinted to her daughter, kissed the top of her head.

"Where were you?"

"I screwed up that you were at Sophie's, not Dad's." Natalie sunk onto the bed. "I was distracted, sorry."

Hadley wiggled her silver earring, imploring, "Okay but, Mom, I told you a hundred times I was going to Sophie's."

"A hundred times?" She smiled at this exaggeration; her girl was still just a girl.

"I couldn't wait to get out of there, and you were *so* late."

"That doesn't sound like you, wanting to leave," Natalie said with a pang of worry. She caressed her daughter's downy skin and made sure not to pull at the same knot in her hair that needed to be combed out every day since she was two. "You always beg to stay at Sophie's."

Hadley disentangled her legs and stretched one out, her calf muscles defined in her black jeggings. She flexed, then pointed, her foot. Her toenails were painted a bright orange-red called *Speak Your Mind*. "Ever since she started hanging out with this senior, Priscilla, and her friends, Sophie's been acting like an asshole."

Seniors? What had she missed? "How long has this been going on?"

"Since the school year began. They party too much."

"What does that mean exactly?"

Her daughter shrugged. "Weed, drinking."

"That's not good." *Jesus. Where have I been?* "I don't want you hanging around those kids."

Hadley scrunched up her brow, an expression that resembled Marc's. "I'm not. That's the point. I don't even like being with Sophie anymore."

Her best friend since first grade. During one of their last fights, Marc had said, "Without your obsession, you'd be left with us, your life now. You'd have to concentrate on *us*. And that's not enough for you."

"Oh, Hads. That's so painful." Natalie reached for her daughter's hand. As always, her child's long, slender fingers came as a poignant surprise, how they resembled her mom's. "Why haven't I heard about this?"

"You've been so sad. It's gotten worse since you got back from your vacation."

Natalie picked at a flap of loose scab on her wrist. "How do you mean?"

"You're, like, more preoccupied. I hear you walking around sometimes really late."

The old nightmare was the culprit, only in this version her mom was driving on a dirt road on a tropical island. She tried to grip the wheel, but her hands kept slipping as if coated in grease. Natalie heard herself say, "Your brain isn't working now." Then the driver's seat was empty. Natalie pushed open her door without resistance. The car sparkled, not a dent on it. Natalie whisked above the road, feet not touching the ground. She saw it lying there, her mother's body curled into the shape of a capital C. When she moved the hair flung over her mother's face, it was gone. Not bloody and bruised but wiped clean of all features: a porcelain plate with three holes where eyes and a mouth should be.

"I'm so sorry if I've been waking you."

"It's okay," Hadley said. "I fall back asleep. Are you upset about Garrick?"

"Yes, of course."

"You, like, never talk about him. I mean I know you weren't close. Are you worried about Aunt Isabel?"

"Not worried, no. She's sad, of course, but she'll be all right."

"It's just . . . I tell you stuff over and over and you just space out about it."

"I didn't realize I was doing that."

Shivering, she hugged Hadley. Even in the winter, her child slept with the window open. Sometimes, Natalie envisioned Hadley freezing in the night, icicles stuck to her hair, her lips bluish. She'd check on her, over and over, creaking on the wood floor until Marc would say, "Come to bed. You'll wake her." He and Hadley used to race out the door of the cabin they'd rent in Vermont, in bulky ski attire, laughing in camaraderie. Natalie would venture out into the village, shoot photographs. She hated the crackle of the air and snow, the swish and roar of speeding down the mountain—that fast motion she couldn't control.

"I'll try to be better." Natalie scraped the skin on her wrist until drops of blood sprouted.

"I didn't want to bother you about Soph. I mean, it seemed so . . . dumb after Dad moved in with Elizabeth."

"That happened to both of us."

"Yeah." Her daughter wriggled free of Natalie's embrace to attend to the polish that was beginning to peel off her big toe. She chipped away at the edges.

"Hads, your relationship with Sophie isn't dumb. Nothing in your life is. Please don't think that."

Hadley nodded, her slim back still bending away from Natalie.

"If you have to nudge me to pay more attention, do it."

The girl turned around, her glare a condemnation. "I thought it would be so much fun being in the Caribbean with Aunt Isabel, going to that resort, getting massages, even those lectures—some of them looked cool."

"It *was* fun."

"Then, Mom, *what's* wrong?"

Natalie shook her head, mouthed: *nothing.* "Maybe Isabel can take you to the conference next year. I know she'd love that. I'm not sure you can go to the events till you're eighteen, but she told me it's going to be in Australia."

Hadley gasped, her eyes wide, prismatic. "Oh my God, that would be the best! I'd be fine hanging out with the kangaroos."

She'd slipped free of the noose. This time.

LATER THAT EVENING, Natalie cajoled Hadley into watching an episode of *Project Runway*, which they always recorded. At eleven o'clock, Natalie followed her daughter back to her room. Hadley, at the edge of her bed, nudged the Kurdish throw rug with her big toe. "This could just be a stage with Dad, this Elizabeth thing. All my friends agree you're a cool hot mom."

Natalie watched as her girl chewed the side of her cheek, a nervous tick usually reserved for trying to solve a word problem in algebra or structure the argument of an English paper.

"That's hard to believe," Natalie said, with a static smile.

"C'mon. You're way younger than most of my friends' mothers, and you have good bone structure. You could do a lot more with yourself. Get highlights. Wear pumps, like, you know, a heel, not those sad looking boots."

The ones with the fake fur lining that she wore when it rained or snowed. Did Hadley believe that if she'd worn stilettos Marc wouldn't have left? She kissed the top of her daughter's head, smelling coconut shampoo. "I don't think it's a stage. But *I'll* try harder. At everything. I really am sorry I've tuned you out."

"Mean it." Hadley raised her head.

"I do." She felt loose and overflowing, a river of apology.

After saying goodnight, Natalie took a moment in the hallway to observe the professional shots of her girl as a toddler, her copper-brown corkscrew curls and hazel eyes with the scar above the right one from stitches she'd gotten after falling off a playground swing. "Here is your life," Marc would say, pointing to these images, when Natalie was caught chasing her elusive past, images not taken by her. She snapped casual pictures of her family on her cell phone, but she hadn't attempted serious portraits since her mother's death.

As a child, she'd loved taking photos of people, her mother's compliments, "That's wonderful, how you caught her expression, how it makes me want to know more about her." They were on vacation, in Muir Woods, the summer Natalie turned ten when she'd started. Her mother observed how the sequoias resembled relics from medieval times, an eerie army of knotted giants with enormous bunions on their trunks, and yawning, cavernous mouths. She shared her Leica with both girls during that trip. But it was only Natalie who'd shown interest, not in nature—other than as background—but in Isabel and her mom standing in the triangular opening of a split Redwood tree. And, oh, the swell of pleasure as the image started to emerge in the chemical bath. It was a trick of timing, luck, and skill producing that ideal shot, the truth behind the person's gaze.

But, after the accident, Natalie stopped altogether, not lifting a camera until college, when she'd dared to try again. Natalie signed up for an elective: food photography, and she'd thought, *Well, food doesn't have a soul, why not?*

She changed into her flannel pajama bottoms and Marc's t-shirt with the Apple computer logo on it, then lifted her engagement ring out of the velvet box on her night table and snuck it on her finger. She only wore it when she was alone. Staring at the small, round diamond, she wondered how much it was worth. Soon, very soon, she would sell it to a jeweler in her neighborhood. Out of habit she curled on her right side, as she had throughout her marriage.

What you do with your time isn't my concern.

Sorrow burned Natalie's eyes, and she switched off the lamp at the side of her bed. She should try Isabel's relaxation app. Instead, she opened the drawer to her night table where she kept her "emergency" bottle of Xanax. Among the coins and Post-it notes and squishy earplugs was a photograph she'd taken of her mom the summer before the crash. In the snapshot, her mother's head was thrown back in profile, mouth open in joy as if trying to swallow the sliver of sunlight above. Grief was an inflammation, a bodily sensation. The flare-ups never stopped. Time, that famous healer, was a quack.

She eased the photo back into the drawer, along with the pill bottle. Then, she saw it, the small silver flashlight, the one she kept in case of a blackout.

Her mother's voice: *The light's blinding me. For Christ's sake, what's going on?*

Her heart fluttered, skipped beats.

Who are you?

five

—

AFTER DROPPING HADLEY AT SCHOOL THE NEXT MORNING, SHE typed: "traits of a psychopath" into her browser. Manipulative: no, that wasn't her. Lacking in empathy. She paused for a second, and said aloud, "shush," the way her doctor did when listening to her heart with his stethoscope and, just for a second, Natalie worried about an arrhythmia. No. She might be forgetful, but she adored her child, her sister Isabel, and for almost two decades, her husband. Egocentric? Marc might differ with her if she protested. She stared at the PET scan images of a psychopath's brain. The black splotches, where green and yellow should be, indicated reduced activity in the areas that regulated aggression and morality. A decade ago, George had ordered an MRI at Natalie's request. He'd reported that the findings showed no lingering effects from her concussion. "Some people have mild injuries but profound memory issues. What you have is retrograde amnesia, meaning erased sections of your past."

But what about more significant abnormalities? Garrick's letter wouldn't provide scientific proof but might reveal her character without it.

Yet, two days passed, and Ellen's FedEx failed to arrive. Natalie checked the vestibule of her townhouse where the packages piled up, then her mailbox for a notice in case it was being held at a facility. She listened to the message again, the assertion that Garrick's assistant would be sending his documents. Future tense.

Before running out to the studio, Natalie sat at her desk. It was like the aftermath of a hurricane: paperclips strewn haphazardly, bills in several piles, lens cleaning cloths bunched in a corner, and Post-it notes stuck on her computer, as well as the stand she used to hoist up the laptop on an angle, with her to-do lists scribbled on them. Marc had wondered how she found anything amid the clutter. But, jutting up from the pottery holder Hadley had made in elementary school were business cards she'd saved for years, including her stepfather's from the university.

When a young man answered, she said, "I'm calling for Ellen Alden. She worked for Professor Walker. He passed away recently."

Ellen must have been reassigned to work for another professor or several in the department. Most of them shared assistants, Natalie knew. Garrick's situation was unusual due to his status and long tenure in the department.

The man said, "Right, of course. Horrible loss. One minute. I'll find out for you."

He put Natalie on hold, and when he returned said, "Ms. Alden hasn't been in all week."

Isabel's words buzzed in her head: *Poor woman has no life outside of her job and my dad.*

"Is she ill?"

"Uh, not sure. Would you like me to ask around and see if anyone has more information?"

"No, that's fine. I'll try her home number."

After a brief search, Natalie located an E. Alden in Cambridge. Ellen's phone peeled in the same interval, over and over, as if content to never stop. Natalie stared at the cracks in her wall and wondered what kind of person didn't use voicemail. Perhaps Ellen had no need for the service now that Garrick was gone. According to Isabel's reports over the years, Ellen's identity was tied to her relationship with him.

I don't think she'll be happy until Dad declares his undying love for her.

This Natalie remembered: there had been a party, the first gathering at their home after her mother's death. A year had passed, maybe two. Isabel was in discussion with one of her father's younger colleagues who fiddled with his miscalculation of a bowtie. Natalie took a glass of wine from the sidebar without anyone noticing. She had no parents, no one to monitor her. That fact was a constant, an involuntary act, like the beating of her heart.

Her friends had tried to reconnect at first. At school, they'd smiled at her in the hallway, invited her to sit with them at lunch, even asked her halfheartedly to join them at the mall or the movies. Natalie always declined their offers. She *had* wanted to be with them. But the hum and hustle, the shrieks of surprise and gasps of laughter startled her. Unexpectedly, she'd feel as if she were hovering above the group, a quivering apparition. Then, in a swish, she'd be suctioned back into the suffering cavity of her body, all thrashing heart and overheated skin. She felt safer alone in her bedroom, or the bathroom stall at school.

But Garrick had expected her to attend his party.

The crisp warmth from the alcohol suffused through her body, which helped as Natalie witnessed her stepfather. His arm was around a woman whose waist was as tiny as a Victorian girl's, sucked into a corset. Otherwise, his date—her name was Iris— was not attractive. Her eyes were rather high on her face, and she had an overbite that she ran her tongue over nervously.

As she drank, Natalie stared into this room of men, many bald or with receding hairlines, a sprinkling of women whose shoulders curved forward as if they cradled heavy textbooks in their arms all day. At some point, she turned towards the window and saw a woman illuminated by the porch light. Ellen, with her trademark knotted scarf, staggered down the stairs then ran to the car parked behind Garrick's in the driveway. Natalie pushed aside the curtains to watch as her stepfather's secretary, in an accelerated fury of motion, scratched her key against Iris's black Audi. When Ellen looked up, her face was stamped with alarm as if stunned by what she'd done. She craned her head from side to side and then started back to the house.

Good, Natalie had cheered her on silently, hating her stepfather for trying to replace her mother. Never mind Ellen's motivation, her wish to *be* the replacement.

FOR THE NEXT WEEK, Natalie was fixated on her mail. When she returned to her apartment from outings, she looked for notes from FedEx saying they'd missed her. Could the wind have loosened the tape, caused the paper to fly off the front door? She checked FedEx.com, but because she had no tracking number, she couldn't determine the status of her shipment. One morning after dropping Hadley at school, Natalie contacted the local center. When the customer service man asked her for the tracking number, she said, "I don't have that. But I know it was sent overnight."

"Maybe there was a mix up. Can you get in touch with the sender?"

"No," she lied. "It was a letter my father wrote to me the night before he died."

"Sorry to hear," he said.

"I'm happy to come pick it up if you verify it's at your location."

"One minute." He put her on hold and when he returned said, "Our records show that package was delivered to your residence." He reported the date.

"No, that's wrong," Natalie insisted, her bare toes tapping the floor. "I never got it."

"It says here—"

"I don't care what it says. It's a mix-up."

"Well, there was no signature required. Perhaps your spouse or roommate picked it up?"

"No. There's neither." But she wondered. Could Hadley have gotten the package without her knowledge?

Natalie quickly dismissed this idea, as her daughter was never home when FedEx packages arrived. Even if she had been, Hadley would have left it on the dining room table or the hutch, as usual. Her daughter would have no reason to suspect what the contents contained, the crushing secrets inside.

When the conversation with the representative ended, Natalie mumbled, "Idiot."

She attempted to reach the old woman again on her way into the studio. She tried the law department first, and this time the young man was more abrupt. No, Ms. Alden wasn't back. Would she like to talk to another assistant who could help her? "Yes, please," Natalie said, on speaker. This second person explained that Ms. Alden had tendered her resignation abruptly. "I can check the date if you need me to." Natalie took a sharp right onto a narrow, European-style street, the white steeple rising above an elegant brick church. The woman explained she was not at liberty to disclose further private information.

Isabel's words buzzed in Natalie's head. *I won't be surprised if she dies of a broken heart.*

Natalie wondered if that were possible as, at a standstill on the road, she entered the digits of Ellen's now memorized telephone number. She heard a click and the sound of a woman's slightly startled voice. "You have reached the home of Ellen Arden. I am not here at the moment, but if you leave your message at the tone, I will get back to you shortly," then a beep.

"Hi, it's Natalie. I'm so glad to have finally reached your voicemail! The folks at the law school said you're no longer working there. I hope everything's okay." Before she had the chance to explain about the documents, there were three beeps, followed by a dial tone.

As soon as she parked her car, she called again. This time no message played.

WHEN ELLEN HADN'T replied by that Sunday morning, Natalie decided to take action. Hadley would be at Marc's till after dinner, which left her plenty of time to ride over to the secretary's home. She knew the address in North Cambridge by heart, as well, and could use the GPS on her phone to navigate.

She pulled on the boots Hadley disliked, zipped up her coat, and grabbed her scarf. On the drive, she imagined Ellen lying face up on her bed, her skin waxy and whatever hideous hue an un-embalmed corpse turned, her body bloated.

"Don't overreact," Natalie repeated Marc's scold aloud. She felt disjointed, her limbs floppy, the usual prelude to panic. She tightened her hands around the wheel and narrowed her eyes on the road to concentrate.

Ellen's street was tree-lined with a suburban look to it: all houses, no apartment buildings, and small private yards enclosed behind wood fences. Natalie parked in front of a two-family beige Victorian with maize-colored trim and side-by-side brick-red doors. The lights were out in both homes. Natalie surveyed the area—up the street, down, across, where a pine tree towered next to a row house, seeming to pierce through the dull sky—and saw no one.

She turned off the engine, left the car unlocked. Even in leather gloves, her fingers burned from the dramatic dip in temperature. She walked up the three steps, which were icy but salted. Someone was taking care of the upkeep. On the narrow porch, she peered through the identical glass doors of both homes, first the neighbor's, just to ensure that no one was in the front of the house. All she could see was a coat rack with a couple of jackets and a red plaid scarf draped over it. Faded lace curtains hung in Ellen's window, blocking the view. The light under the stained-glass fixture in her hallway was off, and the wood blinds on her slimmer window were drawn. Natalie rang, just to be certain. "C'mon, Ellen." She rang again. A loud, furious barking: the sign she needed. A dog in the house meant Ellen was alive.

Or most likely.

Of course, she is.

But what if the dog was alone, without food or water? Another animal Natalie would leave to die? Natalie turned the doorknob. Locked.

She searched inside her bag for the pen and notepad she'd carried with her. She wrote quickly: "I hope you're well. Please call or email me when you get this. I never got Garrick's package. Thanks, Natalie." The lid to the metal mailbox creaked when she opened it, and inside was empty other than the crumpled pieces of a dead leaf. She stuck the note inside.

"COME IN, WELCOME," George exclaimed as he opened the door to his and Isabel's Back Bay apartment. "Happy Thanksgiving."

Natalie and Hadley had arrived mid-afternoon to the brownstone near the French Library and Cultural Center, with twin, potted mums adorning the front steps. They'd brought a bottle of white wine and one of cider, as requested. The minute they stepped into the apartment, Natalie hoped the calm ambience would work its magic on her. There was a still, cathedral feel to the place, with its high ceilings, lack of clutter, and low temperature that warranted sweaters in winter.

George hugged her, a stocky man with milky brown eyes, slightly disheveled looking with his lock of hair hanging over his face and his creased Brooks Brothers shirt. Pressed against him, she smelled the mix of cigar and orange tea on his breath. She watched Isabel rush from the bay windows, sleek in her black pants and silver sweater with leather pockets.

"Hey, kids!" Isabel kissed her niece on both cheeks. "Look at you, Hads! You're so beautiful."

"Thanks, Aunt Belle."

Hadley had become more aware of quality clothes in the last few months: from Merino Wool to the unattainable Vicuña. She'd spend hours perusing shopping sites online, scouting for sales.

"Is that coat a Belstaff?" Isabel asked, sliding her hand over the waxed cotton fabric.

"An impracticable gift from Marc and the girlfriend," Natalie said. "Way out of our price range."

"That doesn't sound like him," George frowned. Frugality was a quality the two men shared, despite the difference in their circumstances. "Sex and baked goods, that's how I get him to do what I want," Isabel once had joked to Natalie.

Isabel asked, "Did you pick this out, Hads? It's so sophisticated."

"Yes, thanks. Oh, I love your shoes, Aunt Belle! They're super cool."

Natalie glanced down at Isabel's snakeskin pumps that almost crackled with animal life. There was something obscene about them, their seductiveness and opulence. They must have cost upward of five hundred dollars.

Isabel smiled as she gazed at her purchase. "Decadent, right? I wasn't going to buy them. But with all the pressure from my seminars and then my dad's death, I needed to treat myself. You like them, right, George?"

"Not the price tag," he said with a stiff smile. "But you're working non-stop on this new blockbuster book."

Natalie chewed the inside of her cheek. The editor had slammed the last draft of Isabel's manuscript. "She hated the direction it was going in. First time that ever happened to me," Isabel had confessed. "I'll fix it." A paper cut on the skin, stinging but barely visible. "Don't tell George. I already spent the advance on my business, building a brand." Attendance at her lectures was down. She shrugged it off, plaited hair swinging. "That happens between books, my PR team says."

"I meant how they look," Isabel said in a flirty voice.

"Well, sure," George said. "You're beautiful in them."

"See, Mom?" Hadley turned towards Natalie, the spray of pink on her cheeks reaching down to the part of her chest exposed by her wide shawl neckline. "Men like heels."

Isabel said, "Hads, your mom has her own style."

"Yeah, boring."

"Hey, enough," Natalie snapped. "That's mean."

Isabel said, "Your mom isn't boring; she's classic. George, would you mind getting the gifts in the bedroom for my favorite niece and stepsister?"

"Why did you get us anything?" Natalie asked, exasperated. "It's not Christmas yet."

"We've all had a tough year. I wanted to celebrate early."

"I'll do it. You can hang onto mine. I'll get Hadley's," Natalie offered, slipping her phone in her pant pocket.

Not every man finds me undesirable in my flat shoes.

"It's the bigger box," Isabel said.

The bedroom was long, airy, and fragrant with the scent of Isabel's tea rose sachets. A shiver ran through Natalie, not just from the temperature. It was the sense of the forbidden. She could poke around the drawers or the boxes of Isabel's jewelry. In her closets hung cashmere sweaters Hadley would covet, light as meringues, her crepe de chine shirt-dress, her gray suede pants. Natalie wondered what it would be like to don these clothes, the soft wool and cool silk against her skin, to feel what it was like to be Isabel. No wonder Hadley admired beautiful things; she'd acquired that trait from her. Natalie fingered the fabric of her drab tunic. She would not let herself tank.

Until we meet again.

She could email Simon Hotmail Drouin right now, wish him a "Happy American holiday." Not that much time had passed, a couple of weeks. He'd remember her. It would be her secret, as luxurious as one of Isabel's shimmering scarves. An antidote to feeling like the dreary stepsister, the rejected wife. But then she thought of her photos, the leaves with the reddish-brown splotches, and tucked her phone back in her pant pocket.

"It's chilly in here," George said when Natalie reappeared. "Maybe I should turn up the thermostat."

"Yes please, Bear," Isabel said.

The intimacy of the nickname made Natalie think about pressing her lips against Marc's cheek, of the smell of his skin, cedar and sandalwood from his aftershave.

How ironic. The first time Natalie had met George, she couldn't figure out her sister's attraction to him. Isabel's previous boyfriends had been sinewy, charming men with the stamina to work long hours, then stay up making love half the night. Natalie was proud she'd nabbed the more desirable mate, with his lanky build and sloping height, his large hazel eyes, and his expressive mouth that she wanted to kiss while he talked. But what did any of that matter in the end?

George is the keeper.

"Can I help with dinner?" Natalie asked her stepsister.

"The turkey's cooking. The crust for the apple pie is in the fridge. I have to make the mashed potatoes and finish the salad." Isabel smiled.

"Impressive. When did you learn to cook?"

"Don't laugh! I watched YouTube videos. It helps to keep busy since my dad died. Come help me."

"Hadley, you keep me company," George said. "I'll make a fire. That's cozier."

"Be careful." Isabel wagged her finger at him. "Last time he almost burned down the house. Can you imagine if he'd gone into neurosurgery as planned?"

"Surgeons are glorified plumbers," George said with mock outrage, palm splayed on his chest. "I'm too scholarly to spend my days slicing into brains. Researching how they work is more intellectually taxing."

"I'm glad you chose so wisely." Isabel bowed towards her husband. "I'm lucky to have an in-house consultant for my program."

Natalie witnessed the adoring look Isabel gave her husband. She rarely loosened up like this in front of others. Natalie envisioned them, when alone together, as engaged in parallel play, like toddlers building their block creations without awareness of their buddy's construction. Working, always working. Perhaps grief was an emollient, loosening Isabel's emotions.

Natalie followed her stepsister down the hall on the Persian rug runner. Everything was polished and gleaming: brass floor lamps with sleek hoods, the coffee table with its slender vase of white roses, and the bronze bookshelves with medical and psychology tomes. The kitchen was a showstopper with its granite countertops, the herringbone backsplash, and the glittering silver range.

Isabel opened the refrigerator door and took out a bag of arugula, one of mixed greens, and one of rainbow-colored baby carrots. She handed them to Natalie and gestured for her to put them on the counter. "Did you get the letter?" she asked, peering back inside the fridge, pushing away neatly lined plastic cartoons and emerging with several potatoes. She dumped them next to the lettuce.

"No. Ellen must not have sent it."

"You're kidding! Do you think she forgot?"

"No idea. I found out from the department, she retired."

Isabel shut the door with her elbow, arms full of tomatoes and peppers. "Big surprise. She was only staying for my dad."

"I can't reach her. I keep trying her at home, and she doesn't answer. I'm worried something happened to her."

Isabel shrugged. "Maybe she went on vacation. God knows, the woman barely took off a minute for forty years."

"Does she have anyone, family, friends, who'd know where she is?"

"I think my father mentioned she has some family in Boston, a nephew maybe."

Natalie asked, "Did you talk to her at the funeral?"

Isabel's eyes were pearlescent with tears. "Briefly. She was wrecked about my dad. She hung onto this fantasy of a life with my dad forever. She didn't even ask how I was."

"Ugh, sorry."

For a while, Natalie sliced endives, yellow and orange peppers, purple and white carrots on the cutting board. Her stepsister chopped potatoes into wedges and then threw them into the pot of boiling water. Then, George poked his head into the kitchen. "Do you need any help? I don't want you to think this is women's work."

"We have it covered," Isabel said.

Hadley was out of earshot, but Natalie spoke in a low voice. "I did want to ask you something, George, about my scan. I read something, an article about inactivity in certain parts of the brain."

Isabel put down her knife. "I thought you'd stopped looking that stuff up ages ago. There was no structural damage, no bruises."

"I'm wondering if you found this pattern." Natalie went back to sprinkling sunflower seeds on the salad. "Too many black areas, meaning problems with empathy and moral reasoning."

"Are you talking about the Fallon study?" George asked, pressing down on Natalie's wrist as if checking her pulse. "How he made a correlation between reduced ventromedial prefrontal cortex and or- bitofrontal cortex activity and psychopathology?"

"Yes," Natalie whispered.

"Why are you reading about *that?*"

"To torture herself needlessly," Isabel said.

They heard Hadley squeal. "Oh my god, I love this!"

"We can take a break while the potatoes cook," Isabel said.

Releasing Natalie's arm, George shook his head. "Fallon's reason- ing is flawed and, anyway, has nothing to do with you."

When they went back into the living room, the girl was holding up a black leather satchel with a lovely sheen to it.

"Belle, it's too much!" Natalie scolded.

"Mom! C'mon."

Isabel said, "From a doting aunt."

One extravagant gift from the doting aunt, another from the new girlfriend. And, she, Natalie, was just the "boring" single mom on a budget.

By the time they began the meal, dark had gathered outside, broken up by the gas streetlamps lining Marlborough Street. Hadley asked Isabel about the conference in Australia—not bold enough to try and solicit an invitation. Natalie smiled at her and mouthed, "I'll talk to her about it."

"I have this friend, Priscilla, whose mom teaches at Emerson, Media Studies or something," Hadley said.

"Isn't she the partier?" Natalie asked, an uptick in anxiety. "When did you and Priscilla get so friendly?"

"Mom!" Hadley cried. "So embarrassing."

Isabel put down her glass of wine and reached across the table to cup Hadley's hand. "Being a professor is a lot harder than working just two days a week. You have to publish to get tenure."

"Which you got," George crowed.

"Priscilla's mom is right, though," Isabel said. "Professors rate high on careers that make people happy. It just wasn't a good fit for me, writing for academic journals. I thought I could be more helpful sharing with the general public."

The girl tilted her head so that her hair fell, in a chunk, to one side. "Do you miss teaching?"

"What I do now is still teaching, only I make the rules. I left academia for the freedom, even though I was raised with certain prejudices. Scholarship was one thing, but 'pop psychology' another."

Hadley asked, "You mean Garrick called it that? Wasn't he excited that you're a best-selling author?"

"No, my father wasn't pleased," Isabel said, hoarsely. "Only certain fields were acceptable to him."

Natalie recalled Isabel showing her father her report cards, the string of As lined up like good soldiers. Garrick would nod and fold it carefully, handing it back to her. There was an air of ceremony in this exchange, every time. He never displayed her accomplishments the way Natalie's mom would do. Natalie received some As, but also Bs in Math and B pluses in Gym, and there had been that humiliating C in Home Economics the semester she'd sown her apron into a triangle. Yet her mom had insisted on taping each girl's final report card onto the refrigerator.

"What about you, Mom? What did he think of Photography?"

"Garrick let me go my own way," Natalie said. She gazed at the white vases filled with the same color roses on the white tablecloth, the fine crystal and gold-plated flatware. So much beauty on the outside, but Belle was more injured by her father's disapproval than she'd let on while he was alive. "He was never that interested in the choices I made."

Isabel said, "You were lucky that way."

"I wouldn't call myself *lucky*."

"No, of course you're right. I only meant avoiding my dad's pressure."

Hadley studied them, first Natalie, then her aunt. "It sounds like you two grew up in different families."

AS SOON AS they got home, Hadley raced to her room.

"What are you up to?" Natalie asked, following her. She'd hoped that the two of them could watch one of their TV series together.

At her door, the girl pulled her arm at the elbow, as if stretching before a run. Another newly acquired hobby, thanks to Marc and Elizabeth's fitness routine. "Mom, still spying on me?"

"I'm just curious about you, that's all. I thought you didn't like that Sophie was hanging around Priscilla."

Hadley sighed and switched to her blasé, cool-girl voice. "Chill, Mom. Priscilla's fine. I'm not walking around high or binge drinking, because she has some power over me. Anyway, since Trump, they sell Klonopin in the school cafeteria."

"Very funny."

"Can I show Soph my new bag now?"

Natalie reached out and looped her daughter's arm around her in a reluctant hug. "Go to it," she said.

Alone in the hall, her eyes filled with moisture. Natalie recalled how, as a toddler, Hadley had developed the habit of sneaking into her parents' bedroom with her blankets, sheets, and floppy stuffed cow. One morning she woke to find her daughter's warm forehead touching her cheek; Hadley's breath came evenly, pushing out soft shushes. Her eyelids fluttered, and her small hand rested, as if in benediction, on the top of Moo's head. Hadley smiled at Natalie upon opening her eyes, and said, "Hi, Mommy. I miss you at night."

Time was a ruthless thief.

On her bed, Natalie checked her phone messages. There was nothing from Ellen. No email either. She wondered if she should call the police. Of course, that was an alarmist response. Isabel was probably right. The old woman was most likely on vacation. She noted the new emails: an inquiry about work, five political cries for donations, and one in her junk file from a bbGodfrey@gmail.

Natalie clicked on the unknown sender and read: *You were lied to about that night. Have you asked your sister about the blood on the car? The guy who was there knows.*

six

———

HUGE WINGS SEEMED TO FLAP IN NATALIE'S CHEST. SHE
experienced a blurry disorientation. Like the first walk down the
corridor of the hospital, after her concussion, with its chemical odors,
the sight of the patchy-skinned sick from their opened doors, the
grim discussions among the bevy of medical staff. She bolted out of
bed, bent her knees, squatting into a dip position, as if readying herself to fall on the ice. Leaning forward, fists on her floor, she breathed
deeply.

Get up. You're fine.

How was this person privy to her identity, her email address, her
relationship with Isabel, she wondered as she scuttled to the kitchen
to get a glass of water, an excuse to keep moving. Hadley, who was
most likely plugged into the synth and stomps of Beyoncé, wouldn't
hear her. Her mind charged with questions. The Caribbean night had
been so dark, and the only other car on the road had been Simon's.
Maybe another vehicle had arrived soon after they'd left the scene,
and the driver had noticed that someone was wounded, which somehow, the three of them had failed to see.

Exhale!

It could have been someone from the conference who'd recognized Isabel when they'd first left the party. This bbGodfrey could
have been following them, just not too closely, and gotten the license
plate number, tracking them down through the rental company. The
car had been registered in Isabel's name, so discovering Natalie's
connection was another loose end.

Why shadow Isabel? Why the spooky mystery?

Halfway down the hall, she spun around, dashed back to her computer, hit reply on her mail. *Who are you? What do you want?*

Then she typed into Google: "Car accidents in Grand Cayman," and filtered for November of this year. She read the one brief report: "Surgery for Motor Bike Rider." According to 27 News, an eighteen year old had been hospitalized after colliding, at 9:00 p.m., with a Jeep Cherokee on the East-West Arterial. There was a Royal Cayman Islands Police Service website that Natalie scanned. On the news link, she speed-read about crashes in other areas of the island than where they'd been heading, at various times of the day and on different dates. She skipped over passages but got the gist of what was on the screen. Nothing correlated with the night that she and Isabel had been driving from the Happiness cocktail party in the West Bay area of the island back to the Grand Reef Resort on the quieter East End. *Good. Good.*

Natalie changed the search phrase to include "hospital reports." The first result was a Wikipedia entry, followed by a list of irrelevant information. She tried "deaths on Grand Cayman," and extended the filter in case the victim took a while to die. *God, gruesome.* Nothing.

Her eyes burned. She hunted for the old eye drops—most likely expired—she kept for summer allergies in the hall bathroom. She passed Hadley's room again; the door was three-quarters shut, neither a deterrent nor a welcome sign. Natalie longed for a diversion, but she was too keyed up to engage in a casual conversation with her daughter. And it was still too early to say goodnight. While Natalie's pulse had been hurtling, time had slunk along. It was only 9:30 p.m. How could that be? There must be some equation in physics to explain this phenomenon.

She flipped on the light in the bathroom and avoided the mirror above the sink. She knew how she looked: wan, glassy-eyed. She searched the vanity cabinet for the eye drops. Inside, along with a communal box of tampons, was her panoply of over-the-counter medications for stomach upset and headaches, for sinus congestion and menstrual pain, sunscreen, and a tube of cortisone cream for her skin. Among the mess lay her Visine, like a tiny bowling pin knocked over.

Natalie uncapped the Visine and squeezed two drops in each eye. *Have you asked your sister about the blood on the car?*

Back on her bed, she pushed the star icon for "Favorites" on her phone. When Isabel picked up, she blurted out, "I got a really strange email. About the accident at the conference. It freaked me out."

"Nat, slow down," Isabel said. "Who was it from?"

"Someone named bbGodfrey. Do you know him?"

"Godfrey? No. I meet new people all the time, but I don't recall that name."

"He mentioned the guy on the road, Simon."

"That is creepy," Isabel said, her voice thicker.

"Did you ever call the police?"

"I told you I did. And you said you checked the newspapers?"

"Yes, nothing."

"The emailer could be some crazy stalker I upset."

"How would he know who we are or about the accident?"

Isabel hesitated. "It might be from someone who came to my lectures, who wanted to get my attention. Or who I unwittingly ignored. Simon could have mentioned it to anyone in passing."

"I'm upset."

Natalie wasn't certain, anymore, if she were referring to the message, that there had been a witness in the Caribbean, or to the rest of what she'd learned about herself, all the revelations like a girdle tightening around her, cutting off her air.

"Of course, you are. Listen, if this Godfrey contacts you again, we'll investigate. I'll take care of this, okay?"

"Yes," Natalie said with a rush of reassurance.

"NORWAY BEAT DENMARK in the Happiness ranks this year. It came in second, after Finland," Isabel announced from her seat on the desk. "My mother, Sigrid, was Norwegian, so it's a matter of national pride to me."

Natalie stiffened. The last time Isabel had opened up about Sigrid was two decades ago in their Cambridge apartment. One evening, Natalie recited the blurb on the back of a book she was reading. It was about a girl who'd been on a class trip when her mother was murdered.

Isabel had stopped eating their Chinese take-out, oily on her paper plate. "I was at nursery school and the classrooms were in a basement of a church that faced a cemetery. I tried very hard not to look at the graves. But sometimes, I'd do it anyway and get upset with myself for not being more careful. I'd made a valentine out of red felt for my mother even though it was April. She'd just gotten back home after traveling."

Natalie stayed very still, not wanting to cause a disruption. She asked, "Traveling?"

"To Norway, to visit her family. My dad said she'd needed 'time off' from me. Motherhood was too much for her. I'd been a colicky baby. My dad said she hadn't gotten sleep for months."

"But you wouldn't have had colic anymore at four."

Isabel shrugged. "Obviously. But, my father said, 'Don't cry when she comes home.' So, I didn't. She was home a few days and was supposed to come get me at school. I was so excited." Isabel's nostrils had flared. "But she didn't come for me. *Ellen* raced into the room."

Natalie knew the rest of the story. Instead of picking her daughter up at nursery school, Sigrid had a sudden cerebral aneurysm and died immediately.

Now Isabel uncrossed her legs and leaned her hands on her knees. Her voice lifted, no hint of sorrow there. She was herself again, not the girl in nursery school whose mother had forsaken her, not the graduate student who still felt the effects of that wreckage. Natalie's shoulders fell. Isabel had transcended a tragic history; so, could she. She had to believe that.

"Tonight, we're going to focus on some of the things we can learn from the countries that got the highest ratings from this year's World Happiness Report."

The man with the tortoise shell glasses and the messy hair cried out, "How does anyone quantify the mood of an entire country?"

Isabel laughed. "I can hand out the OECD's two-hundred-page package, which will explain the qualitative and quantitative indicators used, Mr. Sonnenberg."

He waved this away. "Jeremy," he said. "Don't you chalk up the good mood of the Scandinavians to their excellent social programs, great healthcare, family leave, free higher education, the whole she-bang?"

"Absolutely. There's a section this year on how the United States has fallen from third place to nineteenth."

Hands on knees, he said, "No surprise why. Positive thinking, what we're learning here, is all about one's attitude, not real-world problems."

Natalie listened to this interaction, her attention dragged down like a flat stone skimming a lake until it sank into the muck below. She pulled out her phone and checked her email messages, as she did hourly: nothing from Ellen. Nothing from bbGodfrey. The *what did I do?* chorus temporarily silenced.

"I'm not talking about denial," Isabel said after Jeremy recited the litany of the country's ills. Natalie realized she was nodding as his list lengthened, like a string of spittle from a sick man's mouth.

"Don't you think this excessive navel gazing—all our selfies and Facebook posts and Instagram pictures—have led us to this predicament?" he asked.

Isabel shook her head. "You are conflating self-care with selfishness."

Prama said, "You can't just stare at the duhkha, you have to work through it. Find those doing good in the world, the light that has been turned on in the darkness."

Oh, for fuck's sake.

Natalie locked eyes with Jeremy who was making small circles around his ear: cuckoo.

The college girl called out, "What about those of us who struggle with mental health issues?"

Yes! Or worse, so much worse. Natalie thought of those brains with the black smudges, the marks of a killer. *That could be me.*

"That's an excellent question, Ms. Anshaw."

Isabel referred to studies, quoted statistics and promised that, utilizing cognitive techniques, anyone could reign in personal demons and "enjoy their lives."

How? How? How?

Natalie had asked herself that question so often, over the decades, it creaked, worn and overused, like an old rope bridge. Did she even deserve contentment?

After the group ended, Natalie lingered behind with the usual crew of women. "I was surprised you brought up your mom," she said as soon as she had her stepsister's ear. Once again, they huddled on the other side of the room and spoke in low voices.

Isabel nodded. "I surprised myself. I've been going over this business with Ellen so much, my mom's been on my mind. I don't think there was anything sexual between my dad and Ellen. But maybe my dad had an emotional affair with her. Maybe that was part of the reason my mother needed to get away, to visit her family."

Natalie reached for Isabel's hand. "You think Ellen was a problem for *your* mom too?"

"Yes. I think Ellen was an issue in both of my father's marriages.

Anyway, I should go talk to Prama before she loses her Zen." She winked. "Let me know if that nut job emails you again."

"Oh, I will."

When Natalie left, she found Jeremy Sonnenberg still in the vestibule, looking out the door's glass panels. He wore a long rancher's sheepskin coat with the fur-lined collar pulled up and a turtleneck sweater underneath.

"Hi," Natalie said.

He swung around. "Hey, I was waiting for you. Time for coffee?"

She felt a twitch of pleasure. "Sorry, I have to get home."

"Ah, my big mouth got me in trouble again. I admit I got carried away. I promise to reign it in next time."

She smiled. "You were a bit of a hog. But that's not the reason. I have to get back to my daughter."

"Babysitter waiting?"

"Ha, no. Hadley's fifteen. I don't want to leave her too late, though."

"Wow. Did you have Hadley when you were in Kindergarten?"

Natalie liked that he'd repeated her daughter's name. He was listening. "Nope, second grade."

"Overachiever I see. I'm Jeremy. Well, you know that." When she introduced herself, "Natalie Greene," he asked, "I'm headed to the T, you?" She nodded. "Walk together?"

"Sure."

The wind was a bully swatting her across the cheeks, pulling her hair in front of her face. She hurried east, towards the Orange line. "How about you—any kids?"

"Nope. Just a Golden named Reed, a Retriever, not one of those fancy doodle dogs."

"I love Doodles."

Jeremy slapped his hands over his heart in mock pretense.

"All Retrievers. I swear! They're my favorite."

"Reed's a good boy. Do you have a dog?"

"No, my husband—soon to be ex, isn't a dog person."

"Sorry to hear, the dog, not the ex. If you don't mind me saying that. No harassment, I swear."

She laughed. "I think, legally, you're fine."

"So—clever change of subject here—how'd you hear about this workshop?"

"Isabel's my stepsister." When his eyes widened, she said, "Please don't tell anyone else in the group."

"Not a problem. I don't talk to Prama or Feather or Hemp."

She deadpanned, "I'm pretty sure there's no Hemp."

"Okay. Virasana."

"Ah. I see you're not a yoga virgin."

"Only a couple of times, very painful. Got stuck in pigeon pose, needed to be airlifted out, limped for a week."

She laughed. "Duly noted, no pigeon poses."

"No cat or cow either. The animals are dangerous. I'm wondering if it violates some shrink code, though, you being a relative."

"Isabel wouldn't do anything unethical."

"What about selling her wares at the group?" Her book and journal and *Happiness Doctor* mugs in daisy yellow and Aegean Sea-blue. Trying to promote her brand, please her publicist, "play the game."

Natalie said, "There's nothing wrong with that, everyone does it. The Obamas got a zillion dollar advance for their memoirs, and they are the good guys. Sickening, though."

"Yep, pretty disgusting. Anyway, sorry. You guys are on the same team."

"This isn't a sport," she said, thinking of Marc and his team building.

Jeremy's face glowed under the pharmacy's lights. "I do find Dr. Walker's ideas seductive. We're in charge of our own destinies. Changing our outlooks can alter our lives."

"I'm sensing a 'but.'"

"I don't believe that being an optimist guarantees love, or a living wage, or affordable health insurance. Especially now, in this country, and this city. It just strikes me as smug, the idea that pessimists cause their own diseases and bad fortune."

Natalie started walking again, chased by the cold. "That's not what Isabel believes. But there are plenty of studies on how attitude affects your health."

She felt the thrum of her heart.

"It's hard to be jubilant when you're ill and can't pay for a doctor or medicine or are unemployed or homeless."

She heard Hadley's voice, "White privilege, Mom."

"Agree. I'm lucky," Natalie said. She wasn't going to reveal that, without Marc's monthly payments, she'd be living far away from Boston, that once the divorce was finalized, she'd be strapped for money. She thought of the high sticker price for the workshop, which she couldn't pay, but Jeremy obviously could. Noting his expensive leather getup, the Frye boots and jacket, she said, "You look like you do okay for yourself."

"Don't be deceived," he said. "I come from a long line of indigent cowboys—Montana cattlemen."

"Uh huh. So why did you join the group if you're so cynical, Mr. Cowboy?"

"You first."

Natalie peered into the pearl-gray sky spotted by snowfall. "It's been tough since separating from my husband. Then my stepfather died; brought up old things."

Accompanying her stepsister to Grand Cayman, which stirred up the misery of many names.

"Dr. Walker's father died recently? I'm sorry to hear—"

"Don't say a word. I shouldn't have blurted that out. Anyway, I thought I'd give Isabel's techniques a try. Up my serotonin levels or whatever levels need upping."

He inched closer, slapped his gloves together. "Wouldn't it be better to see someone more. . . qualified?"

"You mean a shrink, that first world luxury?"

Jeremy's eyes rested on her for a moment. "Touché. I won't say another word. Sisters, huh? I don't see the resemblance."

"We're not technically related."

"Right. Stepsister. Gotta remember that."

They were standing next to the Copley station entranceway. Natalie hugged her arms tightly, second-guessing herself for confiding in him. "Why'd you drop so much cash on something you think is bullshit?"

He grinned and his sword of justice fell away. "Just a little personal investigating."

Her throat felt constricted. What if the Cayman police had contacted him about the crash? "Are you a detective?"

He laughed. "Just a working stiff, ma'am. See you next week?"

"Yes. Goodnight."

Seven

———

"DON'T OVERREACT," SHE QUOTED MARC TO HERSELF.

Natalie was alone in the kitchen the following morning. Her suspicions about Jeremy seemed farfetched now, the chance he had a connection to bbGodfrey or knowledge about the crash in the Grand Caymans. "Personal investigating," was a cryptic description. It could mean anything.

Natalie rinsed out her daughter's cereal bowl with the puddle of milk and floating flakes, the spoon resting on the side like an oar. Coffee cup and breakfast bar in hand, she sat at the butcher-block table. It had been scarred over the years by knives and pens, and she stared at these marks as if answers were encoded in them. Forget the email for now, the island mishap. What were Ellen and Garrick's roles in both his wives' deaths? Maybe Ellen hadn't sent the envelope out of fear there was something that would incriminate her tucked away inside it.

Natalie sipped the still burning drink. When she was old enough to wonder, she'd asked her mother about Sigrid, poking around for clues about this mysterious figure that the family never mentioned. Laura answered, "She came here from a place called Bergen, to go to college. In the winter, the sun is out for less than six hours where she grew up. I think that must be very hard. It can make a person feel sad."

Natalie had pictured a woman with delicate features like Isabel, with the hair and skin of an albino from living in the dark. "Was she happier here, with more sun?"

Her mother's response was sucked up into that void of lost memories.

About a year before her mom's accident, Natalie had been loung-
ing on the couch, book in hand. Isabel was next to her, painting her
toenails so expertly not a drop of the polish spilled on the fabric. Above
Isabel's head hung a Kandinsky lithograph, all sharp angles and lines in
rich colors. If Natalie looked at it too long, it made her dizzy.

They heard her mother's voice from another room: "Half a pill!
Don't confuse me with Sigrid."

Garrick said, "Shush, the girls can hear you."

"What does he mean?" Natalie whispered to Isabel.

Isabel clasped her arms to her chest and rolled her eyes so that
only the whites showed, then shuddered, as if convulsing.

"Zombies?"

"Crazy!"

"Why does your dad think your mom was crazy?"

Isabel had shrugged. "Better than blaming himself."

Natalie typed in "aneurysms" on her phone. High blood pressure
could cause them, and severe stress contributed to high blood pressure. Theoretically, Ellen's relationship with Garrick could have killed
Sigrid. Natalie bit into the peanut butter bar with its medicinal after-
taste. She'd been patient. She wanted answers now.

She tried the secretary's home number and, as usual, it rang un-
abatedly. Just as she was about to hang up, a young-sounding woman
answered, "Alden residence." This was followed by the sucking sound
of a yawn.

Finally!

"Is Miss Alden there?"

"No, uh. . . ." Natalie heard a rustling sound, then a thump. "Hold
on. I don't know how to work this machine. It's, like, from the Juras-
sic Age. Okay, I'm turning it off for good. Jesus. She isn't here."

Who was this, then, the housekeeper or dog walker? "Do you
know when she'll be back?"

"It's open-ended."

"Would this evening be better?"

"Uh, try in, like, three months."

"Months?" Natalie's eyes flew to the time indicator in the corner of her computer screen as if it would measure the twelve weeks in minutes.

"She's on vacation."

"I wouldn't bother her if it wasn't important."

"Are you from the law school?"

"Indirectly. I know her through the university."

"Uh, huh." The girl paused, as if considering. "She's visiting her friend who moved to Costa Rica. She plans a long stay, playing it by ear."

A young house sitter then? "I can't wait that long."

"Sorry. She retired, so she's not obligated to you guys anymore. She deserves this time to chill."

"Well, maybe, I could reach Ellen there." Natalie heard a dog's triad of barks in the background.

"They're in the Galapagos. The Wi-Fi is non-existent." The barking increased in intensity. "I gotta take out Malcolm. He's old, can't hold it in."

"The thing is, I'm looking for something she was supposed to send me. It's pretty urgent," Natalie insisted. Maybe if this kid thought it was a legal brief, she'd take her request more seriously. "There aren't any documents she left at home by mistake, are there?"

"Not that I've seen. Ellen's really careful about work stuff, super organized and reliable. Which you should know if you're at the university."

"Yes, I just meant, because she was leaving."

"That she flaked out?"

"Of course not. Can you give me the tracking number so I can hunt this down?"

"I wouldn't know where she keeps anything like that. Anyway, I promised not to bother her unless there was, like, a major emergency. You need to ask the department. Ugh, gotta go. Malcolm just peed. If Ellen checks in, I'll tell her you called."

After hanging up the phone, Natalie realized the girl hadn't taken down her name. Or asked for it. She tried back, but the phone rang and rang. Even if she did reach this girl again, it was doubtful she'd pass on her message while Ellen was in the Galapagos.

An impasse. *Damn.*

She dumped her mug into the sink, the wrapper in the garbage.

Natalie had time before she needed to leave for her studio. What she didn't want was to ruminate in her apartment, which was so quiet she could hear the ticking of her thoughts. They hurt, as if coming in thrusts, muscular punches. She could listen to Isabel's *Wired Happy* app, a massage for the mind. But what she craved was the sound of laughter, a hand covering hers, eyes alight.

She imagined Cate, her friend since childhood, with her vivid smile, who always smelled of cinnamon and nutmeg from her job managing Brookline's herb and spice store. By high school the normal chatter and giggles of friendship, the politics of seating in the cafeteria, the exchange of notes and passing of Tic Tacs in class, the choosing a lab partner in Bio, all these interactions had felt unendurable to Natalie. She lacked the swagger and daring of the other girls. But Cate McAllister persisted, inviting her to sleepovers, meals, even holiday parties with boisterous relatives. At the McAllisters', Natalie never felt like Jane Eyre locked in the red room.

Cate had moved back to the Boston area after college in the Midwest, married, eventually settled in Brookline, and had three sons. Her home was teeming with neighbors and friends of her boys, her vegetable garden abundant with Crayola red-orange tomatoes and peppers with skin shiny as rain slickers.

Natalie had avoided reaching out since the conference. She'd retreated into her worries. *Egocentric?* One characteristic wasn't enough to doom her. She dialed her friend's number and heard the lilt and laughter in Cate's message. She said, "Call me when you get a chance."

An hour later at her studio, Natalie was fixing the white balance, highlights, and shadows on the image of a strawberry crêpe, when her phone rang. Normally, she'd ignore the interruption. But Caller ID read: "Spice It Up."

Natalie pushed the green button with the image of a receiver on it. "Hey!"

"Hey, kiddo! Haven't heard from you in forever. I wanted to give you space after Garrick . . . you know."

You know how you get.

"I'm sorry. It's been hectic."

"How was your vacation?" Cate gasped, as if she'd rubbed through to a winning number on a lottery ticket. "The island is supposed to be beautiful."

"It is," Natalie said quickly. "You won't believe what I did. I joined one of Belle's workshops."

"Good for you!" Cate had talked to Isabel at a local reading of *Get Happy Now*. While signing copies of the book, they'd discussed crystals and herbs, joked about how Cate had gone "all Wiccan." She hadn't, of course. But Cate *did* meditate, journal, and adhere to a vegan diet.

"Neuroscience of spirituality is all the rage now. It might help," Cate said. "What else have you been up to?"

"You mean besides resetting my brain's neural pathways?" Natalie said.

"Ha! That would explain why you've been so busy," Cate laughed. "Resetting can be very time consuming."

"Yes." Natalie stared at the vibrant red strawberry slices on the side of the plate, the swirl topping the crêpe, all the effort it took to get the best image. "I'd love to catch up. Are you free to get coffee at Mindy's Corner after dinner?"

"Only if you split a dessert."

~

MINDY'S CORNER COFFEE SHOP was in a perpetual state of disrepair. The red vinyl seats on the booths were ripped and patched with gray duct tape. The walls were decorated with landscapes that could only have been found at the bottom of a sales bin at Stop & Shop. Even the waitress, with her puffy eyelids and tight lips painted with candy pink lipstick, looked as if she could use renovation. But the food—home-cooked bread, thick slices of turkey breast, flaky crusted pie—was wonderful.

Natalie arrived first and chose a booth near the front window so that her friend would see her immediately. The seat's jagged edge of torn fabric gnawed into her thighs. She tapped her fingers on the table, calibrating how much to divulge, what not to say. Her friend resided in a moral universe populated by decent people not undone by calamities of their own making.

Cate rushed through the door in her bulky down jacket and distressed leather boots. She wasn't wearing any pentagram jewelry or black lipstick or a purple, hooded cape. She wasn't a Wiccan practitioner carrying a satchel of crystals, but an upper-middle class Bostonian mom who used hair gel to keep her long brown curls from frizzing and 100 SPF sunscreen on her freckled face to ward off skin cancer. She was carrying an expensive Frye pocketbook.

"Sorry," Cate said. "Had to sign two homework thing-a-ma-jigs at the last minute, then Danny couldn't find his math book, which only I had the magic power to do, and then Foxy threw up on the rug." Foxy was the family's Collie-Husky mix.

"No problem," Natalie said with a flutter of longing. How she coveted Cate's happy, messy family life. How she wanted not to be this person, envious of those she loved. "I just got here."

Cate unwound the wool scarf from her neck and ripped off her jacket. "So great to see you."

"You, too."

The waitress moved quickly on her thick, short legs. "What can I get you ladies?"

Cate exclaimed, "I've gained six pounds cooking for Thanksgiving. But I'm dying for the winter fruit pie. Can I have that and a decaf?"

"I don't see why not," the waitress said. "And you, dear?" she asked Natalie, who ordered chamomile tea.

When the waitress headed back to the counter, Cate grinned, causing laugh lines and crow's feet to burgeon. "Thanksgiving weekend was crazy. Matt's sisters and their families flew in from Seattle, and Richard and his wife and two kids. We had people sleeping everywhere. Tess pulled out her back from the couch—you know the one in our den? It broke! The springs gave out when the poor thing was asleep. She was literally bent over for days."

Natalie listened to the escapades of Cate's holiday with her husband, Matt; his sister, Tess; Cate's brother, Richard; the eleven children, the tumble and roar of a packed house. She pictured the living room: the battered sofa with kids' sneakers poking out of the skirted bottom, children's schoolbooks flung on the coffee table, photographs of the family lining the fireplace mantel along with candles in glass holders. There would be suitcases open to reveal rumpled clothes, sheets and blankets draped on furniture. The home would be fragrant from the meals brewing in Cate's slow cooker, sage, thyme, leeks, and parsnips.

Envy was a toxic arrow to the chest. Energy-sapping, bad for wellbeing and relationships. What would Isabel advise?

"You're so lucky to have them," Natalie said.

"I am, I know. You're lucky to have Hadley and Belle."

Yes! I am!

The waitress appeared with a slice of the dessert and two mugs. "Here you go, ladies."

"Thanks," Cate said. "Yum. I don't know how you resist eating this."

"Do I look like I resist?" The waitress pinched a roll of skin around her waist.

"You look great," Cate touched the woman on her arm.

Natalie smiled and agreed weakly, "You do."

But she was a terrible liar. Really, she meant the compliment for Cate with her clever eyes and mutable face registering every glimmer of emotion.

"You gals are too kind." The waitress winked and strutted back to the counter, the nylon pants stretched tight across her butt.

Cate stuck her fork through the thick helmet of crust. "Enough about me. Tell me everything that's been going on."

"I don't want to dump on you so much." Since Marc's departure, Natalie had been careful not to lean too heavily on her friend, not be that girl again whose skin felt burnt raw and blistering.

"You know you always can, no matter what—even if I'm so over-loaded with relatives they're hanging off the roof." Cate slid the plate to Natalie and frowned. "Eat some. You look like you lost weight."

She had. The skin around Natalie's waist felt tight as if sewn to the bone. The narrow pouch of fat that had stretched around her waist since Hadley's birth, was deflated. "Just a few pounds." She lifted a bite of the pie onto her fork.

"I feel like a cow, yet here I am with no willpower. See, that's something you don't want, believe me." Cate patted her stomach, well hidden by one of her usual bulky sweaters. She had a slight paunch from giving birth to three sons weighing in at over eight pounds each. Natalie loved the way her friend looked, but Cate was in awe of Natalie's extra six inches of height. "Are you all right, I mean with the holidays and Garrick's death . . ."

"I'm fine, even if my life has become a soap opera."

"I love soaps! You know I was addicted to *The Guiding Light* all through high school. What's going on?"

Natalie took a sip of her tepid tea. "It wasn't a big deal at the time, but . . ." She described the accident, the message, and Isabel's take on it.

"That *is* totally bizarre," Cate agreed. "And creepy. Isabel's probably right, that the email was from a disgruntled fan, someone wanting attention. Occam's razor. The simplest solution tends to be true."

"That doesn't explain what the person saw. What if it wasn't a dog I hit? What if, in that split second when I couldn't see anything, a body flew into the bushes?"

"You would have felt the impact."

"It happened so quickly. I was being so careful, going slowly. It was *his* headlights."

"I'm sure, it wasn't your fault." Cate tilted her head, her eyes large and warm and seeking goodness. "I've been with you in a car. You go forty miles an hour on a highway."

"That's an exaggeration!"

"I'm not judging. It's just the way it is. You're afraid of speed. You were a fantastic skater and gymnast. But when Mrs. Corrigan asked if you wanted to join the gymnastic team you said no, you didn't want to get hurt."

"That was because of Ally Lee!" Natalie cried. A girl in the high school who fell on the uneven bars during a competition with another school and took a semester to recover. "I agreed, if Corrigan needed someone on the mat."

Cate laughed. "I know. You didn't want to be on the uneven bars, even though you were amazing."

"I couldn't deal with that," Natalie said and stared at her yellow-ish tea, "not after everything."

"*Exactly.* You wanted control after your mom died. No one could blame you for that."

Years ago, she'd revealed to Cate the ritual she'd performed after her mother's death, one that continued until pregnancy, when her body changed in ways she could no longer govern. She'd observe herself in the mirror each morning and run her hands down her stomach, the insides of her thighs, the cords in her neck. It had been important to check that she was lean and fit, ready to out-chase disaster. People could disappear in a flash. The body was just a vessel, one that required vigilant attention. The touch of her own skin and muscles had pacified her. She'd told Cate and no one else, not even Isabel, whom she didn't want to worry further. Certainly not Marc.

Natalie asked, "Was I like that before my mom died, a control freak?"

Cate closed one eye as if to improve her vision into the past. "Never a freak. You were prepared and focused, not afraid. You did double axels like a pro."

"I've been trying to get those six months back, the ones leading up to when my mom died. I'm wondering if I seemed already different to you before, more stressed than usual?"

"Umm. You were private about what went on at home. But, yeah, you seemed tense."

"Did I ever say anything about going to boarding school?"

"What?" Cate asked, voice pitched high. "Nothing like that. Why?"

"I had a weird memory." Natalie lied, glimpsing at the rooster clock on the wall behind the counter. She couldn't risk losing Cate's respect. "I probably mixed things up."

"You were worried about your mom. You said she and your stepdad were fighting a lot."

"Was I fighting with my mom, too?"

"Not that you told me."

"Anything else . . . from that time?"

"You did say you overheard your mom and stepdad arguing about her taking pills." There was a nervous edge to Cate's tone. "You were scared about that, that something bad would happen to her."

"I guess I was right. It was a self-fulfilling prophecy."

"That's not what I mean. Your mom, that wasn't your fault."

Wasn't it?

eight

ON CHRISTMAS DAY, NATALIE WAS ALONE. ISABEL AND GEORGE had invited her along to George's parents' home in Wellesley, but she'd declined. There was only so much charity she could accept and, truthfully, she preferred her plan: eating leftovers while binging on Lifetime movies about single corporate managers hitting their heads and waking up in another life as a wife and mother, humble and happy. These sorts of mindless films would run one after the other, blotting out the hours.

Natalie had spent the night before with her sister and brother-in-law, a quiet dinner, prepared by Fresh Direct. Since Hadley was born, this had been the tradition. Her husband and Isabel tolerated each other, but Marc adored George. His brother-in-law, with the spiffy Harvard MD and comprehensive understanding of the nervous system, would ask Marc to reset the cable box or rejigger the mail program on his iPhone, and they'd discuss the newest MacBook Pros. Was Marc helping Elizabeth's brother or uncle or mother with their gadgets now?

Even before the anemic sun tapped the window with its fingers, Natalie was inspecting her phone for texts from Hadley. The last one from her daughter she'd already seen: *Merry Xmas Eve. All good. The cousins are nice.* Nice was bland and unrevealing, meant to avoid stoking pain in Natalie. Hadley had exhibited her practiced nonchalance, shrugs and slumping shoulders, and monosyllabic answers if prodded about how she felt. This would be her first time spending the holidays surrounded by strangers. But Natalie knew.

The single child role in the family, Hadley was bestowed with lonely "princess" status. Isabel always lavished her with expensive gifts: a collectible Barbie in a pink satin gown, a signed first edition of *Harry Potter and the Sorcerer's Stone,* a bison leather backpack. She'd engaged her in discussions of her favorite characters, starting with Ariel from *The Little Mermaid,* then Meg from *A Wrinkle in Time,* and, of course, Hermione Granger—right up to Emma Woodhouse. But still, there were no cousins, no brothers or sisters.

So, the prospect of Elizabeth's relatives, the promise of nephews and nieces close to her in age, caused Hadley to squeal on the phone. "There are, like, dozens of them. No idea. Could be hot. Are there hot guys in Ohio?"

Natalie stared at the screen. Nothing new from her girl yet— well, for God's sake, it was too early. Marc was supposed to bring Hadley back in the evening so she could go to Sophie's annual party, but still—she'd be in Brookline, in Natalie's territory.

There was the usual junk in her inbox along with a Season's Greetings e-card. It was a photo of a sliced fruitcake laid out on a holly-lined platter with the text: *To my favorite Food Mortician. Hope to see you again soon. XO, Simon.*

Natalie grinned and slid her hand under her pajama pants. She might be a mortician, but she wasn't dead. But, then, she stopped herself. The email address. No, it wasn't bbGodfrey. Of course not. She typed the words she hadn't meant to say. *What does the guy on the road know?* Just as she was about to hit send, she saved to drafts instead.

Take a breath. Don't get mixed up with this man.

Natalie pressed the ten-minute meditation setting on the *Wired Happy* app. Seated on her bed against her backrest, she started the relaxation routine. Her legs were slightly apart, arms away from her body. Her shoulders sank and her feet flopped to either side of her. She "observed the belly as it rose and fell. You are being healed, cradled by the sky. You are floating on the wind." She felt the strain in her muscles lessen and focused hard on pushing away the clack and clutter of her thoughts.

Isabel's voice called her listeners to attention with the swirl of chimes, the swish of a breeze. "Imagine you are in a place you love."

That would be her childhood home when her mother was still alive, the two girls decorating the Christmas tree, always a tall, dignified pine whose long branches swooped into the air. She and Isabel hung the strands of popcorn and tinsel, the candy canes, and the red and green balls. Isabel would unwrap the two glass figurines that had belonged to Sigrid's family in Norway. One was female with long yellow hair and wings so sheer they seemed like they might break just from the weight of fingers pressing against them. The other was an elf with a round belly, a white beard, and a red pointed hat with a tiny Norwegian flag in its hand.

A dull beeping replaced the hypnotic sounds. Natalie opened her eyes. She'd forgotten to turn off her phone and saw her daughter's name and number on the screen. It was only 7:45 a.m. Quickly, Natalie paused the meditation. "Hads, you okay?"

"Can you come get me soon?" Her daughter's voice was small but serrated with anger.

"I thought you were having fun with Elizabeth's relatives."

"Yeah, I was."

"What happened?"

"I just want to come home."

Natalie swung her legs over the bed. "Did Dad say it was okay?"

"I don't give a shit what Dad says."

"Hads, what's wrong?"

"Dad asked Elizabeth to marry him at midnight."

Natalie gasped, the sound of a swimmer who'd held her breath under water too long. Her eyes darted around the room at yesterday's coffee cup and the heap of pants on the floor. A sweater had caught in the drawer of her dresser, a black bit of wool peeking out. She'd been passing a house aglow with holiday lights when her husband had proposed to another woman. Was Marc a polygamist now?

"We aren't divorced yet."

"I *know,* Mom."

"He did this in front of you?"

"I was in my room."

Her room. As if Hadley lived in this other house.

"I saw it this morning, the ring."

"I'm on my way," Natalie said.

SHE DROVE THROUGH her ex's quiet suburb, wiping her eyes and nose on the sleeve of her jacket. Sobs burst forth, as if a valve had loosened in her.

Up the block from the house, she parked the car without turning off the engine. She texted Hadley, *I'm here.* When she received the response, *K, coming,* she eased her car forward. She stared at the twin pine trees guarding the red door. The house itself was the creamy white of a wedding cake. Why hadn't she noticed this before? The trees were the bride and groom figures. For their ceremony, she and Marc had opted for a dessert buffet of cookies and petit fours. But would Elizabeth wish to go the more conventional route: a tiered cake with garlands piped into the fondant? Maybe they'd marry in a quaint colonial church, the pews filled with her legion of relatives. The family he'd never had and had sworn he neither missed nor yearned for.

Natalie wanted to shatter the engagement ring with a hammer—while it was on Elizabeth's finger. She wanted to smash every digit of the woman's hands, so she'd keep them off of her husband. She thought of those black spaces on the Pet Scan images and didn't care if her own brain lacked cheerier colors.

Natalie closed her eyes. *You are being renewed and regenerated.* When she opened them again, Hadley was on the pathway, Marc by her side. She clenched her hands together. *You are being eviscerated, crushed into dust.*

Hadley tugged at her hair as she walked. "Thanks, Mom," she said as she slid into the passenger seat, backpack by her feet. She quickly closed the door, a gesture of solidarity.

At her window, Marc knocked lightly. Natalie noted with satisfaction that his face was rounder and his chin less defined than the last time she'd seen him. "Elizabeth loves to bake," Hadley had announced. "If I lived there, I'd have a stroke from all the fattening crap."

Maybe Marc would have that stroke.

Natalie pushed on the button until the glass slid an inch down, no more, as if face-to-face with a dangerous criminal.

"Sorry you had to come all the way out here," he said. "I would have brought her back."

"Obviously, she didn't want to stay till you were ready."

"I guess Hads told you our news."

Our.

She felt so diminished, a speck of a woman viewed from an ascending plane.

"Yep. Didn't know you were into sister wives."

"Huh?" A look of confusion flashed over his eyes.

"Polygamy, Dad. It's a Mormon thing."

"Obviously, I mean, we're waiting till after the divorce," he stammered. "Elizabeth is fine with a long engagement."

"I'm so relieved," Natalie said, above the Congo drum of her heart. "Are you for real, Marc?"

"I was going to tell you myself."

Hadley raised her voice. "Can we go now?"

"Sure can," Natalie said.

She tore from the curb without waiting for Marc to say goodbye.

Hadley slid her seat to a reclining position, everything long, legs and neck, mass of curly hair. She shut her eyes, not even bothering to stick in her ear buds. "Maybe I won't go to Sophie's party tonight."

"You're definitely going."

"Mom, what about you?"

"Jessa invited me to come over," she lied. "She's having some friends for dinner." Jessa, the food stylist she worked with, who would be spending the day with her husband, child, and in-laws. Natalie was determined, no matter what it entailed, not to be a burden to her child. She would not be the stone around Hadley's neck pulling her to the ocean floor.

"I like her. She's good for you, Mom."

Natalie noted her daughter's sad smile and felt wounded for her.

LATER THAT EVENING, after her daughter was gone, Natalie dragged her quilt from her bed to the couch and draped it over her knees. Dust particles danced under the standing lamp. The area rug revealed a hole the size of a quarter. There was none of the adornment—stockings and garlands, wreaths and potted poinsettias—she envisioned at Elizabeth's house.

She reached for her phone, paused a moment, then sent Simon a different message, one of her photos of Crème Brûlée, the torched burnt sugar on top, a spoonful of the rich, luscious custard scooped out. *Happy Holidays to you, too* was all she wrote.

Isabel was at a celebration in Beacon Hill given by George's wealthy colleague at Mass General. She would be standing in the living room of the doctor's row house, champagne flute in hand, perhaps wearing her new snakeskin pumps. Isabel's cell would be tucked away in her leather clutch. There was a good chance she wouldn't even hear Natalie's distress signal.

She texted: *Marc proposed to E.*

Immediately: *What? Sister Wives!*

Laughter bubbled up. Natalie drew the phone closer to her face.

She typed back: *Sorry to bother u @ soiree.*

Please. All beta-amyloid & tangle talk. Sushi good though.

U talking to big docs?

Isabel sent an emoji of a toilet. *Conversing with nice towels, Matouk, EC, very fancy.*

Here Natalie had pictured her stepsister in a glamorous pose when she was with her panties around her ankles, peeing in an upscale bathroom. *EC?*

Egyptian cotton.

She smiled at the thought of Isabel checking the labels for fabric, trying to distract her. *So sick of Marc. Ready to start over.*

Good! Isabel shot back with an accompanying smiley face.

Thx for helping me rewire my pathways!

Ha!

Enjoy dementia.

Love you.

You too.

She turned on the television and flipped through the channels. There were hundreds, newscasts and football games, reruns of *NCIS* and *Storage Wars*, endless movies with Santa, elves, and Scrooge in the titles. Changing images quickly was relaxing, like staring at a hypnotic black and white spiral. It was a quirky habit Marc found endearing until he didn't.

For years, they'd sit together on the couch, watching either the news or a dramatic series they'd stream. Some nights he rubbed her feet, others she draped her legs over his lap, and that was enough. She should have suspected he was already gone when he positioned his computer across his thighs, leaving no room for her. She'd had trouble deciding among all the services to which he now subscribed.

"What can you possibly be looking for?" he'd asked during the final months. "That you haven't passed over ten times already?"

Even though she'd switched off the heat, Natalie was perspiring. The blood was hissing in her veins. Would Hadley be in the wedding, a bridesmaid in a pastel pink dress with a crinoline and lace hat chosen by Elizabeth? Would Natalie be required to take her daughter shopping for her husband's wedding, or would Elizabeth micromanage, schlepping Hadley to bridal boutiques on Newbury Street and beyond?

When her front bell rang, Natalie startled. She wondered if Hadley, upset with Sophie again, had gotten a ride home.

"Who is it?" she asked into the intercom.

"It's me," Isabel said.

"Hey, what are you doing here?" Natalie buzzed her in, almost giddy with gratitude.

She opened the door and peered out into the hall.

And there was Isabel in a liquid silver cocktail dress under her unbuttoned calfskin coat, the scent of her perfume filling the vestibule. "I come bearing gifts. Merry Christmas!"

She smiled, motioning to her stepsister. "Don't be silly. You gave me that wonderful book last night. And that incredible bag for Hadley at Thanksgiving, which she can't get over."

Natalie's gift was an edited version of a landmark book, a tribute to a famous photographer. She'd rifled through the pages of erotic portraits, many of bare breasted, ropey-thin women. She stopped when she came to a nude model lying in bed, the sheets stripped away. This image, the hollow of the belly under the ribcage, the long legs and swing of hair, kindled something in her.

"Your mom loved her work," Isabel said. "We cracked up when she dragged us to that exhibit of the nudes. You were only eleven, but I was old enough to behave."

Her mother, at the museum, lozenges of light on the pine floors from the slatted window roof, pointing to the pictures hanging in front of them. "Now these are art."

Natalie had giggled at the sight of the woman's asymmetrical breasts, the nipples staring straight at them, like a horse's eyes. Next to her, Isabel had squeezed her hand and mouthed, "So gross."

Now, Isabel reached out her palm upon which sat a small box wrapped in holiday paper. "Go ahead, take it."

Natalie tore off the red ribbon and twinkly foil. Inside was a velvet box that sprang open to reveal a black stone with a greenish tint, held in place by a wispy white band. "Jesus, Belle!"

"It's actually not Jesus. It's just a diamond. I didn't think a clear one was appropriate. But you deserve one more than the woman I shall not name."

"I can't keep this. It must have cost a fortune."

"Not so much," Isabel waved away the discussion of money. "Anyway, it's for fun. You can always take it off when you start entertaining gentleman callers."

Natalie laughed at the Katharine Hepburn imitation. She slipped the ring on her finger and held out her hand in front of her. Her eyes brimmed again. "How did you manage this? All the stores are closed."

"I got it last summer and was waiting till the right time, when you were ready to ditch Marc. I had it fitted for you. The band was too big. But you always had the tiniest fingers."

AFTER NATALIE WALKED her stepsister to the stairs in her building, she paused on the landing. She remembered hearing that phrase before: *the tiniest fingers.*

So many years ago. The sound of howling had woken her in the night. When Natalie tiptoed towards Isabel's room, she'd realized the noise was coming from the TV, one of those horror movies her stepsister loved. She'd edged open the door to see Isabel lying on her stomach on her area rug. A pile of clothing towered near the bed. It was a worse mess than usual: dirty sneakers under a standing lamp, schoolbooks scattered all over the floor, a mug with the residue of milk in it, and a plate with crumbs balanced precariously on a canvas chair.

"Shush," Isabel whispered and hopped up. She took Natalie by the hand. "Let's get a snack."

They padded their way into the Newton kitchen with the canary-yellow wall phone, which matched the sunflower wallpaper and the canvas on the stool seats. Natalie poured milk into a bowl of Honeycomb cereal. Isabel swiped a dishcloth from the handle of the refrigerator and tortured it into a tight knot. She was barefoot, her toes polished a blackish red color so that they looked banged up.

"She wants us to be apart, but I won't let her."

"You sure the school was my mom's idea?" Natalie asked. Her gut was bunched up like the towel.

"Of course," Isabel said, leaning on the Formica countertop. "Laura makes all the important decisions. My dad would never come up with it."

"But things aren't that bad, are they?"

"She said it would be better for you, 'a calmer environment.' Those are the words she used."

Natalie couldn't let the riptide of fear pull her under. "I'll tell her that's not true."

Isabel picked up a dry piece of cereal on the side of the bowl and bit down on it. She edged off her own mother's wedding band. Isabel hardly ever discussed Sigrid, but she'd held onto keepsakes. "For you, so you don't forget me." She eased it over Natalie's knuckle, which wasn't big enough to prevent it from slipping off. "Wow. You have the tiniest fingers."

"No," Natalie said and returned the band. "I'm not going to forget you. I'll convince Mom or figure something out. Don't worry. I'll do whatever it takes for us to be together."

nine

———

SINCE THE HOLIDAYS, NATALIE HAD STARTED USING THE *WIRED Happy* app daily. Chimes. Breeze. The sound of Isabel's voice: "Sit or lie down and focus on your breathing. Place one hand on your stomach and one hand on your chest. Observe the belly as it rises and falls. You are in a place of tranquility."

Natalie was too far from that place. Sitting with the pillows wedged between her and her bed frame, she spun her foot around and around as if drawing geometric circles and tried to ignore the racing interference of her thoughts. But disturbing images crammed through. A dark street, a sudden burst as if a strobe light were aimed in their direction, her mother's car veering—then losing time.

She thought of the memory that had come back to her. She'd told Isabel, "I'll figure something out. I'll do whatever it takes for us to be together." Was it because Natalie was so desperate not to be cast from her home, away from Isabel, that she'd caused the crash, an impulsive act by an impulsive girl? She pictured the flashlight in her drawer, right here next to her bed, and was certain it was a token, a recognition of the child who needed a school for troubled teens.

There was no one else she could ask about the girl she was before the crash, the one teeming with fury and fight. Other than Cate and Isabel, there'd been only her stepfather. And his message to her had been lost with Ellen somewhere in South America.

Isabel proclaimed, "With each breath you are being renewed and regenerated. At this moment, there's no sense of time. You are being healed, cradled by the sky. You are floating on the wind." Natalie imagined the cradling sky loosening its arms and dropping her—whoosh—until she splatted onto the street below. One eye open, she viewed the glowing green numbers of her clock change to 3:53 a.m.

Natalie snapped the wires from her ears and wrenched them free of her cell. She switched on her table lamp and padded to her closet. On a high shelf was a shoebox stuffed with loose Polaroids of her childhood and a couple of her mom's old albums. Quietly, she tiptoed to the kitchen. She filled the kettle with water and turned up the flame on the stove, the room partially illuminated by moonlight. At the table, she studied the plastic-covered album pages.

In snapshot after snapshot, Natalie was surprised by her mother's youthfulness, the candor of her smile, flyaway hair, casual in her clothes and poses with only the peachy-orange lipstick as a concession to beauty. While the sense of her mother was always with her, Natalie could no longer summon up her mom's features on demand. Her brain, that unreliable organ, had erased the exact details: the hazel tint of her mom's eyes, the slope of her cheeks, the olive skin and curly dark hair of Natalie's great-grandparents who'd left Kiev in the late nineteenth century.

Here was a picture of Isabel at maybe fourteen-years-old: her hair cut so that it kissed the middle of her neck, her eyes staring straight into the camera, exhibiting the usual sense of self-containment. Isabel's intensity and superior intellect had garnered her the respect of other students, but not their friendship. There was one odd girl who'd come to the Newton house and watched TV while Isabel did her homework. Natalie couldn't conjure up her name but recalled the girl was chunky and wore gobs of concealer over her chin acne. Later there were others: a pack of slim-hipped boy-men, and a few young women in breast-hugging shirts, drinking from bottles of beer in the low light of the living room. Where were her mother and Garrick who, certainly, wouldn't have allowed these kids to drink alcohol in their house?

Natalie paused when she came to a portrait of herself at what must have been close to the age of the crash. She was skinny in bell-bottoms and a t-shirt, her eyes wide and her curly hair awkwardly parted down the middle. She was wearing a chunky turquoise ring on her index finger. Natalie examined this girl who was smiling dreamily. Beneath her preteen languidness, had rebellious rage hid? No answer. Her fickle memory refused to cooperate.

The room was still. The whirring, coming from the refrigerator, had temporarily stopped. Natalie felt an ache in her abdomen, a longing like homesickness. She shuffled to the couch and scrunched one of the pillows under her head.

What did I do?

HADLEY'S VOICE WAS tinged with concern. "Mom, why are you out here?"

Natalie blinked awake. "Hi, Hads."

"I went into your room and you weren't there."

"Oh, I got up to get a glass of water and must have conked out."

Hadley's eyes rested on the photos scattered on the floor. She shifted her weight from one foot to the other. "Did you have that nightmare again?"

Natalie startled, felt a flutter of heat. "What?"

"Dad told me you dream, sometimes, about, you know, the accident."

"He shouldn't have done that."

"It's okay, Mom. I'm not a little kid."

"I'm fine," she chopped down on the words. Glancing at the Roman numeral wall clock, she added, "Hey, I better hurry and get you to school."

January third. First day back to their routine, thank God.

"Yep." Hadley gnawed on her lip. "I'll get my stuff."

Natalie hurried to start the coffee, shower, and grab a pair of jeans and sweater from the hamper. She towel-dried her hair so at least water wasn't running down her back and frowned at her reflection. Since the Caribbean, she'd dropped ten pounds, and it showed on her drawn face, her sunken cheeks. She touched a small constellation of brown freckles near her mouth. "You look like crap," she said.

In the car, Hadley asked, "Don't you have a job today?"

"Best Pastries of Boston. Want me to bring you home cannoli?"

"Sure." Her daughter slid the wand out of her lip-gloss applicator and dabbed it on her bottom lip. Through a mouth glistening like mango sorbet, she said, "You had that same sweater on last night."

Natalie turned right onto Washington Street, snow dusting the trees. "Hads, when did you become the clothing police?"

"Mom, it's gross. You promised you'd make an effort."

How much of Hadley's new habit of inspecting flaws was normal teen behavior? Hadley might be fuming at Marc for his engagement to Elizabeth, yet she wasn't going to let Natalie off the hook. Natalie hadn't paid enough attention to her presentation, her daughter's comments scolded, the way she dressed, her unkempt hair, her disheveled home office—all of it a symptom of a disordered life. Natalie was tempted to ask if Elizabeth ate breakfast in pearls and lipstick, if she rolled her underwear into neat compartments and stacked them in rows. But the argument wasn't, never could be, with Hadley.

"My job isn't till ten. We had to get going. Next time I'll wear my diamond tiara."

"Yeah, thanks, Mom."

Natalie slowed down the car, as she edged closer to the school. She reached out to touch her daughter's arm. "Listen, Hads . . ."

Don't blame me for Dad's behavior.

"I'm going to be late," her daughter said, pulling away.

It struck her then, after her night of studying photographs. "You have my mother's eyes."

The girl's expression softened. "Grandma's?"

How could her mother, dead at thirty-eight, be a grandmother? Natalie nodded. "The exact shape and color."

"Wow. You never talk about her."

Natalie stroked her daughter's cheek. "It's hard for me."

"Mom? They're your eyes, too."

SHE ONLY HAD a few moments to check her email before getting ready for her shoot. Natalie's throat clutched. There were three new ones: an inquiry about work, one from a political fundraiser, and one from bbGodfrey@gmail. She placed her hand on her stomach and watched it expand as she slowed down her breathing. *You are in a place of tranquility.* Not so. She clicked on the message. It read: *Doesn't it bother you what they did, that you were lied to? That guy witnessed what happened, the blood on the car. Why haven't you done anything yet?*

There was no sign off or name. It felt like a clap to the cheek, the soft spot under the bone and above the teeth that hurt the most when hit. She tapped reply: *I'm asking again, who are you and what do you want?*

She read the message over and over until the words thumped like a headache: *What they did. You were lied to.* She envisioned the emailer squatting in the bushes, balancing on his haunches, the warm dirt beneath sandaled feet. She thought of action movies in which kidnappers send a ransom note, followed by intricate, explicit instructions. There were no clear directions here. If Natalie went to the police, gave herself up, who would she save?

What if bbGodfrey was actually outing himself, if the emailer was Simon, who'd acted helpful, then flirted with her the next day? Many people had more than one online address.

Is that why Isabel had warned her against Simon who had flirted with her in his charming British accent, had asked her to dinner, and sent her a Christmas greeting? *A little perversion never hurt anyone.* If he was hiding his identity behind subterfuge, he'd need a motivation. Extortion, a monetary payoff to keep him quiet, was the most likely one. He knew Isabel was successful, maybe figured he could blackmail her to save Natalie. No, that made no sense. He would have asked for money already. But what if he *had* contacted Isabel and her stepsister had kept this from her for the same reason she'd shielded Natalie from learning about Dr. Strout?

Her mind jammed on images of those moments in the tropics: the thump of the car, the sliver of moon, the man's startling eyes and his easy walk to search the bushes.

In the moments before Natalie joined them on the road, Isabel could have pleaded with him to keep quiet about the wreckage. An injured or dead child, not an animal. "She's been through enough. Please. How much will it take?"

Quickly, Natalie rushed to her bedroom, pulled open the drawer to her night table, and reached for her Xanax bottle. She stared at the oval pills inside, which reminded her of blue Pez candies. Rather than cleaving the pill down its fault line—*"Half a pill to help me sleep! Don't confuse me with Sigrid"*—she stuck the entire thing in her mouth. She held the Xanax on her tongue. When the medication kicked in, she'd stop worrying.

Great. I need drugs to get me less anxious about taking drugs.

Natalie spit it out into her palm. She had photo editing to do before her pastry shoot and couldn't be foggy headed.

An idea germinated. Her fingers aquiver, she wrote to Simon: *Thank you, again, for the Christmas card. You told me to write if I was ever in NYC. I'll be coming in. . . .*

Was she serious? She took a second to consider and confirmed that, yes, she was. It would mean withholding her plans from Isabel who would try to discourage her with warnings about this man, warnings that she'd be justified to make. Natalie mustn't do that push-pull thing she did, doubting herself, her every choice, turning to Marc or her stepsister for confirmation. She would imitate that girl she once was before her mother died, the one Cate described to her, who was prepared and focused, not afraid. The next day was Friday. Natalie couldn't arrange to get away so quickly. Chances were he had plans already. She chose the following Saturday's date, even though it wasn't Marc's weekend to be with Hadley. She could work it out at the last minute.

Let me know if you're available for coffee or a drink. Best, Natalie.

ISABEL WAS CONDUCTING the workshop from the center chair in the semi-circle, not perched on her desk, as she usually positioned herself. She scanned the audience, eyes ablaze, her face aglow from whatever cream or peel she'd used to refresh her skin. "Physiological problems can arise from chronic stress: the production of cortisol and epinephrine and the rise in levels of a neurotransmitter called catecholamine. This particular neurotransmitter affects your central nervous system and hormones. It sets off a chain of events that can suppress your immune system, cause poor sleep and appetite, even depression."

Isabel's voice was melodic. How could she make grim medical jargon sound like poetry?

Natalie was perspiring in the heated loft. Her eyes wandered around the room, observing the usual crew: a college girl wearing a tie-dye shirt, a chubby, middle-aged woman, and a bearded man wearing Birkenstocks with socks who appeared to be dozing. She stared at Prama/Heather in black leggings, Uggs, and a hibiscus pink pullover, and felt a flash of annoyance.

"Remember our innate negativity bias? Tonight, I'm going to talk about how this works. If, right now, you're thinking this doesn't sound very scientific, blame your brain! Two-thirds of the neurons in the amygdala are programmed to receive bad news. So, doubting my research means your brain is doing its job." Isabel grinned.

Natalie watched as Jeremy strode into the room, ten minutes late, in the same rancher's jacket and cowboy boots as last time. She couldn't believe her own carelessness at confiding intimate details to a stranger. Even if they did have an easy rapport, even if she liked the way his hair jutted out, his agate brown eyes with the creases and soft pouches beneath. He winked at her and, suddenly, she had the urge to photograph him. When was the last time she'd felt *that*? Quickly, she looked away, stifled the urge.

Isabel said, "We can consciously train ourselves to focus on and store positive experiences, to increase our compassion for others and for ourselves."

Ms. Anshaw raised her hand, and Natalie noticed that she had gray sludge marks under her eyes. She felt a swell of sympathy, an unlikely camaraderie. When Isabel nodded in her direction, the girl asked, "What if someone has done something so truly horrible that the negativity isn't a bias but is . . . justified?"

Yes, exactly.

A woman with hair the color of peach pulp, so closely cropped to her skull it looked like a side effect of chemotherapy, recited, "'Do not judge, and you will not be judged. Do not condemn, and you will not be condemned. Forgive, and you will be forgiven.' Catholic school K-12."

"Thank you, Ms. Demsey," Isabel said with a grin.

A ripple of laughter throughout the room.

"I think it depends what you mean by horrible," Isabel said crisply. "Most of us are much harder on ourselves than we deserve."

The girl frowned. "Not always. What if someone has done something unforgivable?"

"Such as?" Isabel asked, eyes steady on the girl.

"I don't . . ." Ms. Anshaw faltered. "Those school shooters or the white supremacists, you know, those men marching with the tiki torches."

"I doubt they are signing up for happiness seminars," the chubby woman chimed in. "And I'm sure whatever you feel guilty about is nothing like that."

Some things were indefensible. Like murdering your mother.

When Isabel directed the group to consider the various materials she'd distributed at the beginning of the meeting, Natalie picked up the first pamphlet without reading it. After Isabel laid out the exercises to do, the group broke up.

Isabel's most fervent disciples were congregated around her. When Ms. Anshaw tapped her on the wrist, Isabel snatched her arm away—a sign of stress. More flack from her editor to hurry up? With a wave, Natalie ducked out. As she reached the vestibule to the building, she noticed Jeremy's back to her. She was ahead of the others, but once in the entranceway, she aligned herself with the crowd.

"Hold on," Jeremy said as she passed him in the narrow space.

The woman with the cropped hair turned with a questioning look.

Jeremy gestured with a tilt of his head. "I was speaking to Natalie."

The woman glided out the door with the rest of the group.

"Hey, good to see you," he said to Natalie. "Sorry I bolted so quickly last time at the T."

She slid on her gloves. "I've been curious. What is it you do? We've eliminated policeman. And I take it you're not in your family's cattle business."

He smiled. "You asked last time what made me join the workshop. It's my work."

"Are you a psychologist?"

Jeremy glanced up the stairs. "How about I walk with you again?"

She shivered as she hit the ruthless night temperature. "Only if you stop with the twenty questions."

"I'm a Metro editor at the *Globe*," Jeremy said, "and a former investigative reporter."

She hugged her arms around her waist. It was the wind, raw and relentless, that threatened to crack through bones. "Are you investigating Isabel for the paper?"

Not me. Not the Cayman Islands.

"Nope. I'm simply an open-minded observer curious about Dr. Walker's philosophy."

"Please. You think what Isabel says is bullshit. Why are you really coming?"

Jeremy yanked a black wool hat from his jacket pocket. "You got me. It's research for a book I'm writing."

"What kind of book?"

"An exploration of the happiness movement."

She sighed, relief forming a puff of cold air. "So, your intention isn't to try and hurt Isabel?"

"Why? Is there something to hurt? I'm a journalist. This is what we do. We get at the truth."

Natalie thought about how the editor had rejected the first draft of Isabel's new manuscript, how the advance was gone. She couldn't see why he would care about these details, but she'd never disclose them. "You can't use anything I said in your book, about me, any of the personal stuff."

"I wouldn't do that unless you agree to let me interview you on the record."

"Well, I'm *not* agreeing. Why would you want to? It's obvious you're looking to debunk what Isabel does."

"Just to get your perspective."

"No," she said, firmly. "Nothing about me."

He held up his hand. "Got it. Not to worry. I'm a professional."

"How do you know I'm not going to tell Isabel why you're coming?"

"I don't. But I think she'd relish publicity, good or bad. It's media coverage and she's very confident in what she does. I'm sure she's comfortable with controversy." Jeremy's glasses enlarged his eyes, so they seemed to fill his whole face.

"Why don't you just ask to interview *her* then?"

"I wanted to listen without announcing myself." Jeremy pulled down his hat, so it covered his ears. "If you decide you want to chat more, email me. You can find my address on the *Globe*'s webpage, staff list." He smiled in a *maybe I have more than work on my mind way* and asked, "Can I have yours?"

She stopped walking. "I think what you're doing is sleazy."

"Duly noted. I apologize for not being upfront with you. I do. It's a bad habit of the trade. Hope you won't hold it against me."

"Only if you don't talk about interviewing me."

When he nodded, she gave her contact information quickly.

Natalie watched him walk in the other direction, away from the Back Bay Station, wondering if he was just another man who would disappoint her.

SHE POKED HER head into Hadley's room. Her daughter was on her bed, curled over her iPhone, texting rapidly. She'd painted her fingernails a greenish gray, an army fatigue color glammed up and bottled: *Armed for Anything.*

"Hey honey," Natalie said. "Texting Soph?"

"Not Sophie." Head bowed again.

"I'll give you some privacy."

"Wait, Mom." She glanced at Natalie quickly. "It's Dad." A coral patch spread over Hadley's cheeks and throat. "Uh, he and Elizabeth decided to sell her house and move to a condo in Brookline."

Paid for by Elizabeth's inheritance no doubt, the one her Kennebunkport grandparents—friends with Poppy and the Silver Fox—had left her. Yet once the divorce was finalized, Natalie would be strapped for money to pay for an ACA plan and, in a few years, her mortgage.

"Dad wants me to spend more time with him, like during the week."

"Is that what you want?"

"No. I mean, I don't know. I'm still pissed. I don't want to be around Elizabeth so much. But he said he'd spend time alone with me."

Slick Marc. Good work.

"Let's not worry about this yet. It takes time to sell a house and find a new place," she improvised. "We'll deal with this when it happens."

"All right."

"I love you, Hads."

Hadley looked up. "You too."

It was only nine o'clock. But Natalie was ready for bed. It had been a long day—shooting ice cream for a magazine feature, a time sensitive endeavor that took concentration, followed by the Happiness workshop—and had ended with Jeremy's admission. She'd thought he was interested in her. But he just wanted to expose Isabel and her work in print. And now this unpleasant surprise from Marc.

She had to wait to go to sleep. Lights out this early would alert her watchful child: *something is wrong with Mom.* Fodder for paternal custody. She headed for the kitchen. The dimmer switch on the panel was busted again and Natalie had to fiddle for a while to get it back on its track. A new dimmer was on her ever-expanding list of home repairs. Even more costly was repainting and fixing the wood paneling on the floor that had popped out, now held in place with clear industrial tape. All the chores Marc used to take care of were her responsibility now.

She didn't bother with the kettle. She filled up a mug with water and thrust it into the microwave. While it heated, she washed out that morning's cereal bowl, stuffing Hadley's soggy flakes down the drain. She needed to stop cleaning up after her child, stop babying her. Could Marc use that in court to prove she was an unfit mother? Impeding the independence of their teenage daughter.

With the steaming herbal tea in hand, she headed back to her bedroom to wait out the hours.

Natalie rested the computer on her lap and checked her emails. There was the usual junk, nothing from the mysterious stalker. But when she saw the address in bold, her pulse quickened. SDrouin@hotmail wrote: *Wonderful to hear you're coming to the city. Would dinner Saturday night work? Affectionately, Simon.*

ten

—

NATALIE EXHALED SLOWLY. SHE HAD SET THIS PLAN IN MOTION and would follow through with it now. She sent Marc a text before bed: *Have work out of town next weekend. Need you to take Hadley.*

She set two alarms to ensure she was up before Hadley. In the morning, she took an abbreviated shower, dressed in clean clothes—nothing special, but at least presentable for her daughter's sake—and with her hair wrapped in a towel went to make coffee. She had ten minutes before Beyoncé blasted from Hadley's iPhone.

Hadley was groggy, in no mood to talk. On the way to the high school, Natalie noted how her daughter's head was on the headrest, her eyes slightly red from the shock of the early hour. Her neck was long and thin—like her father's—her complexion bright with a pink-ish hue, not yet registering lack of sleep in its color or creases. Her lips were lush, a gift from Natalie's mother. Soon, Hadley would be dating. How could Natalie shield her from the pain of rejection when she couldn't even do that for herself?

"What do you think about going skiing with Dad a week from Saturday?" she asked once they were on the road.

"Uh," Hadley grumbled. "Alex B might have a party. Also, Christina."

"Who are those girls?"

"What's the difference, Mom?"

"I don't know them or their parents." Natalie added in a light-hearted tone, "They could be drug dealers or collect guns for fun."

"Alex's mother is a realtor. Christina's dad owns a bunch of restaurants or something. She's rich, has a summer home on Nantucket. Want their numbers and you can see if they have AK-15s or a meth lab?"

"You're in a mood."

A lion's cavernous yawn for effect. "It's cruel and unusual punishment to make me engage in conversation this early."

"Noted. I just thought . . . you love to ski."

"What's this sudden idea? Big date, Mom?"

"Not at all," Natalie said, pleased her kid considered this possibility. "I have to be in New York for a project."

Hadley glimpsed at her skeptically. "Since when do you have 'projects' in New York?"

"First time. I don't even know if it will pan out."

"Whatever. I mean, good for you. But don't pretend it's for my benefit. I would be with Dad *and* Elizabeth."

"Probably. But it would still be fun."

They rode in silence until Natalie pulled up outside the school. "Okay, sweetie. Good luck on your tests!"

"Yep." Hadley's jacket hung over her shoulders in slipshod fashion, her book bag straps halfway to her elbows. "Are you going to make me sleep at Dad's half the week when he and Elizabeth move to town? 'Cause that's what happened when Priscilla's parents got divorced and it sucks, two houses but no real home."

"No, honey," Natalie poked her head out of the window. "Is that what you're upset about?"

"I just don't want to be roadkill in this arrangement," Hadley said. "While you and Dad go off and have your fun adventures."

"Oh, God, Hads. Never."

Natalie sat for several minutes after her daughter left, listening to the reverberating sound of the slammed door.

How am I going to live alone with Garrick when you go to college, Belle? You're all I have. Without you, I don't have a home.

NEW YORK CITY was dark and cold with a bitter gale beating at the people leaving Penn Station, slapping faces and tossing hair, threatening to knock over an elderly man with a cane on Seventh Avenue. Natalie hoisted her weekender satchel over her shoulder and jammed her gloved hands into her coat pocket. She'd booked a room in Midtown East because it was the best deal for a hotel she could find. It was a long walk up fourteen blocks and cross-town—at least in this weather—but she was hesitant to spend money on a taxi and was not acquainted enough with the subway system to tackle changing trains.

Natalie bustled, her scarf unfurling, among the crowds. She was crammed into a knot of rush-hour escapees determined to zoom and zigzag their way in front of the others. By the time she reached her hotel, she was due back downtown near Gramercy Park in an hour. She would have to go over budget and pay for a cab. Her nerves were dancing sprites. She wasn't certain what scared her more, that Simon was sexy or that he might be dangerous.

Natalie showered for a second time that day and then changed into her nicest teal sweater, black trousers, and ankle high leather boots she'd bought on sale for the occasion. Hadley would be mortified she wasn't wearing more of a heel. No, Hadley would be mortified she'd traveled such a distance to meet a man. Or maybe she'd be glad.

Natalie thought about the last time she'd visited the city. It was over two years ago, a long weekend in May, to celebrate Hadley's thirteenth birthday. When they arrived, she'd felt a giddy release, her spirits boosted. The same cool drizzle had been spouting forth for weeks in New England, as if the weather wasn't limber enough to leap into spring. But when they'd walked through Central Park, the air sang with warmth. Tulips dotted the gardens, the flowering white and pink dogwoods and cherry trees in bloom. She and Marc had taken their daughter to Chinatown for an early dinner and then to see *Wicked* on Broadway. They joked and laughed, engaged in familiar banter.

Now she observed her reflection. At least with the help of mascara and blush she looked pretty again, her skin warm, not sallow, her cheek bones sharp. She wondered if her almost-ex would have a reaction to her meeting Simon, an investment banker at Goldman Sachs—and one this attractive. Would he feel a twinge of jealousy, be disgusted? He wouldn't care.

Get that through your head.

Focus. bbGodfrey. He's why you're here.

The restaurant was buzzing, the clinking of ice in cocktails, the chiming of bracelets against the glasses, the jangling of laughter. The walls were painted a rich amber hue and framed with oak wainscoting. The round tables were draped in linen cloths topped with crystal vases, a tall yellow rose in each one. Natalie waited at the bar, chomping on salty peanuts and sipping her seltzer with lime. A woman with a starched expression sat next to her. Natalie noticed her clunky, silver watch and wondered how heavy it was and if the repetitive movements of her wrist would give her carpal tunnel syndrome.

With each passing minute, she felt a little more winded. She'd prepared for this meeting; she'd take it slow, casual. She wouldn't mention the email until she'd gotten a better sense of Simon. The dinner could be some kind of test, although of what exactly, she couldn't ascertain.

Simon arrived, gorgeous and shiny as a block of gold. Such a defined jawline and steady gaze, the crinkles on his face, around his mouth, did nothing to weaken his appeal. He was wearing a gray blazer and an Egyptian blue shirt. He brought to mind Robert Redford as Hubble Gardner in that last scene of *The Way We Were,* when Streisand brushed his bangs away with her gloved hand.

"Hello!" he said when he spotted her. "I hope I haven't kept you waiting long."

"No," she lied, "just got here."

"Brilliant. Right on time."

He instructed the hostess to seat them at a table far away from the door, which, when it swung open, let in the icy night. The waitress, a girl with bleached white hair and blond eyelashes, blushed as she spoke to Simon. She inquired about drinks, and he requested a glass of red wine.

"Just Perrier for me," Natalie said. She noted her companion's expression. He was smiling quizzically.

"A glass of wine, maybe?" he asked.

Natalie had vowed not to drink that night, to keep her mind clear. But she felt the urge to please him. Her weakness was beauty. She'd had the same reaction to Marc from the beginning.

She ordered a glass of Chardonnay.

They opened their menus with the exorbitant prices. It was a three-course, prix fixe menu, which included the sorts of desserts she would prefer to photograph than eat (prunes and coffee cardamom ice cream).

"You'd rather have a plain yogurt for lunch than duck," Marc had laughed early on in their relationship. "How come you like to take pictures of all the foods you hate to eat?"

"I don't hate them," she'd said. "They're works of art."

"But doctored with chemicals and plastic glazes."

What Marc didn't know was: before her mother's death, Natalie had loved to eat, especially homemade desserts—tarts with frangipane filling in a pâte sucrée, topped with pears poached in simple syrup and glazed in a reduction of their juices—her mother's specialty. After her mother was gone, Natalie read in *Seventeen* that anger could be linked to the consumption of too much sugar. She figured there was sugar in just about everything. She grew ever vigilant, monitoring what she ate until watchfulness hardened like resin.

Natalie ordered what seemed the simplest dish: the chicken with polenta and the squash and endive salad. Simon got the black sea bass with fennel and olives and the pea soup to start.

"I thought you'd like it here," he said. "They have chocolate truffles but no mutton, I'm afraid."

Her skin tingled with electricity. Simon remembered their exchange on the beach. "I'm relieved to hear about the mutton. This is great."

He bent forward and Natalie's pulse sped up a notch. *He must sleep with models, actresses, ballet dancers.*

Simon asked, "So, what brings you to the city, some fabulous food show or something more personal?"

Natalie stared at her butter knife's rounded head and gave the answer she'd practiced. "I'm meeting an old client of mine who moved here."

She couldn't say she had a commercial shoot for a particular magazine. He could catch her in that lie—although the thought of his caring seemed paranoid, self-absorbed. "Egocentric?" she heard Marc's voice.

"This is a personal favor, pictures of their home for a design magazine. What about you, your work?"

Simon leaned his head into his palm. "It would bore you into a coma."

"Well, at least you get to travel to the Cayman Islands, that's a perk."

"Nothing to do with the job. I was on holiday."

"Oh," she said, "I assumed you had a business meeting that morning. You know, when I saw you on the beach."

"Early riser. I'm at the office by seven. You were up at that time, too. Ah, thank you," he said to the waitress who brought their wine. He fastened his attention on her for just a second, but it was enough for the girl to turn a darker pink.

Outside, the wind had risen and was pounding on the glass like an angry spouse locked out of the house. The three women at the table to their right gasped. One said, "So annoying! We're never going to get a cab."

Simon peered at Natalie. "Bothersome how apocalyptic climate can interfere with public transport."

"I hear Southern California has been having issues with Uber, what with the devastating wildfires," Natalie said.

"Such extremes." There was a purr in his voice. "Too hot and dry, too many destructive hurricanes, the ice melting . . . It can make you question everything."

Was he still referring to the weather?

The waitress returned with their first courses. Natalie observed Simon's bowl of soup, with the white Parmesan foam on top and the accompanying spoon filled with bacon bits. Soup was a pain in the ass to photograph, and pea soup was problematic because of the color and texture. You had to be careful or it could look disgusting, like green vomit. But, if done correctly, it could be tantalizing, elegant and refreshing. The bacon would give the image a needed pop of color, of meat. Red-blooded.

"Would you like a bite?" he asked.

"Thanks, no. Just admiring."

"I'm jealous of my appetizer."

"Don't be." Natalie said, despite her good intentions, "I like my men less green."

"Good to know."

She felt an ache in her groin and tightened her legs together to squelch it. *Stick to the script.* She stuck her fork into a piece of squash. "I was up before dawn that morning I met you because I was upset—about the accident the night before."

Simon nodded, appearing unfazed. "It was unsettling. Luckily, the road was deserted."

"I'm not convinced that I didn't injure . . . *someone*, not a dog."

"But I checked. There was no one there." He cupped his hand over hers, his skin cool and dry. "You poor girl. Have you been thinking about that all this time?"

"No, just recently. Something . . . reminded me of it."

His eyes on her were so saturated with blue, it was as if they were animated, a Disney prince's or, maybe the villain's. "What about your sister, what does she say?"

"Stepsister. Isabel. We're not related," Natalie said. Same mistake the emailer had made. The muscles in her shoulders and back twinged, like when she lugged her equipment to a shoot, her camera hanging from the strap around her neck. She pulled her hand away. "She's not concerned."

He placed his spoon down on the plate under his soup bowl. "Well, Isabel said she'd call the police to make sure no one was hurt. Did she reach them?"

"Yes. Nothing was reported."

"Well, that should ease your mind."

He sounded earnest, not rattled or conniving. A good sign.

She said, "I hoped to get your take on what happened."

"And here I thought you fancied seeing me again."

"No, I mean, yes."

What could she say? I came here to sleep with you? Had she? She fiddled with the napkin in her lap.

He pointed to her black diamond. "That's enchanting. I hope it doesn't mean what I think. It's the wrong color, but you're an artist, unconventional, I suspect. If that's not too much of a cliché."

Natalie splayed out her fingers and noted the black diamond. "You mean an engagement ring? No." She could feel her face flush. "I'm separated, soon-to-be divorced."

"Sorry. I'm meddling, none of my business."

"It's okay. This was a gift, from Isabel actually."

"Ah. Fascinating choice on her part."

Isabel. She was the glittering star, the energy center. Maybe it wasn't money he was after, but Isabel's attention. *Admirer. Stalker fan.*

"It's from her and her husband, a Christmas present."

Simon smiled seductively. "I see."

What did he see exactly, that the first prize was taken but that she was available, hurting and hopeful, and not sure, in that moment, if she came to confront him about the night on the island? Or not only that?

"Have you ever been married?" she asked.

"Dodged that but came close. More than a year ago now." He slowly sipped a spoonful of soup. It was a pleasure to observe. "You have similar taste in jewelry. Probably why I noticed."

"I'm sorry. About your breakup."

"Don't be," Simon said. "Otherwise I wouldn't be here with you, at an advantage with my not-green skin."

Natalie rubbed her index finger over her lip. Those were not the sentiments of an Isabel devotee.

The dinner arrived, glimmering and sumptuous looking as any enhanced photograph.

"Delicious," Simon said, tip of the tongue to his bottom lip. "Let's enjoy ourselves."

To strengthen your brain, you must savor life's positive experiences.

"Yes, let's," she said.

She wanted to believe: bbGodfrey wasn't at the table.

eleven

———

SIMON HAILED A TAXI AFTER DINNER TO TAKE THEM TO HIS apartment downtown.

"Just one glass," Natalie said, as she slid onto the cracked leatherette seat. "Then I should get back to the hotel."

"Of course." He glided next to her. "Whatever you want."

Natalie could smell the fennel, that licorice scent, behind the mint he was sucking. She glanced quickly at his profile—so close now, two fingers rubbing his jaw—and felt the hunger rise in her. She imagined him stroking the inside of her thigh, the pressure of his mouth on hers. She wanted to wrap her body around his so there was no space between them. His proximity was both luxurious and perilous, like sun tanning with a reflector at the peak of the day. It wouldn't be wrong to get more out of the evening than she'd planned.

For the duration of the short, bumpy ride, Natalie stared out the window at the passing upscale shops and restaurants, flags and bright window shades flashing by, a colorful pinwheel. This chant pealed through her head: *What are you doing? What are you doing? What are you doing?*

They entered his building with the forest green awning and the ornate limestone trim. Simon strode with such an easy confidence, in his slim, gray trousers. On the elevator to the ninth floor, they didn't talk. But he looked at her with a friendly, open smile.

His co-op was ultramodern: sleek wood, a flat screen television, tapered floor lamps, and a floor-to-ceiling modular bookshelf with spider plants in clay pots mixed among the sprinkling of hardbacks.

It was too Scandinavian chilly for Natalie. But that didn't matter. She wasn't moving in.

Simon gestured for Natalie to sit on the couch. Across from her, on the coffee table, was his closed laptop. "What would you like, red or white?"

"White, please."

"Another Chardonnay or Pinot Grigio?"

"Oh, either," Natalie said, picking at the cuticle of her thumb. "Whatever you're having."

Simon ducked out into the adjoining kitchen and Natalie arched forward, running two fingers over the computer's silver surface. She could flip it open, scan his email, rapidly, the way spies or CIA operatives did in movies with the pounding soundtrack playing in the background. Of course, she didn't dare. Instead, she studied the framed photographs on the console table against the wall. One was an older shot of a slim couple, in their mid-to-late thirties, the woman in a sleeveless salmon-pink dress and a strand of pearls, the dark-haired man in an unbuttoned navy suit jacket with a pastel blue shirt underneath. The woman, whose exquisite face was reproduced on the smaller boy, nevertheless had her arms draped over the taller child, also a male, whose features more closely resembled the man's. Undoubtedly: Simon's family. The younger boy with the flaxen hair and the twisted smirk stood in front of his father whose attention seemed inner-directed, while the older brother, straight-shouldered and slim, with a longer chin and smaller eyes, leaned into his mother's embrace.

The other picture was taken in a park, with hedgerows and wide-armed beech trees in the background, a college-aged Simon next to a ginger-haired girl, arms around each other's shoulders, both of them grinning as if they'd gotten away with a prank.

Simon returned with the long-stemmed glasses and handed one to Natalie. He sat in the chair across from her and placed his flute on the coffee table in front of him. "Tell me more about yourself."

Her nerves were jittering. She took a sip. "Like what?"

"Interests, hobbies, that sort of thing?"

"No time. I have a daughter who's a teenager." Might as well get that out in the open. Some men's smiles would freeze and crack. Their bodies would retreat.

Doesn't matter. He's just a . . .

"Hookup, Mom," she heard Hadley say.

Simon edged towards her, his attention so focused it held weight. "You must have gotten married right out of university."

"I was twenty-four. We met at school."

"Does she live with you, at least?"

"During the week. My ex is close by, so she stays with him and his fiancé on weekends." As soon as it was out of her mouth, she regretted that last bit. No need to sound so easily replaceable.

He reached for his glass. "Engaged before divorce, is that one of America's peculiar customs, like baseball hats and guns?"

She laughed. "Not officially. My situation is just . . . odd. What about you, your family? I saw those photos." She pointed and then noted how his expression changed, a warning.

"Yes, that's them, in our salad days. Before life—and death—happened."

"Oh, I'm sorry," she said quickly, glimpsing at the beautiful woman, the preoccupied man. "What about that other one, the young woman? Your fiancé?"

"Ha! Imogen Howe? No, but a good sport, that one. The fiancé was years later and then there was my last relationship, a bit of a shambles. But I shouldn't compare to your situation."

"That's okay," Natalie said, drinking her wine. Would Simon consider her as good a sport as Imogen Howe, she wondered, when this evening was over?

"Your daughter must cheer you up. Less lonely that way."

"There are other kinds of loneliness."

Simon nodded, his eyes on her.

The silence was full between them. She felt the air pulsing like before it rained.

He stood up slowly, almost ceremonially. "You game?"

"I'm not sure this is a good idea."

"Did I misread the signals?" When she shook her head, he asked, "Then, why not?" he asked. "We're both free."

Simon took her hand, guided her, in the shadows, to his bedroom, and then lifted her face in his hands. When he kissed her, his tongue was slow and tangy from the wine. He pressed in closer and slid his hand underneath her shirt, caressing the small of her back. He gazed at her attentively, waiting for her permission. When she leaned into him, they fell onto the bed, and he snapped her bra open in one nimble movement.

Wow, practiced. She was so hungry, she didn't care. Natalie's mouth grazed the skin on his neck.

Simon pulled her shirt over her head and kissed the hollow of her belly. He took her breast in his hand, his mouth slightly open. The ache in Natalie extended from her groin to her nipples. He inched her pants down and she let him, astonished by her lack of shyness. This was the first man, other than Marc, who'd seen her naked in two decades.

Once she was fully undressed, he ran his fingers across her C-section scar, then down and inside of her. When she moaned, he nodded. For a moment she felt tested and observed, like a roast that had reached the correct temperature. But then she was watching as he unbuttoned his shirt and unzipped his pants; the sensation passed. She could see his chest was pale with sandy-colored freckles, even in the dim light from the hall, his stomach firm and his arms sinewy, as if he spent his days rowing on a crew team instead of stuck at a desk. Marc was slender, but his muscles less toned, dry patches on his torso from flare-ups of eczema, the body of a man with a demanding job, mortgage payments, and a child to support.

Don't think of Marc!

But then a passing fantasy: grabbing her phone, sneaking a picture, sending it to her husband. *See, asshole, this dazzling man I'm having sex with?*

When Simon reached for the band of his underwear and tugged, she said, "Don't. Keep them on for a minute. Just lie down with me."

"With my undies?"

She smiled at the word. "Yes. If they're off, I won't be able to stop myself."

"Why would you stop?" he asked with a laugh.

There was a thin thread of doubt holding her back, a holdover from years of marriage, that sex should be an act of love. Before Marc there had only been one other, the college boyfriend, with the eager grin and the knobby knees who had professed his love for her. She'd lost her virginity to him in a dorm room that stank of moldy towels and unwashed underwear.

"Please."

"Of course," Simon said politely as if she'd requested a glass of water. He scrambled to reposition them, so that he was on the bed with Natalie on top of him.

She thought of Marc, of their last months, their sexual struggles. Either he was too tired from work to make love or he'd lose his erection halfway through. "There's nothing wrong with me. I'm under a lot of stress," he'd say. He was forty years old. Work pressure could last another thirty years, she'd worried. But, of course, in the end, his job had nothing to do with it.

She'd had sex without love that last year after all. At least Simon's body responded to hers.

Caressing her with one hand, the other one working its way back between her legs, he asked, "Is now okay?"

"Yes," she said, cravings so strong. She couldn't recall the last time she'd had such cravings.

When he entered her, she thought: *See Marc? See how much he wants me?*

Afterwards, Simon's eyes on her breasts caused Natalie to cross her arms over them, as if his mouth hadn't just been there. He smiled, lazily, at her modesty and then lying on his back, drifted off to sleep. She grabbed her clothes off the floor and scurried to the bathroom. She closed the door and, with shaking hands, tried to negotiate sleeve holes and pant legs, clumsy as a teenager.

In the mirror, Natalie saw that her mascara was smeared. She took a tissue from a container on the shelf above the toilet and rubbed it under her eyes to little effect. "What are you doing?" she repeated, this time aloud. Then, quietly, she peeked back in the bedroom—*still asleep*—before padding into the living room. There, she knelt down to move the laptop closer to her. The screen was a blank blue with a line for the username and one for the password. Deciphering Simon's codes would take time, if even possible. Natalie closed the lid quickly, looked up as if expecting to be caught. She took a full breath and wandered to his bookshelf.

It was half-empty. The book titles had the words "wealth" and "finance" and "money" in them. There was one resting on its side, with the wrong end facing front, the pages rather than the spine. Instinctively, Natalie lifted the book to rearrange it. When she saw the cover, her stomach contracted, the regurgitated wine, putrid in her mouth. She ran to the toilet, spit out, then, everything pumping, heart and lungs, and leg muscles, returned to the bookcase. She opened *Get Happy Now* and read the inscription: "To Gillian, Much Joy and Success, Isabel Walker."

Who the hell was Gillian?

Papers had slipped out and fallen to the floor. Natalie's fingers felt fat and clumsy as she gathered them. She clutched them and the bestseller close to her and made sure her back was in the direction of the bedroom in case Simon appeared. In her hands were a few pages from the downloaded brochure of the annual Happiness Conference on Grand Cayman, with the dates accented by a yellow highlighter. The others were images of Isabel from a Google search, dozens of them, including the Photoshopped one that she, Natalie, had taken for the book jacket. Isabel looked alternatively regal or relaxed, pallid as a Swede in winter or luminous as if kissed by the Mediterranean sun. There was the posed picture from her website and candid shots of her at various events, that he, Simon, probably took himself—a voyeur.

Oh my God. Oh my God.

She bowed down, hands on thighs, head low, waiting for the nausea to abate. She had *fucked*—God, she hated that word, its guttural ugliness—a man obsessed with Isabel. A stalker, a voyeur, and who knows what else? But what was Natalie's role in his game? She could hear the chugging of her own blood when she thought of the splatter on the island road. What to do? Disclose her findings to him or play it dumb? She waited to see how her body would react next. It released the book back in the exact spot she'd found it. She crept to the bedroom, legs gelatinous.

Simon was awake now. The first few buttons of his shirt were undone and his feet were bare, but otherwise he was dressed. He was reclining against the pillows, legs sprawled. When he saw Natalie, he sat up to make room for her next to him.

She perched at the edge of the bed, no closer.

"That was quite nice," he said.

"I'm just wondering," she said, her voice jangly, "what was your girlfriend's name, the one you mentioned in the restaurant, when I told you I was divorced?"

The right side of Simon's mouth curled upward. "Why do you want to know?"

"Just interested in her and, uh, what kind of women you like."

Simon bent towards her. "Isn't that obvious?"

The smell of his skin was a trap, how it made her want to curl into him as if they were a couple. She eased away. "Do you mind . . . telling me?"

"Her name?" He shrugged. "Gillian Monroe."

The name, at least, wasn't a lie.

"Is she English, too, living in London?"

"She works in New York now. Why?" Simon stood up and stretched his arms above him as if preparing for a workout. "You don't need to be insecure, if that's what this is about."

"It's not that, just curious."

"She's not my favorite subject, things ended badly, and all that."

"Was she with you in the Cayman Islands?" *To see Isabel, the two of you, in this together, whatever "this" is.*

His muscles constricted so that his face closed up. His lips formed a straight line. "You're starting to be a little creepy."

She strained to sound nonchalant, but it came out a tremble, the yearning inside her growing. "I just meant, it was a vacation. It would make sense."

Simon shifted his weight even further to the side of the couch. "What's with this third degree? Do you put all the men you have casual sex with on trial?"

The definition of what had transpired shouldn't hurt. Yet she felt a pang between her ribs.

"There's just one more thing." She reached for her socks and boots, which were tucked under the bed. Time to go.

"I'm not sure I feel like answering." His tone had changed, the warmth gone. Natalie felt his desire for her drain away. His eyes had lost their light, and the air was still, nothing flowing from him now.

"I got a strange email a few weeks ago about the accident that night on the road."

"So?"

"*So*, I thought you might . . . know about it."

He didn't respond, the air so thick and cold, as if winter had slipped inside.

"It was anonymous. The person claimed I was lied to about the accident and that I should ask you about it."

He laughed, then, a real laugh, not forced, and glanced from side to side as if an audience was about to pop out from behind the furniture. "Is this some kind of spoof?"

"I thought you might have more than one email address, work maybe or—"

"That it was from Gillian?"

Natalie hadn't even considered that. The ex-girlfriend was a plausible suspect. The book was inscribed to her. Gillian Monroe could have researched the conference, printed out the photos. She could have left the book at his place when they broke up; it was published over a year ago. Natalie was certain that the worldwide annual conference began advertising months in advance. The timing matched up.

"I wondered, yes," she said.

"Is that what our dinner was about?" He drew a line between them with his finger. "Is that the reason you're in New York, to ask me about some odd email?"

She felt the trickle of sweat under her arms, wrenched on her boots. "Yes."

"No family portrait?"

"No, no portrait."

"What else did it say to drag you all this way?"

His face was still an enticing golden color, but she detected a grayish tint under his eyes, the lines fanning from the corners, long and skinny as mosquito legs. She made a quick calculation not to reveal details. "The point is that it meant that there was a witness, someone who saw the accident on the island. Don't you think?"

"I haven't a clue. And here you went to such lengths because you thought I was involved in—what?"

"At first, I thought you might have sent it using another email account," Natalie said. "Did you?"

"Now you've gone from creepy to disturbing."

His indignation seemed credible. But this could be attributed to good acting skills. He was a stranger, after all, a deceitful man hiding his Isabel fixation from her.

"Were you following Isabel to the Cayman Islands?" she risked. *Breath in . . .*

He grabbed his dress socks, charcoal with small white dots, from under the comforter. "I already told you I was on holiday, and I met you two on the road. Now I have to say I wish I hadn't."

"I didn't mean to imply anything. I'm just asking. Do you know anyone named bbGodfrey?"

"I think it best if you stick to your pictures of sweets and Shepherd's pie. You're not doing a very good impression of Sherlock Holmes." He cocked his head. "Is Isabel in on this arrangement, you and me?"

It wasn't just the question; it was the tone, the way it dropped into familiarity. He had contacted Isabel, she was certain. "I didn't tell her I was coming, if that's what you mean. Have you discussed that night with her? Have you asked her for money?"

"Oh, dear, that's pathetic. Would you like to check my portfolio? I'm quite capable of earning a sizable living without blackmailing strangers and for no reason."

"To not call the police, to . . . cover up that I hit and injured someone." She realized how bizarre her theory sounded.

He grimaced and shook his head, as if embarrassed for her. "You should listen to yourself."

Natalie stood up now. All she had to do was get her coat and run. "I found Isabel's book on your bookshelves. I was . . . just looking."

His mouth twisted with rage. "What else did you dig through without a search warrant?"

"It's not like that." She inched away. "There were photos of Isabel in the book, printouts from the Internet."

"That's Gillian's book, not that it's any of your business. I need you and your delusions to leave now."

Nodding, she hurried for the front closet.

He rushed in front of her. His breath was heavier, and he grunted once, not loudly, but enough for Natalie to recognize what he was stifling. She was more than a nuisance.

"I'll get a taxi," she said.

"Brilliant."

Natalie stood for a few seconds at the door, not turning around. She wanted to know more—about Gillian, about Simon's communication with Isabel—but fear clamped shut her throat.

Simon insisted, "Goodbye then."

She heard him walking away, in the direction of his bedroom. She could still feel him inside of her, could still hear his moans.

twelve

NATALIE AWOKE TO THE HUMMING SOUND OF THE ROOM'S climate control and the dull light wedged in-between the hotel curtains. She felt snug under the covers. Blinking into the still air of the immaculate room, she noted the desk in front of her bed, the modern lamp with the rectangular shade and the flat screen TV hanging above. She almost drifted off again. Then it flowed in like a draft under the window, what she'd done, what she'd found.

There was a rotten taste in her mouth and a great pressure on her bladder. She sprang up and rushed to the bathroom. On the toilet, Natalie tried to reconstruct the night she'd smashed the car into the dog—or person—tried to determine what Isabel's reaction was to Simon. But she hadn't witnessed the moment when they first caught sight of each other. And, anyway, even if Isabel had seen him before at a book signing with his ex-girlfriend, even if he'd introduced himself, she would have filed his image away under "another fan," with the hundreds of others she'd met. Chances were that she wouldn't have recognized him.

Natalie's thoughts looped around again: why was Simon there in the first place? Was he in Grand Cayman to see Isabel—and why, if it was his girlfriend who was the Isabel enthusiast, not him? Did Simon have some distorted idea that Isabel contributed to their breakup?

Bit of a shambles.

Natalie washed her hands in the porcelain bowl under the hook-shaped silver faucet, the décor so pristine and stark.

Over lunch that day in the Caribbean, when her stepsister had warned about Simon, she hadn't mentioned a prior run-in with him.

Isabel claimed she didn't want Natalie re-traumatized. But Isabel could have known more about Simon, his potential for trouble. She could have been attempting to safeguard Natalie. Her hand shook as she unraveled one of the rolled towels neatly stacked on the shelf.

Woolly-socks against the cropped carpet, she rushed to the bed, phone in hand. She pressed the sunflower yellow app, shut her eyes, tight. "You are in a place of tranquility. With each breath you are being renewed and regenerated. There's no sense of time. You are being healed, cradled by the sky." Her thoughts kept coming, flip-book picture fashion: Isabel noticing blood on the rented Camry, Simon hunting through the bushes, the claret patches on the road.

You were lied to.

Thumb on the screen, she stopped the sound of chimes, the promises that weren't coming true. Of what could she be sure? Simon being there in Grand Cayman, at the time of the Happiness Conference, and even on the same road that night. These weren't coincidences.

Natalie grabbed her carry-along bag. She could try to discover the role Simon's ex-girlfriend played in this connection to Isabel and whether or not bbGodfrey was the woman's pseudonym. Inside was her iPad. She had time to search the web. Her train to Boston left at one in the afternoon, an hour after checkout from the hotel. According to the phosphorescent clock numbers, it was only 8:10 a.m. Perhaps luck would bestow on Natalie some kind of proof: a Facebook page with favorite books listed or a blog. She had to attempt to smooth things over with Simon in case she needed additional information from him down the line. He'd used her, why she wasn't sure, but she'd used him too. If he still wanted something from Isabel, maybe he'd respond. She typed: "I'm sorry about the last part of our otherwise delightful evening. I should have been upfront with you. I enjoyed our dinner—and afterwards." She clicked on the wink emoji even as she rolled her eyes. "Yours, Natalie."

She thrust herself into the shower and out into another frigid day. Here in New York, Simon's harried city, the swats to her cheeks felt personal. The trees quivered without the coverlets of leaves. She hurried to a café around the corner. Armed with a large cappuccino and a whole-wheat bagel, she reentered the warmth of the hotel lobby with a shoulder-loosening sigh. Her boots clacked against the marble floor. She nodded at the hotel concierge, a stout man with a prominent birthmark on his forehead.

In the elevator, Natalie pushed the silver button that lit up with her floor number. Gillian Monroe. She imagined scenes from films where the detective examined notes written in parchment, the calligraphy and water marks providing clues. Her search would be easier. She'd start with a Google search, and then scrutinize Facebook and LinkedIn. Back in her room, she darted to her computer. There was no return email from Simon.

She scrolled back to the mysterious message that had brought her here. She clicked "reply" again. This time she wrote to bbGodfrey: *Still haven't heard from you. Why aren't you answering? What do you want from me?*

Was Godfrey planning a scheme to blackmail her?

Gulping down caffeine, she typed Simon's girlfriend's name into Google. There was a Gillian Court in Monroe, Michigan, and a solicitor by that name located in Manchester, England. Next, she tried Facebook. There were fifteen matches, including a woman posing seductively in a red lace teddy and fishnet stockings clipped onto her garter belt, a high school student with thick-framed glasses, and someone whose profile picture was a Scottish terrier.

"Help me out here," she said to the terrier.

Finally, buzzing from the double shots, she found an appropriate person on LinkedIn: an executive director at HSBC Bank in New York City, who'd been educated at Oxford University. This woman had held a previous job as an analyst for a company in Surrey, England. Natalie examined the woman's headshot, expecting a starling, shimmering beauty to match Simon's. Instead, Gillian Monroe was pleasantly pretty with her scrubbed face, open guileless smile, and light brown eyes. She didn't seem to be wearing makeup. Peering closer, Natalie pegged Gillian as being in her mid-thirties. The first button of her blouse was open, revealing the slope of her neck, white with the slightest beige undertones. Her cheeks were brighter with a seashell pink cast to them.

Simon had claimed that she and his ex-girlfriend had "similar taste in jewelry." As far as Natalie could see, this woman wasn't wearing any. Her neck was bare; her ears were covered by long, fine, brown hair. Her hands weren't in the picture. Maybe this was the wrong person.

Had Simon's girlfriend—whether it was this ordinary-looking British banker or another one—introduced him to Isabel? She sent this message to Gillian through LinkedIn: "I've recently been in contact with Simon Drouin. I'm wondering if you know anything about his interest in Isabel Walker, the author of *Get Happy Now*."

Natalie bit into her bagel with the vegetable cream cheese, which was bitter with scallion. She wouldn't confess to her exploits with Simon. But she needed to alert her stepsister about the second message from Godfrey. *Can you meet for coffee this week?*

A few minutes later her cell phone hummed. Isabel texted: *Where are you this weekend? Tried you last night.*

Was out, on a date. . . .

Fantastic! I want to hear all about it! Isabel sent her a wink. Just as Natalie had done with Simon.

HADLEY WAS STAYING after school for a meeting of the Save the Environment club, which gave Natalie this opening to meet Isabel. She was early, yet Natalie raced towards Faneuil Hall, a sense of urgency pressing under her ribs.

Towering skyscrapers lining either side of the narrow old European-style streets and the white steeple rising above the dignified brick Old State House filled Natalie's eye. The eighteenth-century granite structure held a bustling, indoor marketplace chock-full of ethnic and traditional New England food. Vendors sold their touristy souvenirs and handmade crafts along the arcades. There were multiple aromas of fudge and curry, of calzones and fish chowder, of garlic, cumin, and picante sauce. Natalie inhaled. She bought a coffee and sat at one of the extended wood tables in the center atrium in back of a couple of girls with BU backpacks, one in a neon pink down jacket, the other with shocking pink streaks in her hair.

While she gazed out of the Colonnade at a patch of overcast sky, Isabel glided in across from her with a paper cup in one hand, the string from the tea bag hanging over the side. "So, tell me about your date! I can't wait to hear."

"Oh, he turned out to be a mistake."

"Details!"

She felt the pull of intimacy: the longing to reveal her date with Simon, the discovery of the pictures in Gillian's copy of her book, and the pamphlet about the Happiness Conference. But she was edgy from shame and didn't want to be chastised, or worse, coddled: *I wanted to protect you. I knew he was stalking me, Simon and his crazy girlfriend.*

"Rather not rehash."

"That bad? At least you're getting back out there."

"The thing is, I got another one of the anonymous emails about the Cayman Islands."

Isabel shook her head, the diamond studs in her ears glinting. "How annoying. What did this one say?"

Natalie wrapped an arm around her waist. "That I was lied to. That the guy, Simon, was a witness."

"Witness to what?"

"He wasn't specific, just that there was blood on the car. I have a theory. Maybe Simon is sending them, using an alias."

"It's possible, I guess. Remember, last year, that woman in Oregon who emailed her mother was sick and asked me how to think positively about euthanasia? I told her to get professional help, but she kept contacting me for months until she let slip she was hearing God's voice speaking from the toilet bowl. Just the upstairs one, the downstairs one was mute."

"Oh, right." Natalie laughed. "It's not funny. But it kind of is."

"I know. Thank God for Debbie. She's helped people find therapists in their areas. Not exactly in her job description." Debbie: her assistant and ghostwriter.

"But Simon isn't mentally ill."

Parallel lines formed between Isabel's brows. "How would you know?"

Natalie stared into her cup, at the cinnamon sprinkled foam. Stupid slip-up. "I don't. But the point is that he, or whoever Godfrey is, thinks what I did is much worse than you're letting on."

"What did *I* do? Be logical. If someone was seriously hurt, he couldn't have just crawled off and vanished."

"I was out of it for a few minutes, in the car, when you were on the road."

Isabel reached out and grabbed Natalie's hand. "So, you think, what, that I quickly dragged a body into the bushes, that Simon helped me?" she asked, an edge to her voice.

"No, no, of course not. It's just that you'd do anything to save me from myself."

"Not let someone who was injured lie in the bushes."

Natalie pressed down hard on her breastbone. "Simon did the searching. Maybe he lied to both of us."

"What would be his motivation?"

"To extort money from you. Has he done that?"

"No, of course not," Isabel said. "That's absurd. No one has asked me for anything. No one has even contacted me. I'll double-check with Debbie, but she hasn't mentioned anything like that to me. Plus, I have no surplus money now, so it'd be a lost cause for him."

"Why message *me*, not *you*?"

"That's a separate issue. Let's reason this out." Isabel paused, rubbed her knuckle over her lower lip. "Okay, so if this Godfrey person actually is Simon, he saw you were more anxious that night than I was. Maybe he's trying to get a rise out of *you* to get me to react, to reach out to him."

Natalie thought of the images crammed into Gillian's copy of her stepsister's book. "That makes sense."

"I think the best course of action is to ignore him. Responding is just what he wants."

"You're probably right."

"We both have enough shit to deal with." Isabel raised her cup, took a sip. "Speaking of which, have you heard from Ellen?"

"No, nothing."

"I was at my dad's the other day. I looked around his home office, for the envelope, in case Ellen was mixed up. I didn't see anything."

The BU girls got up to leave. The one with the pink hair turned around to grab her bag, and Natalie noticed a silver hoop sticking out of her right eyebrow. "Can't wait to get out of this hellhole. Amsterdam will be so cool," she said loud enough for Natalie to hear. "Padua sounds great, too."

Natalie asked, "How's it going with Garrick's place, cleaning it out?"

"Slowly. The will takes up to a year to probate anyway. So, no rush to sell." She shook her head, as if to contradict herself and Natalie noticed there was a new severity to Isabel's face, the jutting cheekbones, the blanched complexion.

"I just could use the money from it right now to replace what I've spent on the business."

"Is the writing going okay?"

"Sparring with the editor on the direction. I need more time to sort it out, but the deadline can't be moved. It's not like I can just focus on the revisions. I have gigs to do, the workshops, travel." Isabel sighed. "My dad dying didn't help. Horrible to say but true. Listen, I'm sorry to bail. I have a four o'clock meeting with my publicist. She's trying to coordinate an interview on the *Faith Redmond Show* with my April pub date."

"That's amazing, Belle!"

Daytime host, psychologist Faith Redmond, had won an Emmy for her television show three years running. National exposure like that could catapult Isabel to the kind of success her publisher was pushing for. Natalie felt a ping of envy.

"Thanks. It's the publicist I'm paying for out of my own pocket so let's hope this works. Have to finish the damn book in time." She waved it all away. "Don't I sound privileged?"

"You have a lot to juggle. Maybe you should take out a loan or talk to George, sell some stocks so you can write full time."

The glance had a hint of a smirk in it. "I can't abandon my brand for months. It's what will sell the book. I'll handle it. If you get another email from this person, forward it to me. I'll give it to Debbie to deal with."

"Poor Debbie."

"Poor nothing. She makes a tidy sum. Please don't worry about this stupid harasser. If I thought he was a real threat, I'd say we should act right away."

Isabel stood up and kissed Natalie, her lips warm from her tea. "Say hi to Hadley for me. Tell her as soon as my schedule clears up, I'll take her to Cornelia's Closet."

Hadley's favorite shop on Newbury Street with its tables of trinkets and potions, racks of sweeping clothes made of silk and velvet, hand-made hats and jewelry hanging from iron hooks shaped like antlers. "Not when money's tight!"

"That's nothing. Keep me posted."

"Always."

She watched Isabel walk away in her calf skin coat, then checked her phone before putting on her hat and gloves. There was a text from Hadley, informing Natalie that the club meeting had been canceled. She was getting a ride home from a classmate.

Where are you? Natalie quickly shot back.

They had a rule—both she and Marc—that Hadley needed to run it by one of them before driving with someone they didn't know, especially another teenager. She wasn't sure if this was adolescent insolence or simply impatience on her daughter's part.

She hurried now through downtown Boston to a parking lot on Washington Street. Waiting for the attendant to retrieve her car, she glanced at her cell phone. No response from her child. *C'mon, Hads, answer me. Where are you?*

SHE WAS SPRAWLED on the couch as if on a beach lounger. Hadley didn't even look when Natalie got home or wiggle her sock-less toes with the peeling pedicure in greeting. In leggings and her *Liberté Egalité Beyoncé* t-shirt, she had ear buds in place, computer planted on her lap. She peered at the screen devoutly.

Natalie's breath slowed as she watched her daughter's fingers click across the keyboard with quick, expert precision. "Hads," she called out. "Hads!"

Her daughter pulled the wire out of one ear. "Yep."

"Why didn't you answer my text?"

"No battery. My phone's charging in my room."

Natalie sunk into the armchair next to the couch. "I was worried."

"What's new?" Hadley mumbled so low Natalie almost didn't catch it.

"Hey. I heard that. It was rude."

"Sorry, Mom." Her head bowed, the girl stared into cyberspace. "It's just this was no big deal."

"Your friends are too young to have licenses. And you're not supposed to ride with strangers."

"Morgan isn't a stranger to *me*. She's a senior."

"Priscilla's friend?" Natalie's thoughts scrambled.

"Yeah . . ." Hadley combed both hands from her scalp down through her hair, glanced away.

"You said those kids get 'wasted.' That's unacceptable."

"Mom, chill! She doesn't drink at school."

Natalie's posture snapped into place. Tall and tight. Maternal ferocity swelled. "I don't want you in a car with any of those girls again! Do you hear me?"

"Yeah, okay, Ma."

"Good."

She observed Hadley hunched over, arms wrapped around knees. For the first time she could recall, Natalie didn't apologize for her outburst. She could fail at everything else, but not at this.

In her office, she set about to follow up on some work correspondence. She clicked on her mail. Among the six messages, there was this:

The only reason I'm responding at all is because you mentioned Simon Drouin. I don't know what you mean by "in contact." If that's your delicate way of saying what I think it is, words of warning: stay clear of him, for your sake as well as mine. "Interest in Isabel Walker," is an understatement. Please don't contact me again. Gillian Monroe.

thirteen

———

"I DID SOMETHING STUPID," NATALIE SAID AS SHE STEPPED IN from the cold, "some detective work on my own."

"What do you mean?" Cate asked.

They entered Cate's place together, having met at the spice store at five o'clock. Natalie's friend switched on the light and dropped her leather bag on the floor next to a coat tree. Much of the house came into view at once, rustic and light and inviting. The high ceilings and back wall were covered in windows, and a glass door led to a small enclosed porch. The second-floor balustrade presented a view of the family room downstairs, everything open, a house with no secrets.

Natalie removed her jacket and pulled off her boots, one arm leaning against the wall for support. "Remember I told you about the last night in the Cayman Islands?"

"Of course. Wait. Do you want me to make tea? I have anything your heart desires."

That night with my mother erased. The one in the Caymans gone.

"A one-way ticket for Marc and Elizabeth to Papua New Guinea?"

"Better! Hibiscus Petals, Chamomile Citrus, Ginger Lemongrass, Ginger Plum, Peppermint, or Green Tea."

Natalie smiled. "Peppermint sounds good." She sat on one of the wood stools at the kitchen island. She glanced down at the scattered mail in the wicker basket where Cate threw her silver keychain of a Zodiac bull's face—long lashed with upward curved horns. Once Cate had said, "Taurus seems so boring, all stability and reliability.

But we bulls have our hedonistic side." Natalie had laughed, admitting she hated that her sign, Cancer, was a disease, ruled by the moon, all brooding and sensitive, clingy if kind. No crab knickknacks for her.

While Cate boiled water and prepared the teabags in stoneware mugs, Natalie revealed that she'd met Simon for dinner in New York. "He makes Brad Pitt look bad. He was funny. Charming. I went back to his place and. . . ."

Cate grinned. "Oh my God, you are so cute! Are you embarrassed 'cause you think I've been married so long I don't remember what it was like to have sex with a new guy? Believe me," she sighed. "I remember it fondly." She handed Natalie her mug and sat down across from her. "You deserve to have a good time."

"I haven't told anyone, not even Isabel."

"We've been friends forever. I'm the safest person in the world."

"Thanks. That part *was* pretty great." Natalie stared as the liquid in the cup clouded, then darkened. "But, then, something freaked me out."

Jaw so tight, fists clasped together, she relayed how she'd discovered Isabel's book with the slew of suggestive images tucked between the pages. Dry-mouthed, she confessed to her correspondence with Gillian. It felt freeing to share with Cate—but also a transgression. Didn't she owe it to Isabel to keep what she'd found a secret?

"That would freak me out, too." Cate lifted up her drink, steam rising from it, and blew on it. "A one-night stand, all for it. But you can't see this guy again. Promise me you won't."

Natalie nodded. "Isabel can't find out what I did. She warned me about him. But I want to tell her about Gillian, so we can figure out which of them *really* is obsessed with Belle and why. I'm thinking of saying I went back to his place and just had a drink."

A stern gash appeared between Cate's eyes. "Maybe leave Isabel alone for a while. She'll be worried about you. She just lost her dad."

Bobble-head nodding, "Of course." How selfish she must have sounded to Cate, not questioning Isabel's role as the caretaker, no matter what the circumstances. "Godfrey's email implicated me and accused Belle of lying."

"Who are you going to believe, Isabel or some crazy person who won't identify himself? It could be someone else from the conference. Did you see any suspicious characters?"

"I'm not sure," Natalie said. "There were so many people there, from all over the world."

"Anyone named Godfrey?"

"People wore name tags, but I didn't read most of them and the ones I did, it's a blur."

With fingers tapping her lip amateur-sleuth style, Cate asked, "Was someone harassing Isabel, or acting like he might stalk her? Or even just needy?"

"I wasn't with her for most of the conference," Natalie said. "At the party, there was one guy at the end who seemed upset she wouldn't spend more time with him."

"Could he have followed you?"

"I guess, but why would he contact me about the accident? I'm not sure how he could have even gotten my name."

"Let's assume he asked around. There were people there who knew your relationship to Isabel, yes?" When Natalie nodded again, Cate said, "So maybe he wants her to notice him and he reaches out to you. Maybe the guy is seriously fucked up and went to this thing thinking he'd meet these professionals who'd fix his life. He could have a huge crush on her. Not hard to see why. She's beautiful, always had guys falling all over her."

"That's true."

Cate smiled, skin crinkling, freckles like lightly sprinkled cinnamon. "Thomas Dean, her high school boyfriend. I had the biggest crush on him."

Filed away somewhere in the recesses of her banged-up brain was that name. Natalie pictured a rangy boy with a languid gait and eyelashes that met his bangs.

"You did? We were just kids."

"Thirteen, raging hormones. I used to want to go to your house so I could watch him play guitar in your living room. He was so hot."

"She always had good looking boyfriends." Until George.

"Exactly. She attracts them in droves. So, say Isabel blows this Godfrey off—or that's how he sees it—'cause his expectations are ridiculous."

"That doesn't mean I didn't hurt someone that night."

Cate said, "You didn't see anyone there and neither did Isabel or even Simon. And you looked."

"Simon did, in the bushes. There was nothing on the road but a few spots of blood, which I saw."

"So, this Godfrey guy might just be trying to provoke you."

Sipping her cooled-off tea, Natalie paused. "Maybe," she said after a moment passed.

"Even if this crazy guy followed you that night doesn't mean what he's referring to is real. I think you should see if he gets more insistent. If he does, you have to call the police. Get him to leave you alone."

Natalie circled both arms around her waist, tight as a cummerbund. "Okay."

Oh, how she longed to be exonerated for her crimes.

NATALIE HEARD BEYONCÉ riffing loudly. "Turn it down," she shouted once inside the apartment. What Cate had argued made sense, and yet, she couldn't shake her worries loose. She'd felt the thwack, animal or person. She'd done that, caused that action, whatever the damage, no matter how disturbed the emailer might be, whatever his motivations.

The music, with its assertive drumbeat, made her think of shiny black boots marching. Natalie rapped on her daughter's door. "Shush," she shouted. When she didn't get a response, she poked her head into the room. "I told you, Hads, use your earphones."

"Yeah okay," Hadley said. A moment later, the wires were dangling from her ears, and the noise had ceased.

Natalie entered her child's domain. Hadley's books were strewn across her desk and her Kurdish rug. She sat cross-legged on her bed, head bowed, thumbs texting. The goddess Durga stared down at Natalie with her black-rimmed, inscrutable eyes. She waved her eighteen arms, creating a juggling effect, snake in one, trident in another, sword in a third.

She walked over to her girl, kissed the crown of her head. "Aren't you going to say hello?" Natalie plucked out an ear bud.

"Hey! You told me not to blast it."

She stooped over, trying to decipher the girl's messages. Before Hadley tilted the phone away, Natalie caught the identifying name. *Dad.*

"Why didn't you want me to see it was Dad?"

"Do you mind? My texts are not public domain." Hadley's voice softened. "He just wanted to know if you were at Aunt Isabel's workshop."

"I skipped it this week to see Cate—which is none of his business. I don't comment on where he goes or whom he marries."

Hadley hunched over defensively.

"Tell Dad he doesn't need to ask about me."

"*You* tell him, Mom. I don't want to get in the middle."

She tousled her daughter's hair. "You're right. Sorry. Not your job."

In her bedroom, Natalie stripped down to her underwear and put on pajama pants and a faded tee. She rooted around her drawer for Marc's shirt with the Apple Computer logo and yanked it out. She carried it down the hall like a balled-up cotton rag that stunk from grease. In the kitchen, she stuffed the shirt into the garbage under the sink.

Once under her covers, Natalie viewed the novel on her end table. She flipped it open and tried to read, but the sentences didn't gel into meaning. She texted her ex: *Stop using our daughter to spy on me for ammunition. You're not getting her.*

Rarely did she turn on the TV atop her dresser. It was Marc's to watch news in bed, left behind, forgotten. Now she grabbed the remote and scanned through channels, settling on a rerun of a medical drama in which a handsome array of male and female doctors was operating on a brain tumor. "There's nothing more we can do. Cognitive function is gone." She switched it off.

When her phone buzzed, she read Marc's response: *What's with the paranoia, Natalie?*

Towards the end of the marriage, he'd sat on the edge of the bed, his back to her. "For so long, I felt terrible for you, the trauma you lived through. I used to think you wanted to recover. I'm not sure anymore. It's as if you like being damaged."

She was sitting, leaning against the headboard, clutching her knees to her chest. "That's a horrible thing to say."

He turned to her. His face was mottled from crying, the whites of his eyes pink. "You can't let go of your grief."

"How can I let it go when I can't even remember what happened? This is my life we're talking about."

"That's the problem. Hadley and I should be your life."

You don't get the right to diagnose me anymore.

The phone vibrated again, and she peered at it. But it wasn't a text; it was another email from Godfrey. Clenching her teeth so hard she felt pressure in her sinuses, she read: *Who leaves someone on the road to die? A person like that should be locked up. The police have it all on file.*

A yowling fury rose up. She hit reply and pounded out the words: *Why are you doing this? Tell me exactly what you know or leave me alone.*

For the next hour, Natalie focused on locating bbGodfrey by using several reverse-lookup sites. But there was no listing for the address. She could call the Cayman Police to call his bluff, to verify that there wasn't anyone on that street; there was nothing in their files. She squeezed her arms, covered by a flannel pajama top. But, what if he wasn't lying? Disclosure could be an admission of guilt, or at least involvement, in a hit and run, could lead to her arrest. She could try the local hospitals instead. But then she'd have to identify herself and her relationship to the patient—that is, if there had been one.

Dead end after dead end. There were no exits leading to a wide-open road.

What she needed was a private investigator, one of those guys with huge, paparazzi zoom lenses. Maybe she was cowardly, maybe immoral, for not coming forward. She couldn't stand thinking about it another minute. She shoved the laptop to Marc's side of the bed, as if it were a snapping turtle. Natalie rolled onto her other side and stared at the streamer of sky under the bottom of her blinds.

In her dream, she was concussed and lying in the hospital bed. There was a gauzy texture to her thoughts and, although she couldn't open her eyes, she could hear the people in the room.

"Poor thing," Garrick said, "had to lock her up."

Ellen said, "It's right there on her scan. Function gone."

"No," she wanted to shout. But she couldn't speak, stuck in this bed, unable to move or communicate. The thing inside her—a transparent slip made of ether—glided towards the ceiling, able to observe her empty carcass.

Simon whispered into Natalie's ear, "We lied to you. It wasn't a school at all. It was a psychiatric ward."

And then Natalie cried out. She heard her own voice shouting, "That's wrong." There was no one else there. It had been a nightmare, nothing more.

She unhooked the blanket that had fastened around her waist like a tourniquet and rushed from her bed into the hallway. She stopped outside Hadley's room. Had she alarmed her child? Natalie pushed open the door, heard nothing but steam shooting up through the pipes. She needed to set things right. Where to start?

Back to bed.

She lay on her side, under the sheet only, and watched the digital numbers of the clock until fatigue carried her back to the watery world of sleep.

In the morning, she bypassed listening to the *Wired Happy* app. Meditation couldn't help her now; it was like trying to ride a surfboard in a tsunami. She slid on wool socks and went straight to the kitchen to start the coffee machine, cell phone in hand. While the liquid dripped slowly into the carafe, Natalie sat at the table and checked for a response from the previous night's communication. If bbGodfrey were Simon, he was an early riser, too, so he might have responded to the questions she'd fired into cyberspace the previous night. No luck. But there were two new missives, one from Isabel inquiring as to her whereabouts the night before.

The other was: *I missed talking to you after the workshop. Hope you're not done with happiness. Jeremy.*

An idea percolated: Jeremy the reporter. She hunted for his credentials on the palm-sized screen. He'd graduated from journalism school and spent five years on staff at *The New York Daily News* before landing as a writer at the *Globe*. What would she be willing to discuss with him in exchange for his investigative services? What could she offer that wouldn't be a betrayal, wouldn't damage Isabel's reputation? A prick of pain in her belly.

She poured the coffee and drank it black, too soon, burning the roof of her mouth. "Shit," she said. Safer to use a neutral party, which Jeremy was not.

Natalie treaded past Hadley's room, careful not to make any noise. She ate a bag of trail mix in the glow of her computer, not switching on a light, as if to hide it from herself, her search for detectives. "Infidelity, Adultery in Boston, Massachusetts," read the first site. On the right side was a list with buttons to press for more information: "Spousal Surveillance," "Online Infidelity," "Traveling Cheater," "Gay Spouse."

She clicked on a one-man operation, a craggy-faced guy, with a gap between his front teeth. He specialized in the "corporate, financial and business industries to mitigate unnecessary risks." A third, purple and gray website boasted that Menotti and Associates specialized in "wrongful convictions," "medical malpractice," "employee/vendor fraud" and "civil rights."

She sucked on her upper lip, tasting salt. She could approach Jeremy without disclosing she wanted him to verify a crime. She could dodge the truth to get what she needed.

Natalie finished the nuts and raisins while composing an answer to JSonnenberg@globe.com. *Thanks for checking in. I'd be "happy" to meet soon.* She included her phone number.

fourteen

—

NATALIE WAS IN THE STUDIO SHE SHARED WITH TWO OTHER
photographers in central Boston. She'd set up a flash unit mounted
with a medium sized soft-box. The tableware was elegant, and the
texture of the ham was good, but the spiral slices were sloped over,
giving the meat a tired look. "We need to drape them better," she said
to Jessa, the food stylist with whom she'd become friendlier since
Marc's desertion. "Lift them up. Also, the glaze works except for this
glob of apricot. It looks too much like ointment spurting out."

"Gross. You ruined the effect for me," Jessa joked.

"Sorry." Natalie's phone rang. "Hold on."

She grabbed her cell from her back pocket for a quick peek at
the number. It was understood between her and her colleague, the
mother of a two-year-old girl, that work could be interrupted if your
kid needed you. Jeremy was not her kid.

"Go ahead," Jessa said, not inquiring about the caller. She flipped
her long hair over her shoulder so it wouldn't stick to the gooey syrup
or the Vaseline she'd used to patch up holes in the ham. "I'll work on
perking up our star."

Natalie dashed into the bathroom next to the entranceway. "Hi,"
she whispered to Jeremy. "Can I call you back in a few hours?"

"Sure thing. Working?"

She thought of his round eyes, how he'd gotten stuck in pigeon
pose, that he had a Retriever. "Trying. But my ham isn't cooperating."

"Funny, my trout is rebelling."

Natalie leaned into the warmth of his voice. She liked the rich timbre, the joviality. "Trout are notorious agitators, not as bad as fried crabs. No matter how hard I try, the legs always make them look nasty."

"Okay, I'm out of my depth here. I'm guessing you're a chef."

"Food photographer. I thought you knew, you being a spy and all."

"Nope, 'cause I'm only a junior spy, got my kit at Toys 'R' Us. But I'm friends with Bob Garvey at *Boston Magazine*."

"I've worked for Bob!"

A thrill ran up from her belly to her breastbone. *No.* He was only flirting and making this connection between them to get to Isabel. It was so hard to trust people, least of all, herself.

"Small world," he said. "I'll let you get back to your ham. When is a better time to catch you?"

"After work. I'm done by 2:30."

"I'll call you this afternoon. Enjoy your meat."

"Thanks," Natalie smiled, despite her apprehension. "I will."

THE CAR WAS idling outside Hadley's school when Natalie's cell beeped. She fumbled inside her pocketbook before noticing that the phone was upright in the cup holder. The text message from Jeremy read: *Is now a good time?*

Natalie typed: *Sure.* She gazed out the window at the American Flag waving from the gabled roof of the building's facade. She wanted to have faith in his good intentions.

A second later, he called.

"Hi," she said.

"Thanks for answering me. I should have told you what I was doing at the workshop upfront. Guess I didn't want you to blow my cover." He laughed, that hardy sound. He was a generous laugher, she decided. "Now I do sound like 007."

Her anger from their last meeting dissipated. She felt the stirring of attraction and thought of Simon. Attraction was dangerous. "Not sure I approve of your tactics."

"But you emailed anyway. Would you like to meet for coffee?"

"Only if you don't grill me too much about Isabel."

"Ah, a food verb! I like it. I promise not to grill or sear. I'll . . . ugh, what's the opposite of grilling? Tartaring?" he asked. "I don't think that can be made into a verb. It sounds like tar and feathering."

She let loose a giggle. "We can stick to a discussion of your book. No interviewing me."

"Excellent. I'll come to your neighborhood. What evening is good?"

"That's a schlep from your job."

"Hey, you're doing me a favor."

"Right," Natalie said. Above the flag was a cloud-filled expanse, sodden with the next snow. *Don't misunderstand like with Simon.* "I have a favor to ask of you as well."

"A cliffhanger," he said. "I love a good cliffhanger."

SHE HAD GIVEN Jeremy directions to Mindy's Corner and was waiting for him, two evenings later, the only patron in the diner.

He opened the front door with a puzzled expression on his face. He was wearing a down park and chukka boots this time. He hadn't shaved, giving him a scruffy look, which she liked.

"Classy joint," he said, sliding into the booth across from her.

"I thought it was fitting, you being a newspaper man."

He smiled and she noticed a pencil-mark scar on the right side of his mouth. "You've seen too many forties movies. Today, we newspaper men eat at hipster, vegan, gluten-free cafés where you aren't allowed to smoke."

"I'm sorry to hear that," Natalie said. "Mindy's specializes in heavy, fattening food. But with real ingredients, like in times of yore."

"Yore! Best era ever." He tugged off his gloves, one, then the other.

The waitress with the puffy eyelids approached them with menus, this time, wearing a shiny fuchsia lipstick. The blond dye was fading from her hair, the roots spreading like an oil spill. She wore a name tag that Natalie hadn't noticed before: "Jean."

"Hi, Jean," Jeremy said. "What's good here for an after-dinner snack?"

"Pie," Natalie and the server said at the same time.

Jeremy grinned boyishly. "Pie it is. What are my choices?"

Once they'd ordered and were alone with their glasses of tepid water, she said, "Tell me more about your book."

He slammed one fist on top of the other. "My goal is to debunk the positive psychology movement, expose it for what it's been since the nineteenth century."

"Which is?"

"Junk, plain and simple. Neoliberal claptrap, now, this idea that we are responsible for our own fate. Mindfulness and finding your bliss and all that garbage isn't a substitute for health insurance or a living wage or the grief of losing someone to gun violence."

Natalie felt the thickness of his indignation, saw how it made his spine straighter, his eyes brighter. His obsession with Isabel wasn't like Simon's, seedy and submerged, but it was an obsession all the same. "Isabel isn't dealing with those political issues."

"Of course not. Happiness, as a commodity, is a luxury of the well-off."

The waitress balanced their two decafs, a small pitcher of milk, and Jeremy's cherry pie on a tray. "Here you go. Enjoy."

Natalie watched her walk back to the counter, her rounded ankles with no delineation from her calves, her tight black pants and white sneakers. She wondered if Jean was happy.

"There are other . . . things," she said, thinking of those brain scans with their ruinous black splotches, "psychological factors, mistakes that linger, that make people miserable—no matter their social class."

"We all struggle with that," he said, peering.

Every word he'd uttered was true and noble and confirmed Natalie's lack of confidence that she could be mended. Perhaps self-forgiveness could only come through good acts, "mitzvahs" as her mother called them. "You don't believe in meditation or yoga, any of those things that are supposed to help you?"

"I believe in anything that gets you through the day. But the notion that it's your own fault if you're suffering is an insidious American concept."

She stared at Jeremy's slice as he cut it so that the crust cracked and the filling oozed out of the top. Food was so safe and quiet, sitting as it did without protest, making no demands. "So, your book is about our pathetic social system?"

"It's about how our American philosophy emphasizes the world of the mind, our obsession with individuality and attitude and can do spirit, exonerating the role of government and corporations. Even the most die-hard liberals have been convinced that if they follow their passions, success will follow. We should all be able to shape our lives in our own selfie images."

"That's not what Isabel's doing." Natalie looked down at the chip on the rim of her cup. "She's just giving us techniques to help us . . . cope, to stave off despair."

He ran his fingers from the top of his head through his hair so that his curls sprouted up like a stream in a water fountain. In a gentler voice, he suggested, "Maybe that's what you need to get from her promises."

An opening she was not ready to take. "Why not just write a book on social policy?"

He fiddled with his fork, scraped it against the gooey cherry that had run onto his plate. "My twin sister, Alex, died of cancer two years ago. The last few months of her life were unbearable."

"I'm so sorry," she said. She felt an urge to caress his stricken face.

"Thanks. When it metastasized, Alex saw these alternative healers who told her it could be controlled through positive thoughts, chanting, talking to the universe, eating kale, all kinds of shit." Jeremy shook his head. "Alex was a smart woman, but when she got sick, she got into all these insane things."

"Poor thing! She was probably grabbing hope wherever she could."

"She parroted back that she wasn't working hard enough at healing, that her suffering was trying to teach her something." Jeremy chopped up his dessert into pieces as he spoke. "Alex wasted a lot of money on people who prey on the vulnerable. My family tried to get her to stop, especially my dad. Five weeks after she died, Dad had a fatal heart attack."

"Jesus," Natalie whispered. She reached for him, touched his rolled-up sweater sleeve above his wrist. He didn't draw away. He stopped butchering his dessert.

"Yeah. So now you know *my* way of staving off despair—illuminating how these disreputable gurus operate."

"That's not Isabel. She would never say cancer was someone's fault or that her program could cure it."

Jeremy pushed his plate forward and leaned back. "Are you willing to talk to me about what she *does* believe? And what you think about it? I'm interviewing people who are drawn to this movement to see how it works out for them. Look, I'll make sure you get privacy. I have plenty of experts who love to be quoted. I'd use your first name or not mention it at all, if that helps."

A swat of disappointing sadness. They were back to business, the exchange of goods and services, the bartering arrangement. Never mind that Natalie liked this man. He had a request, and so did she. "All right. But here's the favor part. What are your investigative skills like? I need someone to get some information for me."

He smiled quizzically. "I'm not a PI. I don't do stakeouts or follow guys around with my camera and catch them in the act. Whattaya need?"

"Someone with better research skills than I have, and resources available to them, to find out something that occurred recently in another country."

"International espionage! Like a coup?" he joked.

"A bit more personal, not about Marc. That's my ex."

"Yeah, I gathered."

Natalie looked directly at him, something she rarely did with people out of shyness. She felt emboldened by his open expression, the shock of intimacy. "There was a car accident in the Cayman Islands last November. The people who witnessed it said a dog was hit, that it ran away. I just want to put my mind at rest. Nothing turned up online. There may be no record of what happened—that's okay. You must have better ways to find out," she stumbled, "if anyone knows anything about it."

Natalie had wondered if Jeremy might be able to trace the car to Isabel through the rental company. But since it had been a hit and run, and there was no evidence that their vehicle was involved, she couldn't see how. Still, she needed to protect Isabel just in case.

"That's you," he said, and pointed to her ringing phone.

Natalie glanced at the name on the screen. "It's my daughter. Excuse me a second."

"Hey, everything okay?" she asked, as she hurried to the back of the restaurant. She ducked into the bathroom with the image of a skirted figure on the door. It was a tiny cabinet of a room, with a dried-out bar of soap on the sink, and a chipped toilet seat.

"Can you talk to Dad for me?" Hadley asked. "I wanna skip my visit this weekend."

A bubble of satisfaction. "Why honey?"

"Cara is having a party Saturday night. Dad said it's his only time to see me. Yeah, well, weekends are my only time to go to parties."

"That *is* a problem."

Should have thought of that when you walked out, Marc.

"I want to see my friends, not watch *Pride and Prejudice* with Dad and his girlfriend."

"*Pride and Prejudice?*"

"Elizabeth's, like, in love with it, her 'namesake' is badass she says. Uh, sorry. Didn't mean to bring her up."

"Hads, it's okay. You don't have to avoid talking about her."

"It's just . . . I told her I've already seen the whole ten hours with *you.*"

"Elizabeth wants to watch the long version with Dad?"

Natalie tried to visualize Marc viewing this Jane Austen marathon, his computer perched on his lap, his foot a maraca. If you asked him about Mr. Darcy or Bingley, he'd stare and ask, "Are they friends of Hadley's?"

"I know. Right?" Her daughter laughed.

"I'll talk to Dad about you skipping this visit."

"Thanks. It's awkward being forced to go to his house every weekend. My friends act as if I'm being locked up in a psych ward."

Natalie hit her elbow against the sink and startled from the pain as a forgotten exchange popped out of its grungy burrow.

In the car, she'd read *Jane Eyre* asking about Lowood, "And why do they call it Institution? Is it in any way different from other schools?" and turned to her mother, her shadowy profile. "This is what happened to Isabel's mother; she was locked away, too."

Her mother's hands clawed the wheel. Her voice rose. "Where did you hear that?"

"What does it matter if it's true?"

"Sigrid was in the hospital for a little while, not a school."

"Mom, I don't want *this*. I don't want any of this."

"I know, honey. I know you're upset. But I need to do what's best for you."

Natalie had imagined it, being imprisoned like Sigrid: grim, dank walls and cold showers, liquid-y cereal or eggs for breakfast and canned beans with fatty meat for dinner, served on tin trays with medications that a nurse ensured wasn't tucked under the tongue, daily lectures on behavior, always being watched, isolation the punishment for misbehaving.

The memory ended there. Maybe stopping her mother from reaching Dr. Strout's office was an act of survival. Maybe she'd been so desperate that she'd thought her own death would be better than the alternative. Or maybe she hadn't thought anything at all. Wrung out from arguing, blood throbbing in her ears, her arm simply might have jerked up, the flashlight flung out like a sword.

Hadley said, "Mom, you still there?"

Natalie rubbed her elbow. "Yes, I'm here."

"I didn't mean to upset you about Dad and Elizabeth."

"You didn't, honey. I'll be home soon."

Back at the table, she blurted out, "Do you think you can get records from the 1970s on someone?"

"What happened to the Cayman Islands?" Jeremy's voice flickered with humor.

"That's the priority. This second favor is only if you have time."

What was the triangular relationship between her mother, Sigrid, and herself? *Half a pill to help me sleep! Don't confuse me with Sigrid. Laura and Dr. Strout thought it was a good idea to send you to a boarding school for troubled teens.*

"You may be in need of a professional sleuth here, not a cowboy newspaperman."

Natalie bent forward as if the waitress with the overly optimistic lipstick color was listening. "I don't know for sure if this woman was ever in a residential treatment program or an outpatient one."

"Context?"

Natalie said, "She was Isabel's mother. I don't want to go into too much more about her, if that's okay. Obviously, this has nothing to do with your book."

"Got it," he said, entering information on his phone.

"Thank you. I promise to let you interview me about Isabel's program, anything you want."

Natalie would be honest about her own struggle with the positive psychology movement. But she wouldn't hurt Isabel, her other mother, the one who would never have sent her away.

fifteen

___

MARC HAD AGREED TO LET HADLEY GO TO CARA'S PARTY AND, right on time, the next morning, he buzzed the intercom to Natalie's apartment. She glimpsed her ex-husband in profile on her building's steps, his hair clipped shorter than usual. He was hatless, and the tips of his ears were a stinging red from the cold. He wore the goose down jacket she'd bought him for his birthday the year before he left her and thick gloves she'd never seen before.

Natalie pressed her finger on the button quickly, then took it off, not wanting to talk to him. "Your father's here," she called to Hadley.

When her daughter didn't appear, Natalie found her standing at the kitchen sink. "Do I have to go, Mom? I'm beat from last night."

"I know, honey. But this was the arrangement."

Hadley kneaded the toe of her boot into the floor tiles, stuffing a flake of cereal into the grout. "Guess I can nap while Elizabeth bakes her 'famous' sugar cookies with M&Ms. Not exactly the Best Pastries in Boston, like you get to shoot, Mom."

Natalie caressed her child's cheek, battling vengeance (*see what you've done to her, Marc?*) and magnanimity (*you don't have to defend me, Hads*). "Where's Dad in all this? I need to talk to him about doing other things with you."

"Nah, not your job."

"It *is* my job. Wait here."

Hadley's sigh was one of a weary elder.

When Natalie heard the knock on the door and opened it to see Marc, she had that strange sensation of his duality. He was her husband

and not her husband, as if this was an identical twin or a clone of the man she'd been coupled with for two decades. His mouth, the mouth she'd kissed more times than she could ever count, was set, a barrier to intimacy. His lashes were dusted with snow. "Hey. Where's Hads?"

"Hiking the Appalachian Trail."

"Is she ready, Nat?"

"Sure. Always at your beck and call."

He pinched the bridge of his nose. "What's wrong?"

Natalie felt an opening inside her, a vertiginous release, as if a bottle of noxious chemicals were uncapped. "She'd like to spend time with her father, not always with his mistress. Oh, I'm sorry, *fiancé*."

"We're very aware of how hard it's been on her. We've been taking Hadley to places she suggests, new restaurants, shows in town. Elizabeth insists on disappearing for part of every visit, so Hadley can be with me." He lifted his chest up. "We're very aware what a hard transition this has been."

We, we, we.

Natalie said, voice wobbling, "Elizabeth has all the answers when it comes to *my* daughter. No more *Pride & Prejudice* or sugar cookies."

"That was Hadley's choice. And she ate half-a-dozen cookies last time. She doesn't want to hurt you by saying she likes anything about Elizabeth."

Fuck you, Marc. Fuck you. Fuck you.

Was he right, were Hadley's complaints and protestations, all for show? Did she like Elizabeth for the ordinariness of her choices, her big Hallmark channel family, her ability to make Marc happy?

"Dad," Hadley said quietly, from behind her. "I'm ready. Let's just go. Love you, Mom."

They left in a hurry, a mash up of Hadley's goodbye hug and Marc's hustling their daughter out the door. The look in her child's eyes: as if Natalie were an injured animal wrapped in a box and left at their front door.

Natalie stood in the hush of her solitude. The only sound was the sizzle of the radiator. The motto from Isabel's latest handout ran through her head: *CURE: Connect (with friends), Understand (your signature strengths), Re-frame (your life story), Empower (yourself).*

The easiest of these tenets was the first one. She called Cate, trembling from heartbreak. Marc's proclamation of his unity with Elizabeth was a deep stab. "Hey," she said when her friend answered. "I'm thinking about going to a gallery later in the city. You up for a trip?"

"Sorry, kiddo. I'm on call as chauffeur all day."

"No problem. Get together soon?"

"Love to. You okay?"

"Yeah. Go ferry the boys."

Natalie rushed to get out. Coat on and bag with Hadley's shopping list inside, she shoved her feet into her boots. The pharmacy—anywhere out in the world—was a good enough destination. When she reached the center of town, this town they'd chosen together—she and Marc—Natalie parked in the village's main artery. She passed the pizza parlor, the bagel place, and The Cow Jumped—an upscale children's clothing store with cotton snowballs, giant paper snowflakes, and scarves in bright multi-color stripes on display. Every single spot she'd frequented with him.

In the drugstore, she retrieved Hadley's piece of paper from her pants pocket, on which was scribbled: deodorant, tampons, Burt's Bees lip balm. Her cell rang, and Jeremy Sonnenberg's name lit up.

"Hi," she said. "This is a surprise."

"I have something for you."

"Wow, that was quick."

"Easy assignment."

Staring at the word "beeswax" on the yellow chapstick in her hand, she said, "I can't really speak now. I'm at the store."

"You have time later?" he asked, so easy. She couldn't gauge anything from his tone. "Want to meet?"

"I was going to go to an exhibit on Commonwealth."

Saying it, she realized this was her plan. Maybe viewing art would help her understand her "signature strengths." It was hard to count her pictures as anything more than good commercial work. But she could try again, someday, to capture personal narratives, aim for life in motion.

Jeremy said, "I'll meet you there. Just name the time and place. We can grab a bite afterward."

"Are you sure?"

"Hey, I'm a sophisticated guy."

She would have smiled but her body was on animal alert, watching for predators.

NATALIE GAVE HERSELF an hour alone before Jeremy's scheduled arrival. Walking down one corridor of the Photography Retrospective on Women Past and Current, she wondered whom she would choose as a subject if she ever dared to try. Hadley? Well, of course, ultimately her daughter would be the most beloved subject. But it might be better to start with someone less precious, a model or an acquaintance. Less at stake if she failed. Thinking of Jeremy's face—the way his eyes crinkled at the edges, his chapped upper lip with just a dab of blood on it, the laugh lines that rippled from his mouth like waves when he smiled—she felt that spark again. Could she try some candid shots of *him*?

She moved slowly through the hall to rest in front of Imogen Cunningham's *Edward Weston and Margrethe Mather, 1923*. The artist's portrayal of the couple—shot from a side-view, both man and woman with their eyes closed, she with her head tipped back in sensuous abandon—had resonated with her mother. Margrethe Mather, with her curved hands and neck, was abdicating herself to Weston. Natalie felt a wave of repulsion: something in Mather's fluttering hands, in her submission, how it appeared to consume her. Hadn't her mother done the same with Garrick, despite his relentless work schedule, her suspicion of an affair with Ellen, her turning to sleeping pills to function?

Natalie forced her attention to the next image in the gallery, Ilse Bing's *Dancers, Ballet Errante, 1933*. An anguished dancer posed, curled on her knees, while a caped female hovered in the background, face in shadows, a guardian angel figure. It was as if Bing had captured the story of Natalie and Isabel.

Egocentric. Personalizing everything.

She moved to another photograph. She could admire this one without identifying with the lip-puckering, wind-blown Marilyn Monroe. She heard a man say, "Nice gams."

She turned to see Jeremy, standing next to a shot of three women walking on a boardwalk in bikinis and high heels. His parka was unzipped, revealing a forest green sweater with the tag hanging from it. She smiled at this mistake, one Marc never would make.

"Very shapely," she agreed. "Didn't realize you were here."

"I'm sneaky that way."

Natalie hugged her arms around her torso. "Should we go somewhere to talk?"

"Let's take in some culture first."

Probably, he was stalling, fearful she would unravel once he presented his findings. He might want to enjoy this time, their easy banter. But, she reminded herself, he didn't know her, what she was capable of.

"Umm," he said as he approached the famous 1899 platinum print, *The Manger,* a nativity scene of a mother in a shawl, which covered her nursing infant at the breast and cascaded to the floor. Sunlight broke through the window of the wood stable, illuminating the headpiece, sheer as a wedding veil.

"I love this one," Natalie said. "It's so peaceful."

"It's pretty, a little too romantic for me."

"You *are* cynical."

"You have no idea," he said. "Now these I love!"

Jeremy opened his hands. Before him hung three black and white shots titled *Incarceration*. Natalie read the plaque below. They were part of a recent series, by a young photographer who'd spent over a month documenting the lives of female prisoners in the California system. The first was of a Hispanic teenager, staring vacantly into the camera. There were deep scars in her arms below the elbows, marks that indicated self-cutting. She was enormously pregnant. The next shot was of an older woman, her face a wreckage of skin, lips pursed in a scowl.

"These are good," Natalie agreed.

"This reminds me of my ex-girlfriend." Jeremy pointed to the third picture: a woman in a kerchief, with a piercing stare, middle finger raised.

"Uh oh. I hope you don't say that about all your exes."

"Nah, just Greta," he said. "This woman looks happier than Greta was with me at the end. Can't say I blame her. I was no prize to live with."

What would the camera reveal that she didn't want to know?

"You guys lived together?" she asked.

"Yeah, for a while. She left me a few months after Alex died."

His sister had died two years before, so maybe Jeremy had recovered from the breakup. Although, unlike Simon, he didn't seem over anything, grief spouting from him like seepage.

Natalie said, "That sounds hard."

"Yep. I was depressed and pissed off most of the time."

"But you got to keep the dog?"

"Nope. Reed came afterwards. He's not even a year old yet." When she said, "Aw," he grinned. "I bet you'd love him."

She nodded, unsure if this was just another sweetener to get information out of her.

"You think these two would profit from Isabel's workshop?" Jeremy gestured to the photos. "They look like good candidates."

Natalie stared at the older woman with the scrunched-up expression, a lifetime of misery shining out of the one eye not in shadow. "I think they're too damaged.'"

"Some people are." He tapped her elbow. "C'mon, let's get outta here."

Natalie followed him around the corner. They descended steps to a restaurant below street level. The place was dark with aluminum furniture and a long, cobalt blue bar. Various beer bottles, with a variety of colorful labels, lined the glass shelves in back of it. Natalie watched the three college-age guys at the next table, drinking and grunting with laughter.

"So, what did you find out?" she asked, jittery.

Jeremy cleared his throat. "I lucked out with Sigrid Walker. She was in MMHC, the most obvious place. For almost a month in '72. Those old paper files should have been destroyed years ago, but no one has gotten around to it. Happens all the time."

"What's MMHC?"

"Massachusetts Mental Health Center."

"What was wrong with her?" she asked.

"Major depression." He drummed his water glass with his fork. "As far as my contact at records could determine, she was only hospitalized the one time. She had a course of ECT."

With a shiver, Natalie realized, "Electric shock?"

"Yeah, intense."

Natalie imagined a mouth guard being inserted between coral lips—the color of the lipstick in the couple of pictures Isabel had of her mother—a set of electrodes being placed on Sigrid's pale forehead, followed by a seizure, which caused her eyes and mouth to clench in pain. Her gut whorled, and she put both hands over her belly. "I had no idea."

"You must have suspected when you asked me to do the research."

"I didn't have any details; no one talked about her much in my family. Isabel had overheard things, whispers."

"What *did* you know about her?"

"Sigrid died when Isabel was five," she said, starting from the beginning. "Her dad never mentioned her, not in front of me."

"What about your mom?

Natalie shook her head. *This* was the real beginning, then. "I asked her once, and she said that Isabel was mixed up."

"Can you bring it up now?"

"She died when I was thirteen."

"Crap. I'm sorry to hear that."

"Thank you. And thanks for cracking the case for me, so to speak." The muscles in her face were sore when she smiled.

"What about Isabel? Is it taboo?"

"Nothing is. But, I don't want to upset her. That day we met for coffee, I remembered something . . . from when I was a kid," she said, unbraiding the knot gingerly, "a connection between Sigrid and me and my mother."

"And Isabel?"

"Well, she was shaped by losing her mom, sure. We had that in common."

"Of course," he said. "It makes sense the field she chose."

"Yes. She's devoted to helping people. I went through a really rough patch when I was a kid, after my mom died, and she saved me. I mean, emotionally."

His eyes were large, a deep umber brown. "No wonder you're so loyal to her."

"Other than my daughter, she's my only family."

"I get it. So, was this helpful?"

"Yes, thanks."

"Not a problem." Jeremy bit into his burger, which the waiter had just delivered. He wiped ketchup off of his fingers with his napkin. A kind of hopped-up energy emitted from him. "I have information about the accident in Grand Cayman. There were a few significant car crashes that night, but only one in the area you gave me."

It seized her, a hand around the neck. She stared into the glass at the lemon wedge. When photographing a slice, she'd dip it first in water to keep it from browning before placing it on the plate.

He asked, "Were you the one driving?"

"Yes," she said, twisting the skin between collarbones. "It was me."

He nodded. "I figured."

"What did you discover?"

"A fifteen-year-old girl named Grace Cooke was out walking not far from Turtle Farm Road in the East End of the island and was hit."

She felt the floor tilt forward as if the room were rocking. "Is she alive?

"She survived the crash. Was that the name of the street you were on?"

"No idea. I went back but didn't see a sign anywhere." Had Isabel? "How badly was she hurt?"

Jeremy flicked a tortilla chip with his thumb and second finger, as if it were a bug he wanted to shoo away. "It wasn't great. She suffered internal bleeding, a ruptured spleen, and facial lacerations."

"Jesus." Natalie was swooped up into the eye of the panic, dizzy-headed, feeble-limbed. She pawed her pocketbook, fingers on wallet, on keys, on pack of Juicy-Fruit, on cell phone and on the bottle with two Xanax jingling when she clutched it.

"Because she was underage, I had to do some digging. Her name was kept out of the newspapers—also, the extent of the injuries."

Natalie remembered the black taffeta sky, and that it was hard to delineate where it met the road. Could the girl have blended into the night so that Isabel had never caught sight of her? Where was Grace when the three of them—Isabel, she, and Simon—surveyed the area?

"We looked everywhere. There was no one on the road," she said.

The plastic bottle was in her lap, and she pushed her palm down, trying to unscrew its immovable cap. It didn't budge.

"Who was with you?"

"Isabel and some man in the car behind us. They thought I hit a dog."

"But you didn't actually see anything there?"

"No, I swear. How did the girl get to the hospital?"

"There's no record of who brought her in, but it wasn't a 911 call. No ambulance was dispatched."

"We didn't call, well, obviously," she said. "It was so dark, even with the headlights on. We never saw anyone. I guess she could have been thrown into the bushes, somewhere we couldn't see."

Was she speaking too quickly?

He studied her for a moment and then said, "This girl was seriously injured and driven to the hospital."

"Maybe she was screaming and someone else heard her, someone out walking?"

He looked askance. "In the pitch dark? I guess anything's possible."

Natalie stared at her soup, the thick bright slices of okra, the shavings of onion, the shiny bits of tomato and bright green peppers, the chunks of chicken and sprinkling of rice. The bowl of food shimmered with beauty. She should eat. It was after two and she'd skipped lunch. She tried a spoonful, which was so spicy she needed to sip her seltzer right away. She ate one more anyway, for strength.

"I've gotten these anonymous emails," she said. "They've worried me. The person claims he knows there was blood on our car and mentioned Isabel by name. The last email was the worst. It said: 'Who leaves someone on the road to die?'"

"Seriously?"

"Yes."

His eyes widened with glee. "That's very Stephen King creepy. Sounds like a prank."

She took a long breath, another trick to calm down. "The man in the car who helped us search . . . he could be the one sending the emails, one of Isabel's stalker fans, trying to get at her through me. I guess it could be a sort of prank."

"You mean that he showed up on this remote street in the Caribbean, out of the blue?"

"He could have followed her. It was *his* headlights in my rearview that made it so I couldn't see the road."

"That's pretty convenient."

"No, listen," she insisted. *Please. Please. Believe me.* "We were there for a big event—well, Isabel was. I was there for a vacation. The conference was highly publicized online, on her website, and other places."

"Has this kind of thing happened to her before?"

"Not this extreme. But she's dealt with some seriously troubled, even delusional people, fans, who try to get her attention."

He stuck a chip in his mouth and finished it in two bites. "I'm sure you've wondered why he wrote to you and not Isabel."

"I saw the man . . . near our hotel the next day and he asked for my info. I was stupid enough to give it to him."

"That doesn't explain why he didn't try to contact her directly."

"She hired an assistant to weed out these people," Natalie said, her blood stirring. All her effort now was on this: validation. "He may have tried, but I was an easier target."

"I'm sure Isabel's assistant can verify that for you."

"Isabel checked. Nothing."

"I suppose he's the most likely person. It's weird, though."

"Exactly." Those photos of Isabel crammed into Simon's copy of *Get Happy Now* fell to the floor like confetti. "Do you know how to trace an emailer . . . if they have a Gmail address?"

Jeremy shook his head. "I can't legally. You can't get Google to cough-up the identity of its Gmail users for something like this. You'd need a court order, and the guy would have to be threatening to blow up the White House. Tech companies are fighting the government on accessibility to their users."

"I'm just not sure what to do now."

"Call the Cayman police," he said. "Be straight about it. If you tell them what you told me, maybe they can put your mind to rest."

"Or arrest me."

"Doubtful."

"I could just let the whole thing go," she said.

"Yep, you could. But something tells me you won't." He cut the air with his hand. "You'll figure out the right thing to do."

"I hope so, thanks."

Natalie felt febrile with dread. She wondered about the repercussions if she *were* at fault. She could lose custody of Hadley. She could go to jail. It would be too much to endure.

Still, she couldn't shake the feeling that she deserved to be punished.

sixteen

"YOU ALL RIGHT, MOM?"

Natalie was loading the dishwasher after dinner, the hum in her head: *internal bleeding, a ruptured spleen, facial lacerations.*

Quickly, she swung around. It was the sharp, high whistle of fear in her daughter's voice that she never wanted to hear again.

"Sure," Natalie said. "Just thinking about a client who owes me money."

Even though Natalie knew her stepsister was conducting seminars in LA, she'd texted her. She'd gotten this response: *It will be late for you when we end. Tomorrow ok?* She agreed, of course. She'd emailed Simon: *What do you know about Grace Cooke? Were you the one that brought her to the hospital?*

"Are we broke?" Hadley chewed the inside of her cheek, her cell phone hanging limply in her hand, like a favorite toy she'd suddenly outgrown. "I'm sure Dad can give more if you ask him."

"*We're* fine. Normal, annoying stuff." She waited a moment, wondering if she should have popped that Xanax, before returning to the dishes. "Do you have homework to finish?"

"Yeah," Hadley said, her voice slipping back into its normal register. "A reader response for lit and trig problems to finish. Mr. Robbins is such a dick."

"Hads, c'mon," Natalie said, her shoulders falling back into alignment. What a relief that her daughter could focus on this lazy math teacher, a middle-aged man, with cottony hair and a cherubic face, who'd worn cargo shorts and sneakers to back-to-school night.

"Mom, he *is* one. He didn't even bother to teach this unit, just gave us pages to read to teach ourselves."

"Do you understand it?"

"Yeah, I figured it out."

"Smart kid."

Hadley rolled her eyes, but the flush of red on her neck showed she was pleased. "No big deal."

Once Hadley left the room, Natalie poked the bits of carrots down the drain, ran the water in the sink. *Internal bleeding, a ruptured spleen, facial lacerations.* If Isabel had any inkling that the creature on the road wasn't a dog, would she have lied to Natalie to spare her the anguish? *Yes.* Isabel could have taken action to save the girl without saying a word.

THE NEXT AFTERNOON, while en route to get Hadley from school, Natalie picked up her ringing phone. She'd waited all morning. *At last, at last.* Isabel said, "Hi there, it's a whirlwind," to the sounds of lapping water and raucous voices and gulls shrieking. "I'm rushing off to give a lecture. I'm so jammed up here, don't have two minutes together till after 9:00 p.m., too late for you. I'll be back for group this week. Want to speak afterwards?"

"Sooner, if you can. Somewhere private."

"Are you okay? Did that guy contact you again?"

"Not that. But there was a girl . . . in the Caymans . . . she was seriously hurt, and I might have done it."

Natalie expected a gentle reprove. Instead, "Let's talk in person. I'll text when I'm leaving LA."

There was no response from Simon that day, or the next, or the one after that. Natalie had been carrying her phone with her everywhere. When not at her desk, she tucked it in the front packet of her pants, as if proximity to her body would prompt a reply. For minutes on end, she'd stare at the rows of app icons—calendar, bank, weather, message bubble, Facebook, mail, Safari, camera, *Wired Happy*—until her eyesight blurred.

Now, the morning of Isabel's return, anticipation dried out Natalie's mouth. "Forget Grace Cooke and . . ." But there was no use finishing the sentence. It wouldn't work. She wanted to know why the accident was kept out of the paper. And she needed proof, one way or the other, if she had been driving the car that ran into the girl with the busted body, torn-up face.

While she was in the shower, the phone pinged just loud enough for Natalie to hear. She imagined grabbing it off the floor mat, then losing her balance, banging her head and . . . peace.

She emerged, wrapped a towel around her waist, another under her hair, and read:

Coming in at eleven. One-thirty, my place? I'll order from Gran de Café.

The Gran was on Newbury, near Isabel's apartment. As Natalie didn't have a shoot, her schedule was flexible. *Yes. Coming.*

ISABEL, AT THE DOOR, was incandescent. Despite her predawn flight, she appeared burnished and flawless, as if she'd been Photoshopped. *West Coast acid peels? Botox?* Natalie felt a prickle of anger over the extravagance of snakeskin shoes and the ones with the glossy red bottoms, like the coating on candy apples, of rose gold laptops slipped into bison leather satchels, of business class tickets with leg room and free champagne. *Have to keep up my image, Nat.* Isabel was so worried about blowing through her book advance on her business, on George discovering the extent of her exorbitance. *Plus, it makes me feel good. Why shouldn't I feel good?* That last question forceful, almost angry.

Natalie's thoughts ground to a stop. Isabel had invited her over to be of help. As she always did. "Thanks for doing this," she said. "You must have gotten no sleep."

"I'm okay. I'm already futzing with this one chapter that's driving me nuts this morning."

"Where's Debbie?"

"I sent her out on some errands. Let's eat in the nook. I ordered the salad you like."

"What do I owe?"

"Don't be silly. You came to me, so I pay."

The breakfast nook was in front of the kitchen under a bay window. It had creamy white walls and a matching white bench that wrapped around a glass table. Isabel had laid out plates, glasses, and silverware.

"Here you go," Isabel said, handing Natalie her standard fare: a goat cheese salad with sliced pears in its plastic take-out container. She placed two bottles of Pellegrino in the middle of the table.

Natalie asked, "How were the seminars?"

"Great, other than the sound bath event on the beach. When the shamanic healer brought out the didgeridoo, and the healer of all light started speaking in tongues, I was done."

"Oh, dear," Natalie smirked. "What's a didgeridoo?"

"It's this huge motherfucker of an instrument that sounds like wild animals moaning. Details to come. So, who was this girl you were talking about?"

Here we go. You are being healed. You are floating on the wind.

"I read about a hit and run on Cayman Island. A teenager was hurt."

"You *read* about it?" Isabel asked, smiling in bemusement. "You Googled this information?"

"I couldn't ignore those emails."

"But we went over this, and you said you were fine."

Natalie poked a slice of pear with her fork. "I was, I was, until I discovered this girl, Grace, was seriously injured."

"Okay, honey, let's break this down," Isabel said. "It couldn't have been us. The road was empty."

"We can't be absolutely certain."

"What did you read?"

Natalie reported Jeremy's information, envisioning it again—the pool of blood sloshing around Grace Cooke's organs, dark liver, twist of tubular intestines— without referencing him.

"Sounds like a severely injured kid who someone drove to the nearest hospital," Isabel said. "No connection to us."

Natalie stared at her jagged nails. She ripped a piece off her index finger and watched as a spot of red spurted from the cuticle. "I can't get it out of my head, what happened to her."

"Listen, Nat." Isabel put her Panini back in its box after a quick bite. "I'm worried about you."

"You think I've lost it."

"I think you're hurting."

"Well, why else would someone email me about it if I wasn't involved?"

"We went over this."

The pear Natalie had yet to eat looked so meaty, like flesh. "There weren't any other accidents reported on the East End of the island that night."

Isabel formed a steeple with her hands and pressed them to her lips. "If we'd hit someone that size, chances are you'd have felt it. It's unlikely she'd have been flung into the bushes—and, even if she had been, that Simon guy would have seen her. And, let's say he didn't, how would another driver, on this dark road, have managed to?"

"I'm thinking of calling the Cayman police. Do you remember the name of the road we were driving on?"

"It was some side street. I can't recall," Isabel said, lifting her Panini again to her mouth. "You're not eating your salad."

"I'm not hungry."

"That's a bad sign, too. You've been so anxious lately."

"Wouldn't anyone be, if they thought they'd done these awful things? First my mother. Now this. You said it would be triggering, and it has been. I remembered something . . . from the night my mom died."

"What, Nat?"

Isabel's gaze was so fierce, Natalie imagined being lifted in the air by it. "Our conversation in the car, well, just snippets of it. We were fighting."

Nodding, Isabel said, "You cried about that at the hospital."

"It was weird. I said something about *your* mom being locked up, how I didn't want the same thing to happen to me."

"Why were you talking about *Sigrid?*"

"I don't know. My mom said I was mixed up about her. But I wasn't, was I? Something happened to her."

Isabel's mouth twitched, just a tiny movement. "She suffered from postpartum depression. She was given different medications, even electric shock. Nothing worked, not well enough, anyway."

"You never . . ." Natalie felt herself blink; she'd been staring so hard at her stepsister's familiar face. "Did I find out from you?"

"No. I overheard my father talking to Laura. It was really late, but they were loud. You must have overheard it, too."

"I think you talked about Sigrid to me, at least the part about her being sent away."

Isabel sighed, faint lavender crescents under her eyes. "I might have. I tried to hide my dad's real concern from you. He didn't want another depressed wife on his hands."

Natalie felt tricked, even though she hadn't been, not really.

"You never shared that with me."

"What would be the point? Laura was never going to be like *her.* My father was only worried for himself."

"What was he so afraid of?"

"It's much worse than anyone ever told us." Isabel's voice was thick. She drank out of her bottle of sparkling water. "Sigrid didn't die of an aneurysm. She overdosed on Seconal. My dad confessed the night before he died. He'd wanted to shield me."

"That can't be right!" Natalie reached for her stepsister's hand, caressed the smooth, cool skin, the sharp bones of the knuckles.

"It is."

"Why didn't you say anything to me?"

Isabel shook her head. "You've been so devastated since Marc left. I couldn't dump this on you."

"That's not fair. I'm not *that* selfish." Was she? Was she really so egocentric, so fragile? "What about George?"

"Yes, he knows. You're not selfish. I'm just not good at being vulnerable." Isabel smiled wanly.

"You *do* like being in control. But if I were different, stronger—"

"It's not you. You're there for me, Nat. You're a great sister."

Natalie bristled. "You don't require anything."

"But you always offer. And you're a wonderful mother, which is something I never had. Hadley is so lucky."

"Thanks. I'm no Elizabeth with her M&M cookies."

"Enough! You should be so proud of yourself, give yourself a break."

"I'm reckless." *A nice word for manslaughter.* "I can't forgive myself that."

Isabel clucked her tongue. "There's no shame trying a psychiatrist again. There are new meds on the market every day. And if one of them gives you relief, you could take it for a few months." She touched her glossy lip, deliberating. "I'll let you in on a secret. I started seeing a shrink after Dad died."

Natalie swayed backwards in her chair. She couldn't imagine the logistics of the scene, Isabel in the comfy patient chair, yielding authority. "*You did?*"

"Yep. I'm not invincible. You shouldn't hold me to such a high standard."

Marc once said, "The way you idealize Isabel, go to her for everything, there's no room for me, for our marriage."

"Maybe I've put you on a pedestal," Natalie said. "Is this because of Garrick?"

"I have regrets when it came to Dad." Her eyes were wet, shiny, her voice ragged. "He'd never say it—too much like me, or me too much like him—he was deeply hurt by my book."

When she read *Get Happy Now*'s chapter on "flexibility and resilience," Natalie's leg under the covers had shaken so hard, Marc looked up from his book. She didn't disclose that published on these pages was an example of someone with a rigid perception of the world who dealt with obstacles by emotionally isolating himself. Although Isabel never referred to Garrick by name, everyone who knew him guessed the truth. Isabel shared with Natalie that her father had accused her of "unprofessional conduct." Weeks had gone by in which he hadn't spoken to his daughter.

"But you reconciled," Natalie said.

"Yes, thank God. It's also things with George have been . . . tense. All my traveling, and then needing to meet this deadline for the book. It's caught up with us."

"You guys seemed so happy on Thanksgiving."

"We are, just a tough time. Dad dying, work pressure." Isabel deflected with a wave. "Anyway, all this stress on *you,* you should try another psychopharmacologist."

"Who are you seeing?"

"We'll find you someone else. You can't see my doc, too incestuous. He's a psychologist, anyway, can't write 'scripts.'"

"Yeah, okay."

Her stepsister said, "Give me the information, and I'll find out about that girl in the Caymans. I've become friendly with one of the conference hosts; he has a place on Seven Mile Beach. I'll ask him to refer a private detective and then show you the report. If you're not involved and you can let it go, that's one less thing to worry about."

"Oh, yes, thank you!" Natalie said. She had the urge to crawl over the tabletop and embrace her stepsister.

"Eat." Isabel picked out a piece of the arugula from the bread with her fork, then bit into her sandwich.

OUTSIDE, NATALIE STOPPED for a moment on the stairs. The air kissed her with its frosty mouth. The magnolia tree, which burst forth with pink flowers in spring, was bare. Sigrid had committed suicide. Isabel was in therapy. Maybe the brain's innate pessimism really was a blessing, a form of protection.

The T was nearly empty, only two other passengers in Natalie's compartment: a man with a deeply furrowed brow and a long nose with a bulbous tip, like a bicycle horn, and a woman who clung to the sleeping child on her lap as if afraid of theft. Natalie closed her eyes and thought of Dr. Katz, the therapist she'd gone to once right before Marc moved out. She'd liked him. He was young, with a mess of coiled hair and a suit that was a tad too big for him, as if he couldn't be bothered to have it tailored. He pinched a pen in his fingers and swiveled in his chair playfully while Natalie spoke. He'd said, "Let's see if we can help you suffer less."

Natalie appreciated the word "suffer," its humanity, as compared to clinical terms like "dysthymia," and "panic disorder."

He'd steered Natalie away from discussing their treatment with anyone, even Isabel. "Can you do other things together?"

"Such as?" Natalie had asked.

He swung around, towards her, and wrote on his prescription pad. "Bowling?" When she laughed, he grinned at her, as if they were friends. "Tennis?"

"C'mon."

Since her mother's death, she'd been colonized by a viral strain of loneliness, an ailment nestled in each of her body's cells. Now her husband was leaving. Maybe she deserved it, this deep-rooted isolation. But asking Natalie to stop confiding in Isabel, even just about these sessions, felt like a too high a penalty—even for a criminal like her.

"Look, this isn't a hard and fast rule. Just for a little while."

Natalie stopped seeing Dr. Katz after that suggestion.

TWO DAYS LATER, Hadley was staying after school to help paint the sets for the musical *Anything Goes*. Natalie was left with extra hours to fill. She'd planned to research new clients and send out promotional emails. She needed to get more advertising work, not just her preferred assignments, to meet her expenses. But it had been a long morning of editing, and her concentration was shot. She dug out her cell phone from her bag and pressed the star icon "favorites." Marc's name was still on the list. She'd told herself that it was because they shared a daughter, but she knew better.

Next on the list was Isabel, who'd vowed to disappear into her work until her book was finished. Then Hadley. And finally, Cate.

She visualized her friend working in her garden, spade in hand, flap hat on her head, smelling of earth. Once she'd held up a beefsteak tomato and smiled proudly. "It's bigger than my boobs." Natalie wished she were there with Cate now, her smell of the good earth. But her friend was in her shop till later that afternoon when she had to drive her sons from one after-school activity to another.

There wasn't anyone else she felt comfortable calling. She *could* get in touch with Jeremy, as long as she treaded lightly. *I owe you an interview,* she wrote in a text. Then she headed for the kitchen to see what chores she could tackle. A dim square of light pressed against the window over the sink as she rinsed out the coffee pot. She heard the ding from her cell, wiped her hands on the dishrag and fished out the device from her back pocket. She read the name on the screen: Jeremy Sonnenberg. His message: *About happiness or normal human misery?*

She grinned and typed: *Isabel.*

The phone rang almost instantaneously, without having to wait, to anticipate his response. *Easy peasy.* Those were her mother's words from years and years ago, when Natalie was very young. "You are such a good girl, easy peasy." How did an insouciant child turn into a killer?

"That was quick," she said.

"Yep, that's me. So, did you find out anything more about Grace Cooke?"

"Belle is asking some people she's friends with in the Caymans to find out the details for me. Hey, I promised you an interview."

She glanced down into the sink, at Hadley's cereal bowl, two flakes pasted with milk to the side. *Say you want to see me.*

"Great. You free tomorrow night?"

"Yes! I know, not a full dance card."

He laughed. "Well, that makes two of us."

They made plans to have dinner and when Natalie hung up the phone, she sang lyrics that popped into her mind, old Gershwin tunes, some remnant from her childhood. Another mom dropped Hadley off from school, and they ate stir-fry chicken with vegetables. Hadley rattled on about her "putrid math class." They settled in together to watch an episode of *Top Chef* on the couch.

"You're in a good mood, Mom," Hadley said.

"'Cause I'm with you, Hads."

Natalie's cell phone pinged. She pushed the green square with the bubble graphic and the number one in neon red.

"What is it?" Hadley asked, in her vigilant voice. "Something wrong?"

"Nothing, honey." Natalie smiled. "Nothing's wrong at all."

Isabel's text read: *You're off the hook! I bugged the detective to find out ASAP. It's good news. He promises to send notes soon. Off to my lecture. Will call when I get the report. No more worries. XO, I.*

seventeen

——

"EVERYTHING WORKED OUT," ISABEL BEAMED. "COME IN!"

George stood behind his wife, his shirt untucked over khaki pants, a stain on one leg. He reached out to embrace Natalie.

Pressed against him, she smelled coffee on his breath, not his usual orange tea. Natalie heard a voice in her head. *He was always so kind and gentle, like you.* Who'd said that? "Good to see you, George."

"Likewise." He released her and asked in a weary voice, "You doing okay?"

"Sure. You?"

The brown spot in the white of his eye had always been there, a tear near his iris. But today both eyes were bloodshot. A displeased side glimpse at Isabel. "Hanging in there. I made another pot of coffee."

Isabel patted his arm and smiled. "Thanks, bear. Have another cup, yourself."

"I've had enough," George said, sharply. "What I need is some rest."

"Bear . . ."

He turned towards Natalie. "If you can talk some sense into her, can you remind Belle she's my wife, not a goddamn brand?"

"I don't—" Natalie said, startled.

Isabel raised her hand at him, a warning. "That's not her job. She doesn't need to be involved in our fights."

For a moment, no one spoke or moved, deadlocked.

"Of course," George conceded. "I was out of line." He slid out of the room, bowed, an actor sneaking off stage.

"Sorry about that." Isabel asked, "You want anything to eat? I got us some bagels from Bobbi and Bubbies."

"No thanks." She nodded in the direction George had gone. "What's going on? I've never seen George like that."

"He's just strung out. I've been flying in at all hours, working half the night. I keep telling him this is temporary, but George has his stubborn side. I've been away too much for him."

"That's sweet, Belle. You're lucky."

"I know. We'll be fine." Isabel scooped up Natalie's coat, gripping it so hard her fingers drained of color. "Let me hang it up. Wow, you look nice! Going somewhere special?"

Natalie was meeting Jeremy in his South End neighborhood that evening. She'd charged knee-high boots and a burgundy cashmere sweater for the occasion. Since Hadley was with her father until the following afternoon, she figured she'd use her free hours to visit art galleries on Harrison Avenue. A reprieve, a distraction from the blitz of the last few months.

"An exhibit," she said.

"You have a date," Isabel declared. She returned from the closet and ushered Natalie into the living room.

"Don't be silly."

Natalie was surprised to see bills and receipts scattered all over the coffee table. Isabel and George were usually so pristine, so private.

"That's okay, you don't have to say. I still remember the feeling— if you say too much, you'll jinx it."

Natalie had airbrushed her meeting with Jeremy into something it wasn't, shot through a rose light, pretty and fun. But talking to him about Isabel was disloyal; even prying into Sigrid's illness had been a breach. Why *had* she splurged when all he craved was confirmation that Isabel's program was a sham? Because no matter what her mind advised, she felt drawn to him.

"There's nothing to jinx."

"If you say so. Sit." Isabel pointed to the gray leather chair that glistened like a wet seal.

Natalie sat. "I can't believe you already got the report."

"Yep. Yesterday. I had to rush him, but it was worth it. This should put your fears to bed."

"Thanks, Belle. I hope it didn't cost too much. I don't want to cause more . . . problems between you guys."

"Drop in the bucket." Isabel rustled through some papers, picked up a fax. "The report verifies that the hit and run involved a fifteen-year-old girl on Turtle Farm Road. She was taken to Health City hospital a few minutes away in the boyfriend's vehicle."

"Does that prove it wasn't my fault?"

Isabel lifted one of the stones and squeezed it like a stress ball. "We were close to the resort, which is a fifteen-minute ride to the hospital. That's the first thing. Then there's the fact that this girl, Grace Cooke, was out with her seventeen-year-old boyfriend against her parents' wishes. They'd gone to a place called High Rock, and the boyfriend claimed he'd left her to walk home after they'd argued. He told the police he felt bad about that and circled back to pick her up when he saw a man on the road outside a compact car. Grace was unconscious on the road. There was no one else there."

Natalie curled forward. "That part's good news."

"Yes."

"Did they call an ambulance?"

Isabel read off the page. "Doesn't say, just that the boyfriend insisted on driving the girl to the hospital in his car. The driver accompanied them, and the police interviewed him. White male, age thirty-eight, London license. Name: Robert Brampton."

"Wait!" Natalie panted. "Oh my God, bb, the first two letters, Bob Brampton."

"They weren't on the same road as we were, and there was no

mention of either of us, no women at all." Isabel handed her the paper. "That's your copy, so whenever you question yourself, you can reread it."

Still, Natalie's thoughts clicked away. "Could Simon have interfered, moved this girl? Could he have placed her somewhere else once we left? The boyfriend wasn't actually on the scene; he didn't witness the accident."

Isabel stood before her, imperious. "Please, Nat, stop leapfrogging to the next possible catastrophe."

"Grace was walking, you said. We don't have the exact distance. It took us at least ten minutes to get back to the resort. She could have walked in the direction of our hotel. What time did she come into the ER?"

Isabel skimmed the paper. "The report says 1:14 a.m."

"That's less than an hour later. Did the boyfriend indicate when they'd fought, if Grace had time to walk to where we were?"

The grayish violet color seeped under Isabel's eyes again. "I'm not even going to ask my investigator. You're contorting the facts to make yourself the guilty party. The driver who hit Grace gave himself up to the police. It wasn't Simon. Do you really think he would go to that extreme to . . . what . . . involve you, to get to me?"

"I don't know," Natalie said. "If I wasn't involved, why would someone send those emails?"

Isabel sat on the couch facing her. For a second, she didn't answer, finger to her lip. "That's a different question. They *could* have come from Simon. I know I said before that he probably had nothing to do with the emails, but I've been having second thoughts. I asked Debbie to look out for anything from him. He actually wrote me a few days ago." She held up her hand. "As himself, not an alias."

"Shit, Belle. You should have called me right away."

"I didn't want you to get worked up, like you are now. And this was literally my first chance to breathe all week. Three lectures and my workshops and a radio interview." She lowered her voice. "I needed to give George some attention."

"Right, of course. I'm sorry."

"Nat, I just handed you the detective report, which verifies the place and the people involved."

"I'm so grateful, really. But, what did Simon want?"

"To meet with me in Boston. He's coming to town for business."

Natalie was subsumed, as if the water level just kept creeping higher, and she couldn't paddle to the surface. "Why?"

"He didn't give specifics, and I didn't ask. I told Debbie to ignore his email, toss it in the trash file. If he contacts me again, I'll have her alert the police." Isabel dropped her stone back into the bowl. "One step at a time."

"What he's doing is harassment. Just be careful."

Isabel said, "I'm always careful."

"Promise me you won't see him."

"I have no intention of seeing him, Nat. What are you afraid of?"

Natalie could smell the wine on Simon's breath, feel his tongue in her mouth, his fingers on her skin. She reached for a pebble, so white and matte, an unblemished eggshell. What to divulge? "I contacted Simon's ex girlfriend, recently. If Simon's not Godfrey, she might be."

"You *did?* How did you know who she was?"

Tracking one's lies was a harder trick than photographing ice cream. With a quick shrug, Natalie said, "He mentioned her name on the beach. It was easy to find her on LinkedIn."

"What did she say?"

"She warned me away from Simon."

"Good advice."

"Yeah," Natalie said. "Maybe he told her he followed you to the Caribbean and brought up the accident. Dropped my name. It's easy to find me by my website."

"Even if one of them is writing you, it's too convoluted to waste time on. Don't get mixed up in their relationship drama. You weren't responsible for that girl. And it was the only crash reported that night. That's the main thing."

"You're right. Thanks. I need to reimburse you."

"Don't be ridiculous. Just do me a favor?" Isabel winked. "Have fun on your non-date."

THE DAY WAS shale gray and the air heavy with moisture. The naked branches of the dogwood outside Isabel's townhouse were extended like a dancer's arms. Natalie pulled her wool hat out of one pocket, her gloves out of the other. Isabel made sense; she was hard-pressed to accept blame even when the evidence pointed to her innocence. Or at least a firm, reasonable doubt. Natalie forced her thoughts elsewhere—the way the Happiness manual instructed—to a talk she'd had with Jessa the day before. Jessa loved "boy talk" even though she was married with a toddler. Yesterday Jessa had given her the thumbs up when Natalie brought up Jeremy at the studio.

Natalie had accompanied her to a nearby bar for a late lunch. They'd sat at a long wood table, sawdust sprinkled on the floor. Two of Jessa's friends had shown up in t-shirts and jeans, one with a huge silver pendant around her neck, the other with a row of piercings—a star, a tiny bird, a peace sign, and a cross—circling down one ear lobe. They'd joked loudly about some party where a married man had hit on the woman wearing the pendant. The one with the piercings had grabbed Natalie's arm and said, "You have to come out with us. *We'll* find you a good guy." Natalie had nodded and wondered if the cross on her ear lobe meant this woman had faith or was mocking it. But she'd felt a flicker of hope, of ease, of being one of the girls. How long had it been since she'd felt that way?

Racing down the street, her cheeks chapped. *Have fun on your non-date.*

Shame snapped inside of her. What did it take to learn from her mistakes?

Jeremy wasn't interested in her. It was Isabel he cared about. Just like Simon. She'd head back to Brookline. If she canceled on Jeremy early enough, he wouldn't be inconvenienced. He could interview her anytime; she could repay his favor over the phone.

The ride was tricky with the tooting horns, the wandering pedestrians, and the cyclists whizzing between cars in their Gore-Tex getups and high-perched helmets. Natalie had to navigate the twists in the roads, to change lanes and merge with traffic, to follow the instructions she'd printed out to avoid listening to that chirping voice on her iPhone. This wasn't a route she was used to, and she cursed herself now for not taking the T. She hadn't wanted to deal with waiting for the train in the piercing cold later that night.

It took forty minutes, twice as long as it should have, to make it back to her place. She passed her neighbor's apartment with the strong patchouli aroma wafting into the hallway. Natalie had seen this woman only a few times, a slender figure wearing oversized glasses. She'd introduced herself, "Vivian," when she'd moved into the building the previous year. Natalie thought about Ellen's package with Garrick's letter, his apology. It had been nearly two months ago now. The FedEx office insisted it had been delivered. Maybe the messenger buzzed her neighbor's bell when Natalie hadn't answered. Once Natalie had taken a package for the previous owner and put it on the top of her hutch, forgetting about it. When she met the man weeks later in the vestibule, he referred to his confusion about his lost parcel, and she apologized for her transgression. Was that what had happened with Vivian?

Natalie paused for a moment outside her neighbor's door, listening for voices or the sound of TV or music—any clue that her knock would be answered. Silence. Vivian was Dr. Franklin, a pain management specialist, at the medical center in town. "I work all the time," she'd said, when she introduced herself. "Barely time to see Waldo." She'd laughed, referring to her cat.

The older couple, on Natalie's other side, wasn't an option. They were snowbirds that spent November through March in Florida. Another dead end.

In her living room, Natalie scrolled her cell screen for Jeremy's information. "So sorry. Must cancel tonight," she wrote. "Promise to talk about your book soon. Thanks again for your help."

When her phone rang, she repeated her apology to Jeremy.

"Listen." He coughed, cleared his throat. "You're not obligated to me. Your stepsister's program isn't something you feel comfortable discussing. Hey, I respect that. I shouldn't have pushed you. This is the official notice that you're off the hook."

"That's not fair to you."

"Nah. It's fine. Not exactly good for the book's argument, me twisting your arm into saying the Happiness Doc makes you miserable."

"But we had a deal."

"Forget it. Let's do something else . . . if you're up for it."

"Sure," she enthused.

You were wrong this time!

"You up for a movie?"

She pictured herself in a dark theater, the hum in her head competing with the booming noise on the screen. Sitting too long was dangerous; brooding would ruin this, an actual date.

"How about something physical?" she proposed.

The idea of movement, of whizzing past her ruminations, appealed to her. She added quickly, "Athletic."

"Athletic?" he laughed. "Sure. Want to shoot some hoops?"

"Umm, no." She laughed back, shucking off her boots.

"Do you ski?"

"Hate it." The snow-dappled mountains in Stowe, Marc and

Hadley soaring in the gondola lift above her head. The frisson of terror.

"Good. Too expensive anyway."

"I can ice skate."

The Saturday morning ritual of going to the rink with her mother began when she was seven. Natalie had taken lessons, learned the basics: how to move with one hand on the rail, to bravely glide away, how to dip and fall onto the freezing surface. She'd conquered forward and backward crossovers, a basic one-foot, and then a two-foot, spin. Soon after she'd turned eleven, she stopped taking classes. All she'd craved was time alone with her mother, spinning together.

Jeremy said, "I played hockey as a kid."

"I have to warn you. I haven't done this in almost three decades."

"Same here. We can be Laurel and Hardy on ice. How's tomorrow afternoon? Too soon?"

She almost joked about his availability. "No, it's great."

NATALIE'S DREAM STARTED out differently that night. She was trapped underground, trying to follow her mother's whispers to the surface, round and round a honeycomb-patterned tunnel. She couldn't reach daylight. Her mother said, "Your dad, if only he hadn't gotten sick. He was always so kind and gentle, like you."

No, mom. I'm not like that, I'm not.

The scene switched to the car, her mother staring into the rearview window. Her cry, "The light's blinding me. For Christ's sake, what's going on?"

Natalie whipped her head around and, in the twilight, spotted the familiar hood ornament on her stepfather's white Mercedes, the radar detector cord bobbing against the dashboard.

Her mother whispered, "Garrick?"

The pulsating lights flooded her vision before their car pivoted.

There was only a moment left in which to react. Natalie might have screamed for her mother or grabbed for the door handle as ballast. Her head swung forward and knocked against a hard surface and everything went blank.

eighteen

——

THEY'D RENTED SKATES AND TUCKED THEIR BOOTS INTO lockers. The locker's key hung from a rubber bracelet around Natalie's wrist, same as it had on her mother's so many years ago. She tied the laces so tightly her ankles ached. Before, when the world was still a safe place, she'd never worried about a lace coming loose, that she'd trip over it.

Jeremy stood up from the bench, which was across from the vending machines. Down the hall was a concession stand where frankfurters, hamburgers, and donuts were sold. "Yum, my kind of food," he'd exclaimed as they passed by. She grinned at his easy nature. *Easy peasy.*

Jeremy asked, "Want to race?"

Natalie regarded him in his rancher's jacket and wool hat with hair flipping out at the sides. "Seriously?"

He clapped his gloved hands together. "Last one on the ice pays for hot chocolate."

Natalie watched him totter through the glass doors. The rink was outside and, as Jeremy approached it, he jerked forward, nearly falling. He reached out for the railing while she slid by him onto the ice. She smiled at his pouty expression.

Natalie listened to the click, swish, click of her body pushing off. She glided and stopped. She was halfway around the ellipse when Jeremy caught up to her. "I used to be much faster," he puffed. "And in better shape. Must get my ass to the gym."

Her cheeks smarted. "I don't remember it being this cold."

"This is nothing. Chicago's brutal. You grew up here?"

"Newton. Then Cambridge."

"Harvard?" he asked.

"No way. That was Isabel. BU." She turned around to brave backward crossovers, and he skated toward her. "I'd never have gotten into Harvard, not that I wanted to. Bad associations with it."

"Cause of Isabel?"

"Garrick, my stepfather, taught in the law school. He wasn't the warmest person."

He faced her as if they were about to dance. "But you must have been close to your family to stick around. Me, I couldn't wait to get away—well, not from Alex."

"It wasn't that." Her body remembered: right foot on the ground. Then push off with the left. "I don't have any family left, other than Belle."

"No aunts and uncles, cousins?"

"Nope. My parents were both only children. I was one—well biologically—so is Marc, and Hadley. We are a long line of onlies. Hads hates it."

"Yeah. I have cousins, but it's not the same. I loved having my sister around." He lowered his voice. "Having someone to complain to about our parents, someone I thought was cooler than me."

Stroke, cross, stroke, cross. "I'm so sorry," she said as she reached his side. "Hadley always complained, wanted a sister, like I had with Isabel."

"You guys seem tighter than most siblings, never mind that you're 'steps.'"

"Here's an example of what she's done for me. I couldn't bear to be alone in our house with Garrick. So, Belle commuted to Harvard rather than live in the dorm. Imagine giving all that up, all that camaraderie."

"That's a big concession."

When he slowed down, Natalie changed direction, moving forward. Her eyes were tearing, and she couldn't say if it was from the chilly air. "That's the thing: she never made me feel like it was a sacrifice."

"I want to know," he said, moving closer, his breath a whisper of wind, "all of it, your story."

What if she tried to spin, round and round, so quickly, no one could stop her? Her *story* was such a heavy weight to carry. How could she spin with that strapped to her back? "Buy me that hot chocolate."

"Let's go."

Indoors, Natalie heard a woman say, "Tighten your laces, Becky, so they don't come undone on the rink." Then the clopping of skates, a child's sigh. Her mother never had issued such a warning.

When Jeremy returned from the snack bar with two steaming Styrofoam cups, she glanced at his hands, at his wide thumbnails and ragged cuticles. They were unselfconscious hands, busy and bitten. Marc's, she loved, so solid and sexy. Simon's were smooth to the touch, his fingers long and thin and nimble. The thought of where Simon's fingers had been made her squirm and shift on the bench.

"Thanks," she said. "So, what do you want to know?"

Jeremy sat down next to her. "For starters, are you still worried about Grace Cooke?"

"Isabel had a private investigator look into it." When Jeremy cocked his head in surprise, she said quickly, "Someone she met on the island." She repeated the information Grace's boyfriend had given the police.

"You must be glad that's been put to rest," Jeremy said.

"Not the emailer's identity."

"Still think it's the stalker fan?"

Was this a test? A way to ferret out information about Isabel and her work? She looked at Jeremy, his olive skin—the suffusion of apricot in his cheeks—the lines reaching from his eyes forming a sideways peace sign under his glasses. He didn't seem to be judging. But she couldn't say what his intentions were.

"Probably."

"What about the rest of your personal narrative?"

She snorted. "Now, you sound like a journalist. Like what?"

He shrugged. "Anything. I could rattle off a list of questions, *reporter-style*. But you'd probably bolt."

"Ask one."

"Okay." He tapped his finger against the Styrofoam cup. "What's the most unusual thing about you?"

I might have killed my mother.

She took a sip of her hot chocolate. It tasted chalky, like a cheap candy bar that had sat too long on the shelf and turned gray. "I had a bad concussion when I was thirteen," she said. "It wiped out a lot of my memory from around that time."

Jeremy reached for her hand. "Same year your mom died."

"Yeah." He was a good listener. "Same accident. I only remember bits and pieces. The doctors say it's not neurological at this point."

"PTSD?"

"Maybe." She licked her lips, which were chapped, and tasted a speck of blood on her tongue. "I've always felt so guilty, responsible for what happened."

"You weren't driving the car, at thirteen?" he asked, his tone incredulous.

"Of course not."

"Where were you going that night?"

She shook her head. "That's the thing . . . It's complicated. I was a problem kid."

"Like what? Drugs? Drinking? Hanging around with the partiers, skipping school?"

Laughter broke out, and she turned to see a group of teenagers,

184

girls and boys, around Hadley's age, sitting in a pack. Most were holding glazed donuts. Their hats and scarves looked glazed too, as if printed on luster paper, the colors bright and sharp. Before her life split apart, she'd had a pack of girlfriends, too. They'd gather at each other's houses, eat chips and ice cream, paint each other's fingernails and gossip about Denise Rappaport, how she was giving blowjobs in her basement while her mom was working her nursing shifts. They'd giggle and fall into each other like a litter of puppies.

"Not that. More, like, just angry. My stepfather wrote me a letter about what happened."

"What did it say?"

"That's the thing. His secretary, Ellen, was supposed to send it to me. FedEx swears it was delivered. But I never got it and, now, Ellen is in the Galapagos."

"Skipped town?" He took a sip of his drink, his eyes beaming. "The plot thickens!"

She laughed nervously. "I'm like one of those Lifetime movie women who feels like she's going crazy but is actually being poisoned by the nanny."

"I'm not acquainted with that particular genre."

"Post-break-up TV."

"You don't seem like either the poisoned woman or the nanny. You sound like someone who's had some tough breaks."

When he hugged her, Natalie felt that ache, so deep, the origin was impossible to locate. It pushed against her ribs, making her breathing feel labored.

AT THE DOOR to her place, Natalie paused for a second before fiddling the key into the lock. Marc would have dropped off Hadley by now. She'd be in her room, on her phone or laptop. There was no possibility of inviting Jeremy into her apartment and not introducing him to her daughter. She hadn't brought home anyone other than Isabel and Cate since the divorce, certainly no men.

What about the condition of the apartment, she wondered? She hadn't vacuumed or thrown out the pile of newspapers on the coffee table or sorted through the junk mail on the sideboard in the dining room. But Natalie was fairly certain that, unlike Marc, Jeremy wasn't the kind of man who'd care about her housekeeping.

She led him into the living room, which was neat enough, where he lingered by the fireplace. He picked up a framed picture of six-year-old Hadley in her Halloween pumpkin costume.

"Can I get you some coffee?" she asked. "Or water? I have a bottle of wine, but no beer, I'm afraid."

Jeremy shook his head so his hair, flecked with snow, flew in front of his face. "Nah, I'm good. This must be Hadley. She's adorable. Looks like you."

"Thanks." Natalie smiled at the floor, the faded varnish on the wood strips. "I should just poke my head into her room, tell her I'm home."

"Go ahead. I promise not to snoop."

The copy of Isabel's book in her hand, the taste of vomit in her mouth, the pictures of her stepsister strewn at her feet.

"You know the worst about me already."

Stop lying. I can always tell.

Natalie stopped for a moment—the memory of her mother's voice was devoid of time or place—then knocked on her daughter's door.

"Yep," Hadley called out. "I'm alive."

She creaked it open to see her girl cross-legged on the bed, earbuds in, attached to her phone. Her math book and notebook were open, and there was a bag of pita chips on her lap. "Two hours of busy work from Mr. Dick," her daughter said.

"Very nice. Hey, there's someone with me."

"Really? Who?"

"A friend from . . . I met him at Aunt Isabel's group."

"*Him?*" Hadley's eyes grew bigger. "Like a boyfriend?"

"No, of course not," Natalie said, pleased at the suggestion. "If I had one, you'd be the first to know. Come say hi."

As Hadley disengaged from her wires, Natalie realized she wanted her daughter to like Jeremy. She wanted them to like each other very much.

Hadley stood up in loose pajama bottoms that fell at her hips and a tight crop top with spaghetti sleeves. Her long corkscrew curls covered her breasts, but Natalie was certain she wasn't wearing a bra. The thought, *Too sexy,* surprised her. The kid was fifteen.

Thank God, Hadley yanked open her dresser drawer and extracted her ever faithful *Liberté Egalité Beyoncé* t-shirt, layered it over the other one. She slid her bare feet with the peeling pedicure into her Ugg slippers—Elizabeth's Christmas present. "Let's go see your boyfriend," she said cheerfully.

Jeremy was seated on the couch reading his own publication. "Hey," he said. He bolted up, banging his knee against the coffee table.

"Careful there, cowboy," Natalie said. "This is Hadley. Hads, Jeremy."

"Hi," her daughter said shyly.

"He's hot," Natalie imagined her daughter telling her friends. Now her child would have something new to report back to Marc when he asked about the workshop, something that wouldn't show Natalie in a bad light for a change. Satisfaction slipped down her throat like a cool, sugary drink.

"Nice t-shirt," Jeremy said. "I saw her in the *On the Run* tour. Pretty amazing."

"Really?" Hadley asked, El Greco-eyed. "I tried to get tickets, but they sold out in, like, five minutes."

"Helps to have a friend who's the music critic." He gestured to the *Boston Globe* on the coffee table.

"Jeremy is an editor there," Natalie boasted. She felt thrilled he wanted to impress Hadley, which meant he wished to please her.

"'Lemonade' is the best music video ever."

He nodded. "It's certainly up there. I can get you tickets next time she comes to the area if you'd like."

"Oh my God! Yes! Thank you!"

Jeremy grinned. "No problem."

AFTER HADLEY HAD said goodnight and scampered down the hall with a backward glance and wave to Jeremy, and after he'd proclaimed, "That was easy," and Natalie had asked, "What?" and he'd responded, "Winning her over," they sat for a while talking and laughing. An hour passed without any mention of traumatic events. Or Isabel's workshops. Or the Happiness industry.

"I'd better get going," Jeremy said. He dusted off his pants as if he'd spilled crumbs on them.

"Yeah, gotta feed the kid," Natalie said. She could invite him to stay for dinner. But she didn't want to appear too eager, too expectant. Jeremy had discovered the truth about Sigrid. They'd solved the mystery in the Caribbean—unless Natalie contacted the investigator with her qualms and alternative theories. But she'd vowed not to hold the events of that night up to a magnifying glass until she found a coincidence, a twist, a timing issue. Which meant: there was no compulsory reason for her and Jeremy to keep meeting.

"Hey," she said, "I still owe you an interview."

"No, you don't." He stretched as he stood up. "I can no longer be objective about anything to do with you. Including your sister."

Natalie walked with him out of the living room. At the door, he was so close she saw a freckle below his right eye she'd never noticed before.

"Can we . . . get together again?" she asked.

The question hung in the air like a spider's silk, but only for a second.

He leaned over and kissed her. His lips were slightly chapped, and his breath smelled of mints. The tip of his tongue on hers moved slowly, as if inscribing his initials. Natalie felt like an abandoned house re-inhabited. Her currents were surging again, her circuits switched back on.

As soon as Jeremy closed the door behind him, she heard a shuffling. It was Hadley in her Christmas slippers. Natalie turned quickly. What had her daughter witnessed?

Down the hall, her kid beamed. When she got to Natalie's side she said, "Nice going, Mom. Guess Aunt Isabel was right, after all. Her group works."

"We'll see," Natalie shot back. It was a wondrous feeling, this lightness and speed, like coasting down a water slide at an amusement park.

Hadley rapped, "'Whenever I feel afraid, I hold up my head and sing, oh, yeah, and whistle a happy tune.'"

Natalie's mother in the kitchen, drying her hands on a towel, her whispery soprano, "'So no one will suspect!'"

"How do you know that?" Natalie asked.

"The kids in the show are obsessed with Kelli O'Hara. They played *The King and I*'s music the whole time we painted sets."

"My mother used to sing that."

"She did?" Hadley glimmered with curiosity. "What was *she* afraid of?"

"Good question."

NATALIE COULDN'T GET the song out of her mind as she rinsed the tomato sauce from the pan and stacked their plates and glasses in the dishwasher. Or as she soaked in the bathtub, the room lit only by her new tranquility candles that smelled like lavender. Or, as she checked her mail, a nighttime habit she needed to break, she told herself the second she read the sender's address.

"I have no idea who Grace Cooke is," Simon's message began. "Poor you. You seem to be inventing scenarios to stay in touch. I'll be in Boston next weekend. Let's meet and have a proper talk. P.S. No more bothering Gillian."

nineteen

———

NATALIE DROVE TO SIMON'S HOTEL, OVERLOOKING BOSTON
Harbor, in the early afternoon. She rushed through the lobby with its
abstract sculptures and egg-shaped vases stuffed with miniature cacti,
all coolly modern, not cozy or inviting, but open, safe. She'd wanted
to meet downstairs, someplace public, maybe go to a restaurant; although, she hadn't wished to share another meal with him. He'd written back: *What do you think I'm going to do, jump you? Pull a knife?*
You can leave my door open. I prefer to be comfortable after travelling.

She'd acquiesced. But, now, alone in the elevator, she grasped her
pocketbook to her chest as if caught in a dicey neighborhood. On his
floor, Natalie ran her hands over the wallpaper as she walked slowly
to his room. She rounded one corner, then another. There was his
room number on the door. There was nothing to do but knock.

When he opened it, she avoided looking at him at first, focusing
on how the bedspread and blankets were stripped away, as if he'd
been napping, yet the drapes were open. One quick glance and she
noted the constellation of tiny freckles on the side of Simon's face,
the same ones she'd kissed when they'd made love.

She swallowed down the acid rising in her throat.

"Hello," Simon said in a pleasant voice. He left the door slightly
ajar and motioned for her to sit wherever she liked: the unmade bed or
the leather chair by the window. "Do you want me to order drinks?"

"No. Thanks."

He pointed to the bowl of fruit on the dresser, next to the television, a vase of cornflowers. "Pear, apple?"

"I'm okay." Natalie crossed the room to the seat by the window, as far from him as possible in the small space. She left on her jacket and scarf despite the warm temperature.

Simon sat on the crumpled blanket. He stretched his arms over his head to rub the back of his neck, then ran his hands slowly down the sides of his pants. It was if he were pleasuring himself. So unappealing this *little bit of perversion* showboat act of his.

"Let's get this sorted," he said. "Just to warn you, I'm juggling two ladies already. And all your theatrics aren't my cup of tea."

He couldn't be serious, being all performance himself.

"I told you why I'm here," she said. "The emails."

"Yes, you've been sending them regularly."

"The ones I've been getting about the accident in the Cayman Islands."

"I'm aware of this obsession of yours," he said. "Bit of a bore, to be honest."

Natalie said, "If you answer my questions, I promise to leave you alone."

"Very well. Let's get this over with."

"Why were your brights on if you saw us ahead of you?"

He met her eyes. "To get Isabel's attention, of course."

She caught sight of the phone on the desk, wondering if there was a panic-button on it. Famous cases of celebrity stalkers ran through her mind: Hinckley and Chapman.

"So, you're admitting you were following us?"

"Yes."

"What were you even doing there?"

"Isabel wouldn't talk to me," he said. "I'd been trying to have a conversation with her for weeks."

There he was, all neat and put-together in his navy shirt with an undecipherable logo on it, designer jeans, and brown loafers shiny as bread glazed with a pastry brush. His eyes and teeth were beacons of good health. He had Oxford-by-way-of-Eton written all over him, insanity aglow in privilege.

"You traveled to the Caymans to talk to her?" she asked.

"Yes, of course. She's been too caught up in her business woes, finance, deadlines to have a decent conversation."

She was blinking too quickly now. Was Simon someone Isabel owed money to, a loan shark with a fancy daytime job?

"You could have seen Isabel at one of her events in New York. She gives lectures there regularly."

"I'm well aware; it's how we met. Gillie signed us up for one of Isabel's silly seminars. Bit of a drag, giving up my Saturday to placate the girlfriend. But, what a pleasant surprise. I went to Isabel's next talk when she came back to town, alone this time, and introduced myself and, the rest, well," a dip in his voice, his false gallantry, "I'll be a gentleman and spare you the juicy details."

Natalie sucked in her lip, so as not to snicker. "That's hard for me to believe."

"Believe what you want." He shrugged languidly. "We chatted for a long time after her lecture. I suggested we get a drink at The Gramercy."

"That was the restaurant you took me to."

"Yes. I like that place."

Disgust had a taste, like old pennies on the tongue. She stared at the linked, octagon-pattern in the carpet, not wanting to see Simon's face as he spoke.

"Getting her to go home with me, that took a little convincing. Interesting how Isabel worries about following a code of ethics in her work life, isn't it? But she wasn't my therapist. I wasn't her student. This was a gray area, and we were both adults."

"Isabel wouldn't have an affair," Natalie said. "She'd never cheat on George."

"You don't seem to know your stepsister very well."

"I know her better than anyone."

A ripple of uneasiness. *Do I?*

Simon broke into a grin. "Isabel and I were seeing each other for months, and you never suspected."

"Why not meet her in New York again?" Natalie said, sticking to her playbook. Facts, what happened when she'd crashed the car, the emails that followed. The rest was rubbish. "Why follow her to the Cayman Islands?"

"Isabel's idea, a romantic getaway. She made the reservation for the two of us. Then she changed her mind, said it was too risky. When I called the hotel, they were nearly sold out but not quite."

Natalie wondered if he was enjoying goading her or truly delusional. "The reservation was for Isabel and me."

"Not originally. She confronted me the next morning, that day I met you on the beach. She wasn't pleased I showed up. But she left me no choice."

"This fantasy . . . " she had to be prudent, "you should try to let go of it."

"That's what Gillie said—later, when she found out. It's not that simple, though. I'm in love with Isabel. She feels the same."

It slipped out. "That's absurd!"

Simon's eyes drained, his mouth slackened, as if he were injured. This only lasted a moment, this look of vulnerability, before he arched his head in her direction. "She tried to end things between us, even after everything we'd shared, so many secrets, things she'd never say to anyone, even her husband. But she still loves me."

Natalie's hands trembled in her lap. She realized her miscalculation, not standing by the door. She'd have to bypass him to leave, no easy exit for her. She turned toward the window. The water in the harbor was choppy, the nearest dock bobbing, no boats in sight. She touched her wool scarf. She imagined Simon's hands pulling it tightly around her throat, as the world shrank to smaller and smaller circles, surrounded by a black background, like in the endings of old movies. Quickly, she untied it.

"What secrets?" she asked.

"You can't expect me to tell you that."

"I'm assuming you didn't mention that you'd slept with me," she said, her voice too loud in her ears. "I'd love to share that information with her."

"No, you wouldn't . . . or you would have already."

"Try me."

He peered at her. "Why do you think I was driving with my brights on? It was a signal that she couldn't fuck around with me anymore. I knew what had happened to you, how rattled you'd become, how that would upset her. Isabel told me what happened the night your mother died."

There was a glitch in Natalie's perception, the room askew, the light too bright. The danger was coming at her too fast, like a train derailed.

"Why would she do that?" she whispered.

"I asked her the worst thing she'd ever done. And she said, not making sure you were safe."

"How could she keep me safe? She wasn't with us."

"She should have convinced your mother not to take you—or gone along to that doctor. She was too distracted by that boyfriend of hers. I told her about my poor brother, Charles, the sailboat accident."

Natalie recalled the little boy in the picture on this table, the derision already etched on his face, how his mother cradled her other son with love, his father's apparent disinterest. "What did you do?"

"Nothing." Simon glanced at her with those lovely, empty blue eyes. "I did nothing to save him that day. Same as Isabel. We were alone in the boat when he fell in the water. I didn't push him. I didn't rescue him either, although I swore I tried."

"It's not the same thing."

"Ask Isabel," he said, "the details."

"Did you meet me in New York to make her jealous? Is that why you slept with me?"

He shrugged. "You seemed satisfied that night—before you snooped around in my things."

"Weren't you worried that it would get back to her?"

"Not then, too angry. But things change."

"Did you want to hurt George, too?"

"I never gave him a second thought. But I wasn't going to let Isabel decide. It doesn't work that way—maybe with her passive, pathetic husband. Not with me."

"Whatever happened between you and Isabel, she loves George."

"She called him her 'old dog.'" He grinned with fury. "The old dog would fall asleep during sex. Can you imagine, with someone like Isabel? He clears his throat when he feels guilty about not doing his paperwork. She hates that noise."

Natalie's hands and legs were quivering. Isabel had told her about the guttural sound George made, his habit of confessing, his time mismanagement, how annoying it was to her. "So, you came to Boston this weekend to see Isabel?"

"Yes. And I did so, earlier. In this very room, in fact. It was delightful what we did."

He's coming to town for business. I told Debbie to ignore his email, toss it in the trash file.

Natalie's throat was so dry it burned. "Why are you saying these horrible things? I've never done anything to you. Why are you trying to hurt me?"

"Don't be silly. All is mended between us, which is why I would very much prefer you don't mention our little fling. I want you to be my sister-in-law."

"That's disgusting."

Simon pointed to her hand. "Strong word. Why wear the ring I got Isabel if I'm so disgusting? We picked it out together, for her, of course, from a place in the diamond district. Isabel thought it brilliant."

Hatred smoldered. *Careful. Don't incite him. Be strategic.* "If you and Isabel are so close, why hasn't she left George for you?"

"She says it would be bad for her reputation. You know Isabel can be cold-blooded when it suits her. Marriage to a nice, dull doctor, whose research she could use to boost her career, is better for business. Never mind the money I gave her to bail her out. I'm not a fool, though. I'm not going to keep giving without a commitment."

"I should go."

"I just thought of something that might help you solve your riddle after all," he declared, with an uptick in excitement.

"What riddle?"

"The reason you're here. Have you forgotten about your emails already?"

Natalie shook her head, even though she had.

"Gillian and I reconnected before I went on my island vacation. Poor girl never got over me. And one does have to look out for oneself, which Isabel is well aware of. When Isabel leaves George, I will do the same. It's agreed upon."

"What does that have to do with the emails?"

"Gillie admitted to reading mine after I returned from the Caymans, harassed me until I confessed everything."

"She knows you were there to be with Isabel?"

"Yep." He slapped his thighs. "You and me, how we met, my trailing you on the road, the minor drama that sent you into a panic, all of it. She grilled me to death, and I gave the girl what she wanted."

"That you're here today, to see Isabel?"

"Well, not *everything*, just enough to keep her quiet. She could be your offender, if you're being truthful, and this email thing wasn't a pretense to see me. Gillie has wanted to get back at Isabel for ages."

Natalie wobbled upright, secured the strap of her pocketbook around her shoulder and walked the length of the room. "I really do have to go. . . work."

"Ah, pictures of the mutton! Aren't you going to thank me for helping you?"

"Thank you. One more thing . . . can you ask Gillian if she's bb-Godfrey?"

"Sorry," he said. "Don't be greedy. Gillie is off-limits."

She wrenched the door free and walked out quickly, hoping she wouldn't heave up her breakfast on the hotel carpet.

ISABEL ENDED THE workshop with, "As you go through your week, keep up in your journals, focus on forgiveness, expectations, your intentional activities, and how they foster positive experiences."

Natalie's body felt loose and jangly. The plan was that Jeremy would wait for her downstairs. Originally, she was going to ask Isabel to lunch. But she'd shared with Jeremy her meeting with Simon, how he'd bragged about sleeping with her stepsister, how he claimed they were in love. "Let me be there for you in case the guy isn't lying," Jeremy said. "You'll be so hurt."

Isabel glanced her way. "Keep in mind what we discussed today, how overthinking is toxic. Okay, everyone. Have a great week."

After the usual disciples lingered, the room emptied of all but the two of them. Isabel was packing her workbook and pamphlets into her leather tote. She smiled at Natalie. "Hey, stranger. You been hiding?"

Isabel had made several attempts to contact her. The day before, Natalie had texted her back: *Busy. See you at group.*

"I've been really upset." Natalie stared at her stepsister's long white fingers, the platinum band tucked under the handcrafted engagement ring.

"Uh, oh, that deadly rumination."

She was standing on the plank near the dreaded end, choppy waters below. Stay still, focus only on the horizon. She jumped. "I talked with Simon Drouin when he was in Boston last weekend."

Isabel made a small sound, like a gasp stopped mid-inhale. She arched forward, anchoring her weight on her bag. And Natalie marveled, as she often did, how stunning it was that someone so beautiful could appear washed-out with the smallest change in lighting.

"Why did you do that?" Isabel asked.

"You know why. To figure out who sent me these emails."

"And did you figure it out?"

"No. He denied sending them." Confrontation always cost Natalie. "Simon told me something pretty disturbing, though."

"Oh, yes?"

"He claims you two are in love."

"Don't be ridiculous!"

"He knew about me, about my mom's accident. He said that he shined his brights on the road because it would trigger me."

Isabel's eyes ablaze. "He's such a sadist."

The moment was frozen, a photo taken at too fast a shutter speed.

"You told him about me. You did! He said you called George your 'old dog,' never mind the stuff he told me about George and sex."

"What do you want, Nat?"

Natalie's chest was so hot under her sweater and winter coat; she felt like she could catch on fire. "What do I want? I want to know why?"

"It's complicated. . . ."

"That's not an answer! Tell me your version or I'll go to George."

"You'd never do that." Her mouth was tight and colorless.

"Try me. You want to risk it?"

"I want forgiveness. I can't forgive myself for what I did, but maybe you can."

"Explain to me how you could do that." Natalie could hear the percussion of her heartbeat. "Not just the sex but confiding . . . and with someone like him?"

"Worst mistake of my life. I was such an idiot."

"Which part: betraying me and George or falling in love?"

"I never said I loved him." The vein in Isabel's forehead throbbed, and she tugged on the errant strand of hair that had strayed from her ponytail. "It was a fling. Nothing. What I said about you, it was only in the context of my feeling guilty that I hadn't been able to prevent you from suffering. Simon twisted it into something else."

Natalie gripped the back of a chair. "You warned me away from Simon for *my* sake, you compared him to that crazy woman in Oregon. You let him search the bushes. It was the two of you against me."

"It wasn't like that." Isabel knocked her palm on the side of her head. "I fucked up so royally."

Natalie couldn't locate the hub of her wrath: the affair, the deceit, or the chaos so uncharacteristic of Isabel. "It's hard to picture, you that out of control."

"You know I used the second advance, pumped it into my business. But, then, I borrowed from my IRA, because the house and stocks are all in both our names. I should have told George what was going on, but I didn't want him to flip out. You've seen how he is, like my dad that way, breathing down my neck. He would have told me not to aim so high, not to gamble. But how else was I going to keep the platform my editor wanted? The first time I met with Simon, we talked about investments, financial stuff. I thought he'd help me."

"He said that he did."

"Not a lot. I figured he was a cash cow, I admit it. I used him for that. But, I'd come to my senses and broken off with him by the time we went to the Caymans. I couldn't believe he'd follow me to the conference."

"You would have kept up the pretense. You're only sorry you got caught."

"I didn't want to lose your respect," Isabel said, pleading. "That night of the accident, I saw Simon outside the hotel after the party. I went to the pool deck." She was pacing now, gesturing. "He was at the bar in the restaurant next door, and I ducked out, thought I'd avoided being seen. Just to be sure, I told you to take that back road instead of the main one. That was stupid of me. I panicked."

"You didn't seem panicked."

A swish of Isabel's neck, like the tail of an agitated cat. "Nat, I'm good at hiding my emotions. You know that. I hardly slept. Simon texted me to meet him the next morning."

"So, you were with *him,* not the Danish guy?"

"Yes. I told Simon I'd call the police if he didn't stop harassing me."

"You said I shouldn't date him because of the car accident." Here were Natalie's tears. "You fucking lied right to my face."

"I was trying to protect you."

"You were protecting *yourself.*"

The ski marks appeared on Isabel's forehead. "You were already dealing with so much."

"You don't get to do that, twisting it around to be about me. You accused Marc of being a horrible person for cheating on me."

Isabel nodded. "It was hypocritical. But, Marc was a total shit. He left you."

"Are you staying with George just because it's good for your career or because Simon turned out to be stingy?"

"Of course not. I love George."

Natalie pushed aside images of his honeyed skin, his hands moving over her body. A clot of nausea jabbed against her diaphragm. "Simon said you slept with him the other day, when he was in Boston."

"That's not true!" Isabel stood still; her body slackened against the desk. "I swear it's over. That's why I started therapy to figure out why I messed up."

"And have you?"

"Starting to. My ambition, greediness, even my tendency to get bored."

"Are you bored with George?"

"Sometimes," Isabel said. "I have to learn to value comfort over excitement. I adore George. But I thrive on change, challenge. A long marriage isn't like that."

"You had so much advice on the subject. About me. About Marc."

"I'm so truly sorry, Nat. Please don't tell George." There was a ribbon of fear in Isabel's voice. "It will only hurt him. I'll never do anything like this again. Please, for his sake."

"Are you going to be honest about the money, at least?"

"Yes! I'm going to ask him to sell stocks so I can get out of this mess."

Natalie reached for the ring finger on her left hand where she'd worn Marc's diamond, then Isabel's. It was a habit, fiddling with the jewel, but now her finger was bare. She rubbed the skin, which had been compressed from fifteen years of the tight band. "Why did you give me Simon's ring?"

"You were sad. It seemed too pretty to waste."

"You could have exchanged it. Sold it for a nice sum."

"I wanted you to have something beautiful. I was sure I'd recoup what I'd lost without having to resort to selling my stuff like a fuck-ing—"

"Person in trouble? Someone not rich?"

Isabel's eyes were bloodshot and wet. "I made a mess of this."

"Yes," Natalie said.

"For months, all I've wanted was for it to be over, for Simon to leave me alone."

Outside the long sweep of windows, the streetlights shone. Natalie needed to be there, away from Isabel and this clean room with the stark walls and the sheen of the wooden floors. "Maybe he will now. He's back with his ex-girlfriend."

"That's good! Nat, how can I make it up to you?"

Natalie shook her head.

"Please forgive me."

Doubt flew up like a bed sheet that refused to lie flat. "I don't know. . . . I'll try."

Isabel's sigh was deep and long. "I'm so relieved this is finally out in the open."

twenty

———

JEREMY WAS OUTSIDE, CLAPPING HIS GLOVED HANDS TOGETHER. "Hey," he said when he saw her. "Ready?"

Natalie felt dazed, like waking from the anesthesia after her C-section. "Yeah, let's get out of here."

"How'd it go?"

She stared ahead at the lamplights and the chiaroscuro sky. More snow was on the way, endless winter. She started in the direction of the T, pushing forward against the weather. "Simon was telling the truth."

"Isabel admitted she was having an affair?"

"Yes. She says it's over. He said it's not. I don't know who to believe."

Jeremy whistled. "Wow."

"I can't wrap my head around it: the lying, saying she didn't know him, all the crap about him being a fan." Her words formed clouds in the frigid air.

"Did she explain or apologize?"

"Both. But . . . hasn't sunk in."

"Yeah, too soon. You up for a drink?"

"I would *love* to. But I promised Hadley I'd help her with an art project."

He nodded, the earflaps from his aviator-style hat lifting like Hermes' wings. She smiled at how sweet and boyish he looked, how easy he was to speak to. "Hey, no problem. I'll ride with you."

"You live in the other direction."

"What can I say? I'm a guy with a lot of time on his hands."

Natalie shifted her weight from one foot to the other. She wasn't sure what to make of his offer, whether he thought her shattered. She didn't want to be the perpetual victim, Hardy's Tess or Richardson's Clarissa—those tragic heroines from her freshman year's Intro to the Novel course. "That's sweet. But I'll be okay. I'm not going to fall apart."

"Of course not. You're a strong person."

Strong.

Had anyone ever used that word to describe her before?

"You're very gallant," Natalie said, tugging her hat out of her jacket pocket. "But I've been taking the T by myself since I turned forty."

He grinned. "Maybe I just like your company."

"'Thanks. I like yours, too," she said. They walked past filthy snowbanks littered with wrappers, plastic bottle caps, bits of newspaper, and splotches of dog pee. A good setting for a morality tale, she thought.

"Did I ever tell you what happened with my ex?" Natalie asked.

"Umm, nope. I didn't think it was my business to ask."

"This has to do with Isabel. Marc fell in love with someone else while we were still married. They're already engaged, before our divorce."

"Geez, not cool."

They turned the street corner towards the train, the high-rise office buildings in the background illuminating the night. She'd done it again, portrayed herself as the dupe.

"We were wrong for each other," she said, surprising herself.

Nat, there's always a reason you can't be happy.

Why do you always make me sound like some failing, nervous creature?

"Marc told me about Elizabeth before he got involved with her.

He didn't go behind my back. And all this time Isabel's been bad-mouthing him to me."

"I get that. My friends piled on about Greta when we broke up. They were just showing solidarity."

"She was sleeping with Simon at the same time."

For a moment, he didn't reply. Then he said, "Yeah, that's fucked up. But it explains her motivation for not telling you. She must have been afraid of your reaction."

"It's worse, though. She tried to convince me he was a stranger, or a fan. She never let on that she even knew him."

At the station now, Natalie eyed the escalator, imagining the heel of her boot getting stuck in the step's cleat and flinging her forward. Nothing was safe. She chose the stairs instead, and Jeremy followed her lead, without questioning.

They arrived at the platform, and he said, "Isabel strikes me as someone who plays it very close to the vest."

"She is, but that's not the same thing as lying. I had no idea, not a clue."

"Isabel's an excellent saleswoman."

Who is fucking up her finances and withholding it from George—a form of lying.

Even now, even after learning about Simon, Natalie wasn't ready, not quite *yet*, to disclose Isabel's business problems to Jeremy. He worked with a newsroom full of reporters, could expose Isabel. And why wouldn't he?

I would if I were him.

Seated on the train, the odd sensation of the world akimbo lessened. Natalie found the movement soothing, that promise of home. The other passengers were preoccupied with their phones, except for one older woman, peering at the pages of a hardcover book through oversized glasses.

"No one belongs on that pedestal of hers," Jeremy said.

"You sound like Marc. Even Isabel has told me not to idealize her."

"I meant," he took her gloved hand, "she shouldn't put herself there. Guess it's hard when you're a Happiness guru."

She squeezed his hand back. "Ever since her publicist told Isabel to work on her brand, she's been obsessed. She suggested I come to her group because I was so upset about Marc, but maybe I was just another recruit. Maybe all of it—her books, her philosophy—they're all just for fame."

"You don't mean that. You even convinced me that Isabel is sincere about what she does. Everyone now is getting crap over their 'brand.'"

She felt a pang of love for him. There was no way to stop it. "She's been more like a mother to me than an older sister."

"Most mothers disappoint."

Most daughters don't kill their mothers.

Fatigue lapped at Natalie. She shut her eyes, but her mind wouldn't rest. It was a nomad, wandering among the shrubs and inkberry plants and palm trees of Grand Cayman. Simon and Isabel hunched together, examining the hood of the car. What had ensued between the two of them, a quick quarrel, an understanding, a cover up? She turned towards Jeremy whose cheek was close enough to rub hers. She tracked the movement of the pencil scar near his mouth, how it curled upward. How much disclosure could she risk? "Can I run another theory by you?"

"Course."

"Isabel could be lying about Grace Cooke. She could have faked that report because she was worried about her relationship." *And her career.* "If she was in the car that hit that girl, and Simon was there, someone could put the pieces together." *A scandal. Could blow up her whole fucking life.*

"That's a big leap."

Natalie gazed at the young man seated across from them who was tapping his foot to the music on his iPhone. He had an afro and was wearing new sneakers, white as Milk of Magnesia. She couldn't name the mixture of her feelings. They were huge and powerful without her usual skittish tempo. What she could do was funnel her emotions into pictures: the contrast of the train's gritty floor, with spilled soda stains and a Taco Bell wrapper, against this passenger's clean shoes, the older woman's galoshes. Everything but portraits. The only one she wanted to attempt was Jeremy's.

He asked, "You have a copy of the PI's report. Can I see it?"

"Yes, of course."

"I'll double-check the information for you."

"That's really nice but . . ."

"Nah, it's no big deal," he said. "I'm sure it's kosher. Isabel had an affair. She didn't bury any bodies."

"I hope you're right."

"Are you going to contact this Godfrey character, tell him or her the jig is up, that you know about Isabel and Simon?"

"That's a good idea."

Jeremy chewed on his lower lip. "Do you think it could be Isabel's husband?"

"Sending the emails? No way."

"He could have discovered Isabel was fooling around."

"George would never do that."

Doubt shimmied its way up Natalie. Two years ago, she'd have sworn that Marc would never leave, that Isabel would never betray her or George, that her mother would never send her away. What did she understand about people, their underbellies?

"They were provocative messages, meant to be passed on to Isabel."

She said, "I can't swear to anything anymore. But I think he's too adult to do something so small."

"Have to trust your instincts." Jeremy added in a bad Cary Grant imitation, "It's something a newspaperman has to be good at. Stick with me and I'll teach you."

"Only if you promise to wear your Stetson next time." She averted her eyes, lowered her voice. "What does your gut tell you about Isabel?"

"What are you asking me?"

"I guess I mean is she a good person, despite this terrible thing she did?"

"What does *your* gut say?"

Natalie shuddered with the realization she wasn't certain. "It's hungry?" she joked.

They exited at the Washington Square Station. Icy flakes flitted onto the pavement and cars, onto their shoulders and hatted heads. At her apartment door, Natalie said, "Let me just go check on Hads."

"Why don't you get me the report, and I'll jot down the information. We can hang out another time."

"But you came all this way."

He grinned. "I wanted to be with you."

She feared it would show, her bright center, like a fish that lit up to attract a mate. "Be right back," she said and dashed into her office. She was still in her jacket, her pocketbook hanging down from her shoulder by its long leather strap. She heard the ping of her phone and ignored it.

"PI Richard Leroy," he read when she handed him the papers. "Let me write this down."

She touched his hand, and they exchanged glances. His eyes shimmered like drops of water on wax paper.

"Keep it," she said. "I trust you."

BEFORE BED, SHE sent bbGodfrey what she decided would be her final communication, with the subject line: *I know now what happened in the Cayman Islands.* She included the salient points Leroy had documented. Afterwards, she debated checking the text she'd received when Jeremy was outside her front door. It could be from Simon: *I spoke to Gillie, and she's your man. Won't happen again.* Or it could be: *Told Isabel about you and me. She's furious.*

She didn't want any part of it, this scandalous life.

It was from Isabel. *I was terribly selfish. Forgive me.*

As if she could will herself to do so. As if forgiveness were a transaction one could obtain through force or entice with pleading.

Mom, Mom, forgive me for the accident.

Grief ruptured in Natalie's chest. She pushed her gadgets away, phone and computer. They frequently occupied her ex's side of the bed. She shut her eyes and watched the yellowish orange light, flickering inside her eyelids. Time passed in a whoosh.

She saw herself in her bedroom of the Newton house. The crows were perched in the branches of the pink flowering dogwood, cawing, the sound that woke her every morning that first awful spring after her mom had died.

In her short skirt, Isabel twisted one leg around the other so that the soft white underside of her thigh peeked out. She was braiding Natalie's long, curly hair. Her sharply delineated wrist bones peeked out from the sleeves of her peasant blouse. She wasn't as gentle as Natalie's mother. Her hands were too quick and impatient, catching the smallest wisps near her neck.

"What's wrong?" Isabel asked. "Why are you so upset?"

"Lisa was whispering about me in the cafeteria again, how I was the one with the dead mother."

"That's unacceptable! Do you want *me* to deal with it? I'll call her parents and tell them they raised an asshole. Or, I can go to your principal, get this Lisa suspended for a few days."

"I don't think so. That might make it worse."

"If someone hurts you, kid, don't just take it. Retaliate."

A thrill ran through Natalie. The sound of "retaliate" was like the click of teeth.

SLEEP WAS A jolt of a ride, stop, start. A setback, she thought, as she bit into the Xanax in the blood-bruised night. At breakfast, that hungover feeling from fatigue, she drank coffee from her favorite mug. It was a gift from her daughter, inscribed with the saying, "Don't Make Me Shoot You," and a cartoonish drawing of a camera on it.

What if Simon found Hadley's number on Isabel's phone? What if he contacted her as leverage? *So many secrets.*

He won't. He wants to keep on Isabel's good side.

Hadley, long-legged in tight jeans and woolly socks, slogged into the room. She yawned and fell into Natalie's chest as if too weak to carry on. "Trig test first period is a form of abuse."

Natalie stroked her girl's cheek, the skin soft as a puppy's ear. "You'll survive."

"Was Jeremy here last night?"

"Just for a minute, to pick something up."

Hadley thrust out her pelvis and raised her palms. "Way to go, Mom. He's so much cooler than Elizabeth!"

"It's not a competition," Natalie said. *He is! He is!* "Let's get going, Beyoncé. You have a math test to take."

"Queen B to you."

At the front of the school, the rush of students entered the building, book bags hanging like baby carriers on their backs. Natalie watched Hadley walk with a girl in a puffer vest and a boy with the slope of a kid used to being the tallest in the crowd. They were a pack. Hadley belonged; she wasn't suffering like Natalie had at that age.

The phone pinged, and she grabbed it out of her bag. Oh, how she wanted to disengage from this umbilical cord that afforded no freedom. Others ignored their messages or, at least, paced how often they checked them. But she was always on high alert. Fear was a hammer. It wouldn't stop banging.

Isabel wrote, *Sorry I let you down.*

Just can't wrap my head around it, Natalie texted back.

Dumbest thing I ever did. I should have gone to George in the first place.

Did you now?

Yeah. He's pretty angry. But I'm hoping he'll agree to speak to our broker.

Good. I still feel like an idiot.

You're not. It will never happen again.

Could Simon have Hadley's phone number? I can't risk her finding out about me, what happened with my mother.

No, of course not! I swear. I'd never risk that, be that careless.

Ok, good.

Please forgive me.

Natalie stared at the school yard, which was empty of all but stragglers. A moment passed in which she put her car in drive. She returned to park and typed: *Give me time.*

Of course. Thank you. Love you.

ONCE SHE WAS at her desk, everything else retreated. She needed to choose twenty images to correct from the sixty she'd shot of the pink, purple, and yellow, fondant-covered Easter cookies. In each photo she wanted the background to appear crisp and unfussy, not crafty— no bed of confetti paper or wicker basket—so that the "stars" would appeal to the sophisticated readership of the magazine. She loved them, then, these pretty edibles, incapable of harm.

At lunchtime she put an English muffin in the toaster oven.

While it heated up, she allowed herself to read her messages. Jeremy had sent one: *The PI checks out. I'll call you later, tonight a good time to talk?*

A shot of relief. One less thing Isabel had fabricated. And Jeremy wasn't hurrying off. She hadn't spooked him with her troubles. She wrote back, *Yes. Good time. A million thanks.*

She clicked on the bird stamp to retrieve her emails. There it was. The name bbGodfrey, for whom this game was not over.

Nothing you wrote made sense. No idea who Grace Cooke is. What do the Cayman Islands have to do with anything?

twenty-one

———

NATALIE KICKED THE CHAIR NEAR HER FEET.

What the fuck?

Are you Gillian Monroe? I know about the affair with Simon. She didn't use Isabel's name in case Godfrey wasn't the ex-girlfriend. Furious as she was at her stepsister, Natalie wasn't about to advertise Isabel's betrayal to some unidentified bully.

She blasted her reply into cyberspace, fingers resting on the computer as if it were a Ouija Board. When no words materialized, Natalie figured she'd have to coach the ghost out of hiding. *Tell me who you are, or I'll track you down. I know someone at Google who owes me a favor.*

She ran her thumb over the track pad, searching her mind for some scripted television verbiage. *I'll give you till the end of the day.*

After sending this second message, Natalie peered at her inbox, then back at the time on the screen—until fifteen minutes passed. This person was desperate for attention. That's all this was, a plea to be noticed, a hoax. Natalie needed to eat, to finish her assignment; she steeled herself with extra coffee and gulped down toast with cheese.

An hour later, she was concentrating on her assignment when she received another alert.

I don't know anything about any of these people. I was only trying to help. It's your life. If you don't want to do anything, I'll leave you alone.

A precarious dip, like a surprise on a roller coaster. Heat and cold ran through Natalie at the same time. If it wasn't Gillian Monroe or a witness on the island writing these messages, who was it? Another sycophant, a stalker? She could chase the questions on a loop in her brain and get nowhere.

Tell me what you're talking about, she wrote back. *Otherwise my friend will find you and fuck up your email. Everything will be trashed. And I'll call the police. Get back to me now.*

She unclamped her teeth, which were biting down hard enough to chip a tooth.

This time the response took minutes. *What can the police do?*

Harassment can get you jail time.

She had no clue if this were true.

After a few minutes of silence, Natalie added a flourish: *I have my lawyer on speed dial right now. Let's see what he says.*

Ridiculous. Her lawyer dealt with divorce, not crime.

Ok, chill out. See you tomorrow at 11:30 at the Aristotle Café in Cambridge.

She closed her eyes. Simon's British slang coming at her: *Gobsmacked.* BbGodfrey had been *here*, in the Boston area, all this time.

ARISTOTLE CAFÉ WAS quiet at this time of day, the mothers and their small children not yet here for lunch, and the college students who still opted for arty atmosphere over Starbucks not yet ready to study. One young man loped to the pastry counter and leaned towards the guy with the bun and goatee who was serving the customers. Neither of these laconic men looked capable of rescuing Natalie from Godfrey if he got aggressive.

She took one sip of her cappuccino, too revved up to drink more. In order not to stare at the door until her eyes burned, she observed the student photographs on the wall. They were taken in foggy, mystical settings and weren't very good, too wistful and obvious. It crossed her mind that she hadn't informed anyone of her whereabouts. She figured she'd be safe here in public. Now, she wasn't so sure.

A girl not much older than Hadley slumped into the café wearing an open jacket, revealing a form-fitting t-shirt that read *Florida. Life's a Beach.* She was so familiar, this kid with small, delicate features marred by piercings: silver studs in her right eyebrow, her left nostril, and a row down each earlobe. Her makeup was overdone: black eyeliner and vermillion lipstick as if, in aiming for sophisticated, she'd evoked the opposite effect.

She glanced up in Natalie's direction—just for a second, enough time for it to sink in. The girl knew her too. Was she a friend of Hadley's?

Natalie's smile was automatic, and she almost called out in greeting. Then it struck her that the kid was cutting school. She could have been a senior—in fact, she most likely was—and they had more flexible schedules. Maybe this was Morgan, who'd driven Hadley home the day they'd fought about not taking rides from students.

She stood up, ready to wave. Glimpsing at the girl's wrist, on which several silver bands clinked together, Natalie suddenly realized who she was. The hair—a wedge cut, dyed brassy red with bangs that fell over one side of her face—had fooled her. It used to be tapered and dark. This was Ms. Anshaw who'd talked about twelve-step programs and Reese's chocolate candy and wondered about people who'd struggled with mental illness.

After one of the recent workshops, Ms. Anshaw had hovered around her stepsister's desk, waiting for the usual stragglers to leave, her mouth a squiggle of anger, her eyes shining. Natalie had felt sorry for Isabel, having to cater to clients who viewed the Happiness Doctor as a wizard, a shaman.

"You're from Isabel's group," Natalie said once the girl stood next to the table.

"Yeah, I'm, um, Lucy."

"Good to see you." When Lucy didn't make a move to leave, Natalie said, "I'm actually waiting for someone."

"Yeah, I know." Lucy fidgeted with the sleeve of her coat. "It's me . . . you're here to see *me.*"

Natalie felt her breath caught between her ribs. "You're bbGodfrey?"

"He's my cat. Big Boy Godfrey."

The pressure in her chest was so acute, she slapped her hand over her heart to ensure it was beating correctly. Fast but regular. She sat down again. "Is this just a prank to you?"

All this time, she'd tried to chase down the identity, Simon or Gillian, the odd man at the Joy & Wellness party, Robert Brampton who'd hit Grace Cooke. And, like the punchline to a joke, the culprit had been a cat.

The girl slung herself into the seat across from Natalie. "You said if I didn't show up, you'd wreck my mail account or call the cops."

"Our car accident, how did you know? From Isabel?"

"No, she never told me anything personal, nothing that she hasn't used as part of her act to get everyone to believe her crap. Her husband's a big deal doctor who helps her with her work, her mom was an unhappy Norwegian."

"That's enough!" Natalie caught the young man at the counter looking her way and modulated her voice. "How did you know I was related to Isabel?"

"From my aunt, Ellen Alden."

Another punchline. "Garrick's secretary is your *aunt*?"

"Yeah, I've been staying with her this year on a break from college after . . . I got into trouble my freshman year."

"You were in rehab."

The girl nodded. "I had to take a leave after the first semester. My parents found this asshole shrink who spouted Buddhist theories and put me on Trazodone, which gave me nightmares and made me barf. I refused to see him after a couple of months; my parents couldn't deal. They sent me to this program for twenty-one days. Then, I came here."

"Did you come because of Isabel?"

The lunacy of the last few months slapped Natalie on one cheek, then the other, like a Three Stooges' routine. She'd visited Simon, slept with him, confronted Gillian, then Isabel, about the affair—all because of this hapless girl and her pet cat.

"I came to chill," Lucy said. "Aunt Ellen's been great, letting me live with her, no judgment. Just for this year, till I'm ready to go back to school."

"So, that was *you* I spoke with about the tracking number?"

"Wait . . . what?"

"You told me Ellen didn't want to be reached unless there was an emergency. The dog peed in the house while we were on the phone."

"Wow, weird! I thought you were someone from the school. A bunch of assistants called with questions about shit they couldn't find." Lucy sat straighter, proudly, and the words *Life's a Beach* rose up. "They couldn't seem to function without Aunt Ellen."

"What does this have to do with your messages?"

"Aunt Ellen wasn't so cool about my taking Dr. Walker's workshop at first. Which was weird cause, like I said, she was totally chill about everything else, completely hands off."

"Can we get to the point?" Natalie's knee thumped against the underside of the table.

"I'm giving you the story. Aunt Ellen got upset when I told her I wanted to join Dr. Walker's group. I thought it was cause of the professor, him being my aunt's boss and everything. But I convinced my aunt, swore Dr. Walker was professional, would never talk about people in her workshop to her father, that she was this amazingly inspiring person, like Oprah, you know?"

This was a girl raised on Twitter and snapchat and Instagram, and she was composing an epic.

"Yes," Natalie said.

Lucy tugged an earlobe, loosening the last stud shaped like a flower bud. It popped off into her hand. "I'd seen her give lectures in Michigan and struck up a conversation with her. She was the opposite of my shrink, totally approachable."

"So, she *was* one of the reasons you came to live here?" Natalie asked.

"Yeah. Dr. Walker encouraged me to do it and join her workshop. Said it would be a safe space for me. And it was at first. I fucking *loved* her."

"Everyone loves her." Knee thump.

"She's good at that. She was so friendly, always available, said I could text her anytime. Once I found out about her, I knew it was bullshit. But I didn't let on."

Natalie stared into the milky coffee; the foam and sprinkled cinnamon had dissolved. "Can you get to Godfrey, please?"

"Okay, so it started after I mentioned Aunt Ellen. Professor Walker had died before the group started, and I didn't know if I should, like, say that I knew about her dad. So, I didn't at first."

Lucy ran her finger over the silver ball in her eyebrow, nervously. "When I finally confronted her, a couple of weeks ago, I wanted to see if she'd crack. She just turned into a whole other person, this icy bitch. She advised me to go home to Michigan. She said Ellen had an unhealthy obsession with her father and would be a bad influence on me."

So, this was a reaction to rejection, never mind how Lucy knew about the island. "What you did with me was payback?"

Lucy rolled her eyes. "I'm not that twisted. Anyway, I sent the first one sooner than that."

Natalie calculated quickly. "That's true. Why?"

"Dr. Walker called the house one night, right before my aunt left for her trip. Aunt Ellen would *never* tell me what was going on—you should know that upfront. She is so loyal and respectful of that man's privacy. But I overheard her talking on the phone, with Dr. Walker. She was freaked out."

"Overheard?"

"Yeah, she was in the living room, and I could tell she was upset. I picked up the extension. Just for a minute."

Natalie nodded, seeing the pictures of Isabel rain down from Simon's copy of *Get Happy Now*. They had amateur spying in common, she and this storyteller.

"Aunt Ellen said Garrick insisted she carry out his last wishes: get papers to his stepdaughter, *Natalie*. She was conflicted, didn't want to hurt anyone. Dr. Walker warned my aunt to forget about the package and stay out of her family's business. A week or so later, Aunt Ellen brought home this envelope from the office." Lucy fiddled with the flower bud on her other ear, a glint of desperation in her eyes. "I knew what it was, and that Dr. Walker didn't want her to have it. I opened it when my aunt was asleep."

"You read my mail?" Natalie had the urge to grab this girl and shake her so hard the jewels would fall from her, like decorations off a Christmas tree.

"Yeah, not cool. Aunt Ellen would *kill* me if she knew. That's why I couldn't say who I was. Also, I was afraid you might tell Dr. Walker. I didn't know you, couldn't risk it."

"Why does Garrick's letter to me matter to you?"

Lucy's face flushed. "It's because of Dr. Walker, the *real* person, not the fake, happy one she pretends to be. She's out there, writing books and preaching to people. She shouldn't be allowed to pretend that she cares when she's horrible."

"This is based on Isabel's conversation with Ellen and telling you to go back to Michigan?"

"Of course not. It's because of the accident."

Natalie shook her head and the confusion was a tug, like her hair pulled too tight when Isabel combed it. "I have no idea what this has to do with Garrick's letter, but you got some wrong information. It turned out to be a mix-up."

Lucy glared at her. "What are you talking about? Your mother was killed."

Like a water main break: that gush of adrenaline. "My mother's been dead for years. She wasn't in the Caribbean."

"Jesus. What's with you and the Caribbean? I didn't understand why you weren't *doing* anything about Professor Walker's letter."

Natalie felt a wave of wooziness; sweat gathered under her arms. "I don't see what you mean since I never got it."

"Right, but I didn't know that," Lucy said. "There was a police report. There was blood on the road. The police couldn't figure out how it got so far from the car. But Isabel's boyfriend must have seen. That's why I told you to try and find him."

"Her boyfriend, Thomas, was there? Did he see what I did?"

"I don't know what you mean."

"The flashlight . . ."

"Yeah, what about it?"

Natalie's mother had peered into the rearview mirror, fear radiating from her eyes. That fear had transferred to Natalie; although, by the time she realized what she was feeling it was too late. She'd asked, "Mom, what is it?"

And she'd turned around toward the car, her stepfather's Mercedes, trailing them. The headlights were off, when just a moment before a glow had obscured the street and sky. How could her tiny flashlight have illuminated the world like that?

Her mother's last word had been her husband's name.

"Garrick was behind us," Natalie said.

"No, he *wasn't*. That's the point."

The pieces were like scrabble tiles, not yet forming a coherent word. And she was playing this game with a screwed-up teenager. *Who'd been locked away.* "Then who was?"

The girl pushed her bracelets up her arm, nearly to her elbow, and rubbed her wrists as if they'd marked her skin. "I'm not going to say anymore. That's why I stayed anonymous and, umm, cryptic."

"You're not getting off the hook this time," Natalie said sharply.

Manipulative, yes. Egocentric, probably. Empathetic: who could say?

"It's all very secretive and, maybe for you, a big laugh at my expense. But I'll tell Ellen everything you said, everything you did, including reading the letters and harassing me, if you don't explain right now. Why was Thomas, her boyfriend, there?"

Lucy's wrist rubbing accelerated, crept down to her hands. She whispered, "He was with *her*."

"Isabel wasn't there. I know that. I would remember *that*."

"Professor Walker wrote to you about how the blood got where it did. Isabel."

"Where is the proof of this?"

"Ellen sent it. I drove that day; we had lunch out after she ran her errands. One of them was going to FedEx. She addressed the package to you, to Natalie Greene."

"I never got it. Why would I even believe you?"

"Believe whatever you want." Her voice softened, almost scared, "Just be careful. Your stepsister is dangerous."

"Watch yourself."

A fissure opened inside Natalie in which doubt could grow.

Lucy slumped in her seat. "You're right. Why should I care? Just promise not to tell my aunt 'cause she's the only relative who believes in me. I can't lose her."

"You should have thought of that beforehand."

Tears caused Lucy's makeup to run into the hollows below her eyes. Her nose was red, which made her lipstick seem even more of a miscalculation.

Natalie realized that for all her bravado, the kid was scared. "I'm not interested in discussing you with Ellen. It's just unbelievably convenient I never got the letter. Did you keep it?"

"I told you. She sent it! Why would I do that and then email you about it?

"For attention."

"You think I'm crazy, fine. Join the club. You and my parents and the Buddhist assholes and half the people at rehab. But ask my aunt when she gets home." Lucy rocked forward. "She's coming back soon, in a couple of days."

"I *will*. I'll ask her about the envelope, if it just disappeared. You stay out of our lives."

Lucy couldn't sit still. She bent down, played with the purple plaid flap on one of her combat boots. "Don't worry. I'm going back to Michigan, working for a while, then to school. Even agreed to see a new shrink. I would have transferred around here. But forget that. I want to be as far from this craziness as possible."

"Sounds like a good plan."

"As soon as Aunt Ellen gets home, I'll let her know you left messages about never getting the FedEx."

"I won't bring you up on one condition. No contact, ever again."

"No problem."

Lucy slouched as she walked away, whether out of a hipster posture or a real sense of defeat, Natalie couldn't say. But, she raised her phone from where it lay on the table and snapped a couple of shots of Lucy and, in her mind, titled the photos: *Lost Girl(s)*.

I'm one of those.

She waited until Lucy was out of sight. Then Natalie rushed out of the café as if being chased by demons.

She clutched the wheel and drove slowly. She switched on the radio for noise.

It was fantastical, this teenager and her convoluted story. The claims might be the tales of a troubled kid, an addict, another of her stepsister's obsessive fans who felt spurned by her hero.

The niggling problem: Lucy might be just a girl adrift, but that didn't make her wrong.

What if . . . I didn't kill my mother?

twenty-two

———

WHAT IF I DIDN'T KILL MY MOTHER?

All the way home, the echo was like words in a whispering gallery.

If it had been Garrick's car—no matter who was driving—why had Natalie believed herself responsible all these years? *Just be careful. Your stepsister is dangerous.* She tried to squeeze out more memories, like water from cloth, but not a drop came.

Natalie had an hour before Hadley's school pickup. She microwaved canned vegetable soup for a late lunch while she uploaded the images of Lucy. She'd examine the pictures of the girl for clues to her character: truly disturbed, just reacting to Isabel's withdrawal of affection, or a teenager with a dramatic flair whose intentions were good.

In her office, she fiddled with exposure to address the dim coffee shop lighting. She was most taken by one shot, a side view of Lucy in motion seen through the glass door of the café, reminding her of the women in the series *Incarceration*. Zooming in on the girl's blotchy face, eyes bleary and lipstick smeared, Natalie imagined how, in another time and place, she would convert it to black and white and use the Hue/Saturation adjustment to change the brightness, even add back a slight color tint.

She'd jiggered the window open to counteract the heat pumping through the old radiator in her office. The fresh air hit, and suddenly she missed being in the darkroom with her mother. Not just her mom's laughter and instruction, the lilt of her voice, her quick, agile movements, but the workmanship involved, the technical precision of adding the developer to the water, preparing the chemicals for the stop bath and fixer, and the anticipation that arose as they washed the film. Those slow, methodical tasks demanded concentration that would help Natalie ignore the siren wail in her head.

But of course, if her mother were here, there would be no siren wail.

When she heard her phone, she reached for it to press "decline." Viewing the name on the screen, she accepted instead.

"Hey," Jeremy said. "Had a minute and wanted to check up."

She burst out with, "I found Godfrey."

"Really? That's great! Was it the guy in the Caribbean?"

"No. Actually, I got it all wrong."

Wait. Wait! Jeremy craved confirmation that Isabel's program was a sham, that she was conning people.

"I'm not ready to talk about it."

"Take your time. Glad you found the guy," he said. "Will I see you in group?"

"I'm skipping this week."

"Ah. Then, I will too. Can we get together this weekend?"

"Yes," she said.

TWO DAYS LATER, Natalie was making color corrections on the Easter cookies when her cell rang. Her jaw tightened. Isabel had texted her several times, the last one: *Why are you ghosting me?* to which Natalie, strangled by cowardice, answered: *Just busy.* She'd spent nights teetering on the edge of sleep, aching for the Isabel she knew, her North Star. A woman who might not exist.

But this call was from Ellen. "Hello, dear."

"You're back," Natalie said.

About her aunt's timeline, the girl had been credible.

"Flew in last night. My niece told me what happened, that you never got the package. I'm so sorry for this fiasco."

"It's not your fault."

"I wish Lucy had contacted me. I could have helped you sooner."

"There's not much you could have done. FedEx insists they delivered it."

"I know, dear. I spoke to a fellow there just now. I gave him the tracking number right away; he said the same thing."

"Thanks for trying," Natalie said, staring at the pink and yellow fondant.

"Normally, I would have required your signature. But it was such a stressful time. I wasn't myself."

"Well, there's nothing we can do about it now."

"That's not so." The older woman made a wheezing sound when she inhaled. "I copied the documents I have them here safe and sound."

A jab under her ribcage. "What?"

"Garrick wanted me to make a copy, said that I'd understand when I saw what's in there."

"Wait! You knew what was in them all this time?"

"You'll want to see them immediately. I assumed that he expected me to at least skim them, see what I was dealing with."

"I'm coming right now."

"PLEASE EXCUSE MALCOLM," Ellen said, at the door. Her face was tanned and dappled, like a starling's feathers. She had on a gray alpaca sweater and her oxblood scarf, the one she'd worn to Garrick's funeral. From somewhere in the back of her house, a dog ruffed, three barks in succession. "He should settle down. He's just excited by company. Can I get you something other than water to drink? I can heat up some tea."

"No. I'm here for the papers," Natalie said, firmly. "I can't stay." She accompanied Ellen into the dimly lit living room, peeking around to see if Lucy was there. If so, she'd locked herself away with the anguished dog, and wisely so.

From what Natalie could see, the place was narrow with beige walls and wood wainscoting. A spinster's home, small and dark and sad. Ellen led her to the living room and gestured for her to sit on the jacquard sofa with the white beech frame. The hostess settled in an armchair upholstered in the same bluish-gray fabric.

"Please, indulge me a moment." Ellen pointed to the platter of brownies and the pitcher of water with the two crystal glasses on the coffee table between them. She had a tremor that Natalie hadn't noticed at the funeral.

The dog quieted. There was only the noise from the street, the crackling of car tires over pebbles.

Natalie said, "I'd appreciate it if you'd get me Garrick's documents."

"There's something I'd like to get off my chest first."

Another storyteller in the family?

"I don't have long."

Ellen nodded. "We were at the conference in Washington DC together overnight, the day before your mother died. He'd never asked me along before, you see. I was there to be useful, that's all. I wasn't the kind of woman who would get involved with a married man. I want you to know *nothing* happened."

"What does this have to do with anything?"

Ellen touched her beaded necklace with nervous fingers. "It's because of the Valium, dear. Garrick blamed himself, felt horribly guilty."

"That was to help my mother sleep."

"Maybe it was the *intended* use."

"That's not your concern," Natalie snapped.

"I wish it weren't." One of Ellen's eyelids was pink and slightly scaly, Natalie noticed. It aged her further. *Good.* "Laura believed that Garrick and I were having an affair. Later, Garrick let slip it was the reason she took the medication in the first place. Marital stress."

Natalie imagined a stack of purple-covered paperbacks, with titles like *The Duke's Debutante* and *The Earl's Virgin Bride*, on the end table next to Ellen's bed. She'd noticed these romance novels in a girl's dorm room years ago and had never forgotten their names. Ellen probably kept a journal, too, of her unrequited feelings and had taken solace in the jealousy she evoked in Laura.

"We worked together for over thirty years." Ellen's eyes moistened. "I had enormous admiration and respect for him. He was a truly great man. But there was nothing more between us, no feelings on either side."

Natalie nodded, not believing a word.

"He spoke so highly of *you*."

"You're mixing me up with Isabel."

"I would never confuse the two of you," Ellen said. "It was painful for him after your poor mother's accident. You reminded him so much of her, you see."

"I doubt that."

"My dear, you're her spitting image." The old woman reached over and patted her arm the way one would a yelping pet· *there, there.*

"Did you know my mother?"

"We'd met, of course, a few times," Ellen said briskly. "But Garrick was always very private, *appropriately* so. Later, he did share with me his remorse."

"About what?"

Natalie couldn't resist the ocean tide pull of Ellen's tale.

"Neglect, dear. Poor man blamed himself so. For years, he was haunted by his part in both his wives' deaths. He wasn't there for Sigrid and your mother; his work consumed him. He felt he'd missed the signs leading to their deaths. He told me that . . . afterwards."

"None of this has anything to do with why I'm here, for Garrick's letter."

"Oh, but it has *everything*. There was Valium in Laura's system at the time."

The air around Natalie buzzed, suddenly on high alert. "No. That's wrong."

"You must read it, dear."

"I'm sure he was mixed up."

"I'm afraid not. But you can see for yourself." Ellen gazed at her hands, curled around each other. "I'll never let myself off the hook for my part in your mother's death. I needed you to know that."

Natalie didn't respond. There was only the sound of the breathing between them. Whose breath was more labored, she couldn't distinguish. Then the animal barked in triplicate again.

Ellen slid open a drawer on her side of the table. She lifted out a manila envelope that had been edged into the slender compartment and handed it to Natalie. "Garrick cared for you, dear. He tried his best to garner the courage to talk to you. I believe he was finally ready. It was simply too late."

IN THE CAR, Natalie squeezed the metallic clasp and opened the unglued flap. She slid out a page that read "Police Report" at the top and a smaller envelope that was taped shut. She felt that surge, the clang of alarm: *Mayday, Mayday*. But she wouldn't repeat her mother's mistake, wouldn't pop a pill while behind the wheel. She put the documents back in their sheath. She turned on the radio's classical music station, the moaning cellos and mournful horns. Switching to the news, a report on the president's refusal to accept climate science, was worse. She drove faster than usual, in silence, staring ahead at the yellow lawns and barren trees.

In her living room, she tossed her coat on a chair, hopped on one foot as she wrestled her boot off the other, sat on the couch and tugged.

Her hand trembled as she pulled out the report—White-Out correcting the Local Case Number—along with a Crash Diagram and the letter from Garrick. She flipped through the report quickly. The second page consisted of boxes for Vehicle Number and Passenger (only if injured or killed). There were two columns and just one filled in.

On the next page was a complicated grid with ovals that resembled a standardized test form with categories such as, "Type of Driver Distraction, "Vehicle Damage," and "Condition of Driver Contributing to the Crash." That last one determined that there were "No Defects." Her mother had no eyesight, hearing, or "other" defect, no known illness.

Natalie's airway tightened. Her mother appeared perfectly healthy seconds before she was irrevocably dead. The Driver's Action column presented forty-three possibilities to account for the accident, including "Blinded by Headlights," which was not the blackened oval. The blackened oval was "Other."

In the paragraph under Crash Description, police officer Burke wrote, "Tire marks indicate recent activity, though no traces of a collision on the deceased driver's vehicle. Blood found on the road approximately 30 feet away."

Had the blood from her mother's head wound flowed, a warm, rusty-red stream, down the road?

She unfolded Garrick's pages, handwritten on his department stationary.

Natalie, I kept this from you out of loyalty to Isabel. You have a child, so I hope you'll understand. Before Laura's death, she and Isabel were fighting constantly. I don't know what you remember, if anything. But Isabel was drinking, smoking marijuana, and stealing Laura's prescription medication. We caught her in our home in bed with an older boy, Thomas James. She was seeing a psychiatrist, Dr. Martin Strout, for months, but Isabel's behavior didn't improve.

The room was lopsided and ungrounded, the furniture tipping. Natalie stood to get a glass of water but didn't make it. She buckled, knees, and then waist, like one of those collapsible thumb puppets her mom once gave her.

Isabel was the patient, the fucked-up daughter, the liar. Not me.

On the floor, Natalie saw the familiar nooks and crannies, the frayed rug and smudged marks on the walls, the dust motes gathered under the lamp like tiny sparklers. Holding onto the coffee table for balance, she rose and, on the couch, drew her knees into her chest. She remembered being awakened during the night by the sound of howling. When she tiptoed toward Isabel's room, she realized the noise was coming from the TV, one of those horror movies her stepsister loved. She edged open the door to see shadows, blankets and sheets wrapped around Isabel and what looked like pillows lined up next to her. Isabel pulled down her bedding. Underneath, she was naked, her body an elegant ivory, with blond pubic hair and faint peach nipples. A boy's head rested on one breast, his eyes closed, mouth slightly open. He was asleep, his penis hanging languidly on her thigh.

She resumed reading; the words scurried like ants she had to rush to catch.

Laura believed it best for all of us if Isabel received professional help away from the family; Dr. Strout agreed. She'd scheduled a meeting with the clinical director of a boarding school for struggling teens.

They argued the afternoon of the crash, and Isabel threw a dish at your mother's face. That's when Laura decided to take you with her to Dr. Strout's. I was away, at a conference, and couldn't accompany her. But on the phone, I told your mother to let you stay home with Isabel. You two girls adored each other. Laura insisted it wasn't safe.

When I saw the coroner's report, they noted the amount of Valium Laura had in her system. It was three times the dose prescribed for sleep.

I can't reconcile the fact she'd drive in that condition. She was distraught but not self-destructive, and certainly she'd never intentionally put you in harm's way. The only explanation I could come up with is that the stress just got to be too much that day, and Laura got forgetful, took more than she'd meant to. Along with the situation with Isabel, I was away on a trip with my assistant. The last part was meaningless but upsetting to your mother.

Soon after I arrived home that day, the police showed up at the house with the terrible news. Afterwards, I was in shock and not thinking about Isabel, where she was. A while later, she came out of our garage, claiming she'd left her book bag in my car (even though Laura always picked up you girls from school in her car, not mine) and that she never heard or saw the police. When I drove to the hospital that night, I noticed a red blotch that looked like blood on the carpeting under my feet. That didn't register as anything suspicious at the time.

Natalie stared at the scrapes on her coffee table leg. It was so hard to get enough oxygen.

But, at some point, I confronted Isabel about her odd behavior and about the stains in the upholstery. She admitted she'd taken out my Mercedes with Thomas, who wanted to drive it. They'd gone for pizza and eaten in the car. She said the boy must have dropped some on the floor carpet. This also explained why she was getting her book bag when I saw her. But the story always seemed too convenient to me. I didn't smell pizza in the car, and that stain looked more like blood than sauce.

All this time, I've suspected my own daughter of some involvement with what happened that day. I told myself it was her boyfriend's doing, a sick prank to scare Laura, run her off the road, for threatening to send his girlfriend away. But I've wondered why they went through with it once Isabel knew you were in the car and why in the world they didn't help you. Even if they'd panicked, they could have called an ambulance when they got home and not given their names. Maybe they were too afraid of being caught.

I'm sorry to foist this on you in such a cowardly manner. It's haunted me that my daughter and Thomas killed my wife and left you injured. But I couldn't expose my child, to confess that I believed she'd abandoned you after the crash. By trying to protect both Isabel and you, I was paralyzed. I hope you can forgive me for my weakness. Love, Garrick.

HER MOTHER HAD worn her wool coat with the fake fur collar and the rubbery boots that squeaked when she walked. "Bring your homework to do in the waiting room." Her voice was gentle. She was steady on her feet. "I'll be out in forty-five minutes."

They'd been driving down a twisty hill when the car began to sway. Her mother said, "Sorry, honey. I'm feeling a little woozy."

"Maybe we should go home if you're sick," Natalie said.

"I'll be all right." Her mother flashed her a smile and reached for the Dunkin' Donuts travel cup she carried around with her everywhere. "That's why I brought my coffee to shore me up."

Natalie had gone back to reading *Jane Eyre* when a huge light loomed outside, and she heard her mother's voice. "The light's blinding me. For Christ's sake, what's going on? Garrick?"

Natalie's heart had broken into a canter. Suddenly they whirled without warning, faster than any spin she'd done ice-skating. Shrieks. Then, the noise and spinning stopped.

It felt as if a heavy helmet were sitting on her head, pushing it down so her chin fell onto her chest. She smelled the bitter coffee and something else, oil or gasoline. Someone was standing above her, lightly pressing fingers onto her throat. She whispered, a female voice, and pointed the flashlight at Natalie. "You should never have done this, shone this in her eyes. You did this." When Natalie looked up, she caught only a glimpse of a hooded jacket and, around the woman's neck, Ellen's red scarf.

twenty-three

———

THE HOTEL LOBBY WAS BUSTLING. THERE WAS A FLURRY OF VISITORS in structured business suits, carrying leather bags slick as seals. Natalie figured many were participants in the Happiness symposium. She'd read about the featured speakers, had scrolled down each of the site menus. Along with Isabel, there were five other psychologists and a mustached-psychiatrist with "eclectic interests in Eastern medicine, Buddhism and strength-based positive psychology." Natalie watched a mother with a toddler clutched to her chest, his sleeping face burrowed into her neck, a man with a cell phone pressed to his ear, shuffling forward as if gum were stuck to his shoes; a woman in a tight skirt and black jacket gusting by in her designer boots.

Oh, to be like them, leading normal lives. Of course, Natalie had no idea what secrets they carried. The mother could be selling opiates to support her child. The man could be arrested any day now for insider trading. Or, like she, they could be trying to unsnarl a constrictor knot of lies.

For days, Natalie had tried to analyze her flashback, the woman jutting above her, checking for a pulse. She could swear it had been Ellen—that red scarf.

Garrick and his assistant could have arrived home from DC in time to follow her mother to Dr. Strout's. Maybe Ellen had deceived Natalie about the events on Garrick's behalf, still loyal to him after his death. But she couldn't square this scenario with her stepfather's confession, the forfeiting of Isabel as a scapegoat. She couldn't ascertain who was the liar. Father? Daughter? Other woman?

Or all of them.

Natalie had dangled the possibility in her mind, like a bright mobile, that Ellen and Garrick had created a fanciful alternative reality for her benefit. *Please, please, please.* Still, she avoided Isabel, didn't attend the workshop that week, responded to her stepsister's calls with cryptic text messages. She didn't share her discussion with Ellen or the contents of the letter with anyone. One late morning, standing over her kitchen sink, Natalie heard her mother's voice, which sounded like the sea captured in a shell pressed to her ear. "Come to me when you're upset, not to Isabel. She's a very different kind of person, tricky and not always what she seems."

Tricky was an ambiguous word. It didn't mean black sludge on a brain scan. But it didn't *not* mean it either.

A planned meeting would be a mistake. A café was too public—the clank and shuffle and chatter—and the phone too distant. She had to track down her stepsister, to meet her someplace unexpected. If startled, Isabel might lose her composure, might even crack open to reveal what was hidden, the fiend crouching inside.

On the far wall of the hotel lobby was a photo of the Victorian brownstones on Commonwealth Avenue, adorned by the dogwoods in full bloom. This regal area was the proper setting for the beatific Isabel, who Natalie now glimpsed walking from the open doors of the meeting room dressed in the soft pink and white of those flowering trees. She was engaged in conversation with two men. When her stepsister noticed Natalie, puzzlement flashed across her face. She smiled, waved, held up one finger as she turned to her colleagues.

Natalie closed the guidebook and stood up, stomach burning. *Here we go.* A crowd was gathering at the elevators, most likely the guests returning to their rooms now that the convention had ended for the day.

"This is a surprise." Isabel materialized beside her.

"I need to talk to you."

"I'm so glad. I was worried."

"Do you have a room in the hotel?"

"Of course not." Isabel's eyes shone with curiosity. "I'm on my way home."

Natalie placed a hand on her belly. "This is where you stayed when Simon was in town."

"Oh, God, Nat. Is that why you're upset? I haven't seen him in ages."

Liar. You slept with him in this hotel.

"There must be somewhere we can speak alone."

"You chose an odd place for that." When Isabel touched her elbow, Natalie flinched. "Sweetie, what's up?"

"Why don't you ask if you can use a room for ten minutes?"

"All right."

Natalie was terribly thirsty. While Isabel strode to the information desk, she considered buying a drink from the shop at the entranceway but determined that was a risk. Isabel might get caught up in an unexpected encounter, run out of time before needing to meet her lover—or a colleague or whomever—and this opportunity would be lost.

"The manager was very accommodating," Isabel said when she reappeared. "Let's go, the third floor."

It was a large space with two adjacent doors. Long tables lined the room, draped in pleated cloth that reached the floor. There was a pitcher of water on each table, slices of lemon floating to the top. Isabel motioned for them to sit, but Natalie poured a glass and took a long sip.

"What's going on?" Isabel asked.

Natalie felt the breath wrenched from her. "I got Garrick's envelope from Ellen. Turns out she made a copy of everything."

Isabel's stare, so hot, it could burn through Natalie's retinas. "Ellen couldn't stay out of our business."

"According to the report, there was someone else on the road. Garrick suspected that you and your boyfriend chased us in his car."

"I told my dad. We went for pizza. Thomas drove us."

"Garrick said you were the one going to therapy with Dr. Strout, you were the one they wanted to send away. Not me."

There was a moment of silence. Even the air was excited. Isabel stood very still and straight. "That's true."

"Garrick said you were seeing him because you were out of control. Sleeping with that boy in the house, that you'd thrown a dish at my mother's face."

"It wasn't at her *face*. Thomas, yes, so what? I was sixteen. You caught us once. You weren't traumatized by it."

"But you twisted it around, said *I* was the fucked-up kid."

"All these years, I tried to convince you that you weren't responsible while you *insisted* that you'd killed your mother. Isn't that true, Nat?"

There was the pull of belief, like a faith Natalie had rejected. It was incredible, this strong habit of love. "Why were you seeing Dr. Strout?"

Isabel fussed with the collar of her silky blouse, although it lay perfectly flat, then pushed through the top button, which had slipped halfway out of its slit. Nothing had been revealed but the scoop of her neckline, her skin the color of bleached bones.

"I was noncompliant. What a joke. It's called being a teenager. But I was the daughter of Sigrid, so it was easy to blame genetics. But your mom . . . no one should threaten to ship off a sixteen-year-old. You'd never do that."

"You're right. But Hadley isn't you. She's clever, but not like you, even back then: the smartest girl in the school, always. The best at everything."

Isabel smiled wanly. "Not everything. You can't imagine how bored I was. I admit it *was* hard for me to follow the rules."

Natalie nodded. "But that's what made you so amazing. You didn't care what other people thought, did what you pleased. You never had to study like I did to get good grades and ace every subject."

"School was easy. All I had to do was show up and impress the teachers with the right answers, with good test scores. But, at home, it was a nightmare. My dad never paid attention to anything but academics. But Laura, always watching, always judging. She should have left me alone. I would have come to it on my own, stopped drinking, and getting high."

"She couldn't. You have to see that," Natalie said in the softest voice she could muster. "I wouldn't let Hadley do those things."

"But you wouldn't send her to a place like *that,* a place that would have ruined her chances. The students there were all classified, Nat. Do you know what that means: mental illnesses and personality disorders and addictions? I'd never have gotten into Harvard or met George or achieved any success, much less this." Isabel waved at the desks, the chairs, as if building hotel furniture was her profession. "She would have taken away my life."

"I understand, I do." Natalie tightened her grasp on her glass, cool from the ice. But a glass was not an anchor; it could shatter.

"Give me that before you hurt yourself," Isabel said. "Sit down."

Natalie listened because that's what Isabel had trained her to do. She sat on a chair. Her arms and legs were shaking. "I thought it was Ellen and Garrick following us. But it wasn't. It was you."

"I just wanted to talk to her, to get her to change her mind about seeing Dr. Strout. That moron came up with sending me to Pine Mountain. Laura never would have had the idea by herself."

"So, explain it. You thought that somehow you could persuade my mother by letting your boyfriend take you in Garrick's car and cornering her outside the doctor's office?"

Isabel studied her, unflinching. "Thomas came with me, but I drove the car. He didn't have the guts to . . . I drove so quickly—I was going over eighty—to catch her. *I could have been the one to hit that tree, but I was sober."*

"You flashed the headlights?"

"Of course not. I never—"

Natalie interrupted her. "If you don't tell me, I'll show George the letter. I bet George wasn't thrilled about your request to cash in stocks, the mess you'd made of things, was he?"

"We got through it," Isabel straightened, thin and taut. "George will forgive me."

"Yes. Reckless about money is one thing. An affair is worse. But murder is unforgivable."

Isabel stared at her without wavering, but her eyes were vacant vessels, like Simon's. She outstretched her arms. "Nat, c'mon. I've always been there for you, never asked for anything. You said so yourself. Now, you need to be there for me. We do that for each other."

"Just say what you did."

"It was impulsive, just a momentary thing. Laura would have crashed anyway. She was swerving all over the place. She was so volatile, reckless."

No. That was you.

"You whispered to me that I did it, that I shone my flashlight in her eyes. That's why I believed it all these years."

Isabel shook her head so that her chic high ponytail swayed. "You must have imagined that; you were concussed."

"You're lying! You lie all the time. But, you can't get away with this anymore."

"There's nothing to get away *with*. It wasn't either of our faults, yours or mine. Laura was driving on tranquilizers. *That* was in the coroner's report. She could have killed you. Do you realize that?"

"You left me there."

"I made sure you were okay. Don't you see how trapped I was?"

"Is that why you didn't call an ambulance?"

Isabel paced between the tables, an obstacle course. "I knew one would come. It was a calculated risk. We'd both be safe—you and I."

"You abandoned me with a brain injury." *Stay even, factual.* Natalie fed the beast with a steady hand. "I saw you there even though everything was blurred. I thought you were Ellen with that red scarf."

"That was a last-minute thing, just in case we were spotted. I wore one of her famous scarves that I'd found in Dad's car, years before. I always wondered what that meant about the two of them. Thomas wore one of dad's old fedora hats."

"What about my mom? Why didn't you check on her?"

"You don't want to hear about that."

Natalie said, "You have no idea what I want."

"I always know what you want!" Isabel stopped pacing. "There was no reason to take Laura's pulse. Her head was split open. There was blood in her hair and on the wheel of the car."

"She might have been alive. How could you be sure?"

"Her face was twisted. I saw it in her eye. She was dead."

There was a terrible taste in Natalie's mouth, a sense she was gagging. "FedEx swears they didn't lose the envelope. Did you have something to do with that?" When Isabel didn't respond, she said, "You stole it."

"I *intercepted* it. For *your* sake. For *your* peace of mind. It was a pain in the ass, showing up three days in a row, making sure you never saw me. I had to clear my schedule and wait around in your building for the truck." Isabel sighed. "I used your key to go inside and ring the guy in, then met him in the hallway."

Natalie wanted to smear Isabel's wan smile into a different shape, the way she would smear butter at a photo shoot. She imagined the dull knife in her hand. The hollow of Isabel's throat appeared so deep, as if punctured.

Her stepsister strode towards her. "People need to master their impulses in order to get what they want. That's what I teach them."

"But you hadn't mastered them when you were a teenager. And, lately, you've fucked up everything. So maybe you're not the expert you profess to be." Natalie stepped back, her hands trembling. She dug her fists into her coat pockets, a ballast, until she strained the fabric. "What did you do to my mother that Thomas didn't have the guts for? It wasn't driving fast."

"Let's drop this. What good can come of it? Do you really want to trigger—"

"I can find out whether you tell me or not. You want reporters around your classes? Around your career?"

"What can you possibly find out? There's nothing else."

Such a virtuoso manipulator, vaulting to success, leaving a chilly wind in her wake.

"I slept with Simon, your cash cow," Natalie said, winded. "You know what he told me? That you were alike, you shared all your secrets. He never rescued his brother that day they were sailing, and you did the same."

Isabel froze, the look on her face when she felt cornered. "It's not the same. Simon wanted Charlie to die. I didn't mean to kill anyone."

"He wanted his own brother to die?" Natalie asked, queasy. "How could anyone want that?"

"Charlie was the golden boy, the favorite. Simon craved attention."

She moved closer to Isabel. "Did you kill my mother? It wasn't just the headlights, was it? There was something more."

"What does it matter?"

"It matters whether I know or I leak my suspicions to George, the media, everyone. Are you willing to ruin your career, your marriage? They're almost ruined now, aren't they?"

Isabel stood still.

The red pulsing muscle of fear beat in Natalie's chest. "You'd go to any lengths, do anything, to save yourself."

"We are the same, you and me," Isabel cried. "You told me you were willing to do anything to stay together. All these years, you thought you caused the accident. That was your guilt talking. It doesn't matter which one of us acted, which of us was the girl they wanted to send away. I did it for both of us."

"We're *not* the same. I wouldn't have—"

"That's why *I* had to. It was always me who had to save us, save you. I've been saving you my whole goddamn life. I knew what to do. She took that coffee mug with her everywhere. I mixed the Valium into her coffee."

This is Belle, my Belle.

It hurt to speak, that's how parched Natalie was, as if all the fluid had dried up in her body. "But how could we stay together if I was in that car? You could have killed me."

Isabel ran her fingers through her hair, over and over, loosening her ponytail. "You weren't supposed to be with her. You were at your friend's down the block. You got home a few minutes before she left. I said you should stay with me, that Thomas would go. But, still, she refused, said she didn't trust me."

"But you let us leave together, let her take the coffee."

"It was too late by then." Isabel's eyes had a faraway look. "I couldn't admit what I'd done. They'd have locked me away for good. But I realized that if anyone tested the coffee, they'd discover the Valium. So, I followed Laura. I had to get the mug from the car, to make sure the police didn't find it."

There was a smell of terror in the air. Natalie was smothered, her breathing hindered, as if death was before her, reaching out a hand.

"You understand that she forced me, left me no choice? I didn't *want* to do it."

"I . . . I have to go now."

Isabel reached for the glass of water on the table and handed it to her. "Drink. It's the shock. You don't want to faint."

Natalie gulped it down.

"You promised not to tell George. Not about this. Not about Simon. We had an agreement."

"I won't say anything. I just have to get Hadley. I don't want to be late, for her to think anything's wrong."

"You should do that."

Natalie watched as her stepsister shape-shifted into her carefully constructed self: the softening of her features, the congenial tone. Isabel drew her into a goodbye hug, the way she always did, marking—Natalie determined in a flash—that everything was settled. Yes, she'd been forced to confess but, now that she had, life would return to normal. All Natalie had to do was comply, to relax into the embrace. But she stiffened, pulled away.

Isabel's eyelashes fluttered as she stepped back with a cold smile. Everything had changed. "I have a few more things to take care of here. But you go ahead."

Natalie rushed out of the conference room and ducked around the corner towards the stairwell. It was dimly lit but a short distance to the street, quicker this way. At the landing to the second floor, she heard the stairwell to the door close, footsteps behind her. There was no doubt who it was; she didn't need to turn around to check. The metal tip of Isabel's spiky heels clicked as she ran after her. There was heavy breathing, her own and her pursuer's, as if in tandem.

Firm hands grabbing her shoulders stopped Natalie from moving forward. "Careful," Isabel whispered into her ear from behind. "You don't want another accident."

Natalie whirled around, her whipping motion throwing her stepsister off balance. A heel snapped off from one of Isabel's shoes; she reached for the handrail, but it was beyond her grasp. As she lunged forward, Natalie attempted to catch her but missed. She saw her stepsister's expression, the "O" of her mouth, the surprise in her eyes.

It was quick: the flailing limbs, then the loud, dull crack as Isabel struck the bottom step. Her arms hit first, covering her face. There was blood in her hair, bright and copious. Natalie stared as it spilled into the yellow strands, like dye. Isabel groaned, a pitiful sound that ripped through Natalie, the sheer animal intimacy of it. She wanted it to stop. She glimpsed at the door, far enough from Isabel that she could squeeze through, run away. Let someone else deal with this, while she rushed through the lobby in a blur of freedom, right into the drizzling snow. But she wasn't that person, someone who could kill. That was Isabel.

For a few seconds, Natalie waited for a resolution, for the noise to abate. *There was no reason to take Laura's pulse. She was dead.*

But Isabel didn't quiet.

She reached inside her bag for her phone and dialed.

The operator answered, "911. What's your emergency?"

twenty-four

——

ISABEL WAS FACE DOWN ON THE CEMENT FLOOR, NO LONGER
conscious.

The paramedic asked if Natalie wanted to accompany them in
the ambulance. But she declined; she needed to call her stepsister's
husband and would drive herself. The hotel lobby swelled with spec-
tators as the EMS workers carried Isabel up from the stairwell on the
stretcher. A large woman wedged herself next to Natalie. "Poor
thing," she said, her elbow jutting into Natalie's hip. "Do you know
what happened?"

Natalie shook her head. "Excuse me."

She ducked into the ladies' room and, from a locked stall,
texted Jeremy with a cryptic explanation, asking if he'd meet her at
the hospital. He wrote back immediately: *On my way.* She stared at
the marble white and gray tiles, as she called George. She considered confiding in him about the monster he was married to. No, at
least not now. She would not hurt this man, whom she was so fond
of, more than was necessary.

George didn't pick up, so she left a short message.

Natalie drove without awareness of road signs or changing lights
or other cars. But, even dazed, she managed to find her way.

At the hospital, Natalie didn't inquire about Isabel's whereabouts or her condition. She sat alone in the waiting room, beneath
the yellow glare of the fluorescent light, waiting for George to arrive.
With the doors shut, the air was stagnant. There were muffin crumbs
on the floor and a Styrofoam cup, with the last dregs of coffee in it,

on the table in front of her. A few seats away, an emaciated teenager sat hunched over, her head bent forward, a heavy ball attached by a string.

An elderly man was arguing with a nurse behind the partition. He had thick eyebrows and a bushy mustache reaching up into his nostrils. Natalie could see he wanted entrance into the ER, which the nurse was denying him. She imagined the desk as a barrier between the land-dwelling rational beings and the panicked victims out at sea.

She unbuttoned her jacket, untied her scarf, but was uncertain how long she could bear to stay. Finally, George rushed through the doors in his tweed overcoat, without hat or gloves, his hair uncombed, winged on either side.

"For God's sake," George said, when he reached her side. "What happened?"

He had the look of a person beckoned to the morgue to identify a loved one, the grayish complexion, the darting eyes.

She reached out, hugged George quickly before he drew away. "We were at the hotel, where she had the conference. She tripped down the stairs."

"How far?" The skin around George's mouth pleated. "How far did she fall?"

"I'm not sure," she said softly. "Almost a flight maybe."

George's eyes lit up like flares. He knew the possible outcomes better than anyone, certainly better than she did. He was clutching the back of a chair. He released it and dashed towards Admitting. Natalie watched as he zigzagged his way to the front of the line, flashing his medical credentials. A moment later, he was ushered through.

Once she heard the prognosis, Natalie would be gone. Free.

Isabel had groaned in the stairwell, a creaking sound like an old garden door. She could be dead by now. Or the doctors could be trying to resuscitate her, paddles pressed to her chest. She might end up paralyzed or worse. At dinner a few years ago, George had described for Hadley the famous nineteenth-century case of a railroad worker who'd survived a thirteen-pound iron rod impaled into his head. "Gage is a celebrity in the neuroscience world," George said, "the first case linking brain trauma and personality change."

"Cool!" Hadley had laughed.

Isabel's essential self, like Gage's, might vanish. Isabel could wake from a coma, buttressed by a mound of pillows, misty-eyed, gesturing for Natalie to come close. Natalie would lean forward, attentive, so that her stepsister would stutter her avalanche of regret.

Don't be an idiot.

Natalie needed to remain leery of her own hopeful heart.

She fiddled with her phone, tapping the home button. She entered her password, then wrote to Marc: *Tell Hadley I might be late tomorrow. Isabel is hurt, at Boston Memorial. More later.*

She wondered how long this day would last, how far into the night she'd have to stay in this place. It was a particular kind of purgatory, filled with moans and gasps and snores. For Natalie, the reckoning would come but not yet, not in this in-between place. She rubbed the back of her neck where it ached. A headache had started, a tiny woodpecker drilling into her temple.

"How you holding up?" Jeremy said, his hand on her shoulder.

"You're here." She glimpsed up at him. He was wearing his rancher's jacket and faded jeans. He seemed so familiar, more so than the people she had counted on for decades.

"Of course." He sat down by her side. His thigh touched hers. "What's going on?"

"George is in there with her. I don't know anything."

"Shit. How?"

"Isabel slipped," she said. She looked in his eyes, the eyes that made her want to photograph him.

He took her hand out of her hair and held it. "Let's leave this between us. Do you know how she is?"

"No one has said anything."

"Would you like me to ask?"

"I don't think they'll tell you. They only speak to immediate family." That might include her. Yet here she sat without apology.

Jeremy sprang up. "Let's see what I can do."

He sprinted into what was now a throng. Her ringing phone startled her. When Marc's number appeared, she pressed "Decline." She texted: *Can't talk now.* And he responded, *So sorry. Hope Isabel will be ok.*

There was nothing else she wanted to share with him.

A moment later, a young Asian nurse holding a clipboard against her chest approached, smiling with small white teeth and a steely gaze. *Bad news.* But the nurse walked past her.

Natalie glanced at the magazines. A lifestyle monthly promised: "Ten Tips for a Happier, Healthier You." *Of course.* She thought of her stepsister's website, the shot of the Greek island Natalie had taken on her honeymoon with Marc, the words "Happiness Doctor" in golden yellow superimposed across the mouth of the Aegean Sea. That would need to be replaced. She turned the page to a stock photo of a tropical beach scene with a hammock. Suggestions were in bold: *Get High on Nature. Catch your ZZZs. Stress Less with Yoga. Donate your Dollars. Turn Off the News. Splurge—a Little. Lean on your Loved Ones.*

A small laugh escaped, and she stopped reading. The man, sitting across from her, glared. An angry purplish patch was visible on his exposed calf. "Sorry," she said.

Jeremy hurried back in her direction. "They're operating on her now."

"Wow, they told you."

Jeremy sat on the adjoining chair and inched it closer to hers. "I met George. Nice guy."

She nodded. "He is. Why are they operating?"

"I introduced myself. He explained what's going on. They did a

CAT scan." Jeremy clasped her hand. "She has a bleed, but they're draining it. He told me to let you know it's not a complicated procedure. It only takes about twenty-minutes."

"Thank you."

At that moment, Isabel was laid out on a stretcher under the glare of lights, as if she was posing in a photography studio. Only instead of having her picture taken, she'd have a tube sticking out of her shaved and bleeding skull. Could they suck the evil out of her?

"How did George seem?" she asked.

Jeremy cracked the knuckle of his index finger. "Focused."

"Did he say anything else?"

"Just that it will be a while before she wakes up. You can see her for a few minutes once she's in intensive care."

"I should wait to see what happens."

"Of course."

"Listen. This was so nice of you. But you don't have to stay."

He pulled her towards him. "I'm not going anywhere."

THE NEUROLOGY-ICU was in another wing, through an L-shaped hallway, and twelve flights up the elevator. It was white and clean, and the waiting area was smaller than the ER's. Watercolors of pink flowers hung on the walls. George led the way. He must have walked these corridors hundreds of times. He was on staff here, even if surgery wasn't his department.

George stopped at room four and tilted his head. "This is it."

He pulled Natalie close and in a hushed voice said, "Isabel told me what's going on. You've been furious over Marc and his new girlfriend, acting erratically."

"What?"

"With all the stress you've been under, maybe you acted impulsively again. I was hoping the money would help."

"I don't know what you mean."

Although she did: once again, Isabel had lied. But what good would it do to explain to George that his wife had deceived him, now, when she might be dying?

"Let's drop this for now," George said, sternly.

A wiry man with deep-set eyes and gaunt cheeks exited the room, easing the door closed behind him. He was wearing the usual white jacket and extended his hand towards George. Jeremy hung back.

"This is Dr. Hahn," George said. The doctors locked eyes for a moment and exchanged a solemn nod.

Dr. Hahn patted George on the shoulder. "Isabel came through fine. No complications."

Natalie's whimper surprised her. She studied how George's expression didn't change, didn't convey relief. This was a language she didn't speak. "No complications" didn't translate into: "she's out of the woods."

Jeremy smiled. "That's great news."

"What about contusions?" George asked.

"You know we can't—"

George's eyes widened. "How bad?"

"We'll have to wait for the Glasgow score. No signs of bruising on the frontal lobe or medial temporal."

"Thank God." George bowed forward and whistled.

"What does that mean?" Natalie asked.

"Your brother-in-law can explain," Dr. Hahn said briskly. "Let's talk more tomorrow, once we lighten Isabel's sedation. For now, you can visit briefly. And George, of course, take as long as you need."

"Thank you, Richard." George gripped the doctor's hand and shook it firmly.

"Is that good, what he told you?" Natalie asked once Dr. Hahn had left.

"Those areas affect memory and executive function."

Natalie pictured an avatar in a business suit, briefcase in hand. "And they weren't impaired?"

"No signs of contusions." George's tone was hard: the whack of a pool ball. "Doesn't give us a definitive prognosis."

"Can I see her?" she asked, "Alone."

"This will be hard for you." This more tenderly.

He was addressing her old self, the person she'd been that morning: sensitive and scared, quick to panic. "I want to. I promise to be quick, not cause a problem."

George turned the handle, pushed open the door.

"I'll wait here," Jeremy said, rubbing her arm.

Inside, the blinds to the window weren't drawn. The evening sky was an enormous black and blue mark pressing down on the glass. Isabel was alone in the room on a narrow slice of a bed. She seemed shrunken, a husk of herself, eyes closed, face ashy, lips colorless. A patch of her head was shaved and partially covered by a gauzy bandage. Sprouting from under the wrapping was a tube bobbled with dark blood.

On the side of the bed was a monitor, keeping track of her heart and respiration, recorded in green, red, and blue wavy lines. A cuff gripped Isabel's upper arm. Both hands were tucked under the tan blanket.

Natalie tasted tears as they fell into her mouth. Once, long ago, Isabel had hovered over *her* hospital bed, made a hushed threat. "Don't say anything if you want a happy life."

Natalie thought of repeating it now. But that wasn't who she was.

She got up close to the very rosy tip of Isabel's ear and kissed it. "Goodbye, Belle."

twenty-five

———

THE FIRST FEW EVENINGS, GEORGE CALLED WITH UPDATES ON
Isabel's condition, and every time he did, Natalie felt the weight of
his disapproval. In the last conversation, he asked, a tremor in his
voice, "Why haven't you been to visit?"

She pressed the phone to her head, shutting her eyes as he repeated what Isabel had relayed to him many times. Natalie hated
hospitals. It was true that she'd avoided them since her concussion
when she catapulted awake, only to submerge back into darkness, as
if someone were dunking her head in and out of a bucket. Those first
moments of consciousness waking up in the hospital room had been
terrifying for Natalie, the doctor clicking his penlight, the clench of
the blood pressure cuff, Garrick's anemic face, the news about her
mother.

"You can't desert someone because of fear," George reprimanded.
"You owe her for all she's done. And what about me? I sold those
stocks for you—against my broker's advice."

"That wasn't for me." A chill ran through Natalie's skin; when
she touched her face, it felt clammy. "Ask Isabel when she's well
enough."

She hung up the phone, turning the volume low.

It was an existential crisis, this grieving for a phantom. Natalie
felt as if she were hanging onto the walls of an elevator whose bottom
was unhinged, leaving her dangling hundreds of feet above the
ground. She pretended, for her child's sake, that her shock was a result of Isabel's fall, nothing more. The fractured relationship would

have to be dealt with delicately, to keep her daughter and stepsister apart without spooking Hadley. When Hadley inquired about her aunt and uncle, Natalie said, "She doesn't want you to see her this way. And George is overwhelmed."

She followed a strict routine of parenting, photographing food, and spending time with Jeremy, whose patience brought her to tears. He stayed over frequently, arriving with Reed, the Retriever, whom Hadley adored. The three of them binge-watched several Netflix series. When alone, Natalie couldn't stop herself from obsessively checking Isabel's website. There were no future Happiness seminars listed, and the publication date of her book was changed to: "Pending."

A month passed, and the tight grip on Natalie's lungs lessened; the gray cast of the sky lifted. The colorful raspberry compotes and florid Mediterranean salads no longer felt like an assault to her eyes under the studio lights—which meant she was sleeping well.

"If you want to include what Isabel did in your book," she told Jeremy, "go ahead."

Jeremy smiled shyly. They sat together on her couch, his feet resting on her coffee table. "Nah. I've put that on the back burner for now."

"But it meant so much to you! Is this because of me?"

"Partially, sure. But it's for my sake, too. Slamming the Happiness Industry would reflect badly on me, now that we're together. And especially after what happened to Isabel."

"Shit," she said, massaging the nub of her neck where it ached. "So being with me ruined your project."

"I could still justify it. But, at what cost? Hurting Hadley and George or the other relatives of these self-marketing gurus? Not worth it to me."

"I'm so sorry."

"Don't be," he said, drawing her close. "That's the irony. I don't care anymore because I'm happy. I love you."

George reached out again. He recited the name and address of the rehabilitation center in Boston, which Natalie's mind brushed over like sand in a Zen garden.

His tone changed, beseeching, "I don't know what happened between the two of you, but Isabel asks for you every day. She wants to see you."

The old yearning rose in her: *Belle.* But just as quickly: *there is no Belle.* There was only the impostor who'd stolen Natalie's past and left, in its place, the never-ending "what ifs." This thief, her stepsister, probably only wanted to make certain that Natalie didn't go to the police with Garrick's letter.

"I'm sorry, George. I can't."

She heard his sharp intake of air before he hung up without a response.

I need a distraction, she texted Jeremy.

He came over with a large box, with a blue ribbon around it, as if awarded first place in competitive gift giving. He grinned when she lifted out the Nikon that was designed to look and handle like an old film camera, and said, "This one is only for your personal work."

Natalie clasped her free hand to her chest as if to catch her leaping heart. "This is amazing. But, I don't *have* any personal work."

"You will."

The camera lay in its box.

Natalie received an email on a rainy May day: *Isabel is being released tomorrow, and we're going away for a long recuperation. I hope when we return, you'll have gotten a handle on whatever is going on with you. George.* He didn't provide specifics, a place or schedule.

If only they'd stay away forever.

For the next week, she felt ill, headachy and nauseous. She slept poorly, Isabel buzzing in her ear, like a fly, waking her every few hours. She trudged through her day, chauffeuring Hadley to and from school, loading the dishwasher, running the dust buster over the fallen crumbs, paying bills, editing her Fourth of July job: red velvet cupcakes with vanilla icing and blue sprinkles, each one stabbed with an American flag toothpick.

Then, one afternoon, Jeremy came over unannounced, "You need a break from this gloom. Let's go out to a movie."

"No, wait," she said. "Let's do something else."

The warning in her head—don't trust yourself to see people clearly, to interpret what you see—quieted as she envisioned her mother in her garage-studio, mounting her Hasselblad on the tripod. "Let me show you what that does," her mom had said when Natalie touched the shutter release, gingerly. "So someday you can do it yourself. A good photographer can capture someone's soul."

She grabbed the Nikon and said, "Come with me to the studio."

Jeremy, it turned out, was a terrible subject. He squirmed and winked and flexed his muscles like a child with attention deficit disorder. Squinting through the eyepiece, she yelled at him, "Co-operate!"

"It makes me too self-conscious," he said after a few hours were lost. "What you need is a professional model."

"No," she said. "I want to do something more dynamic."

"I can do that!" he exclaimed, extending his arms and swaying backwards. "Baryshnikov in action!"

She laughed, an idea brewing: something much bigger, darker, conceptual.

But she developed the ones of Jeremy, pleased with how she caught his comedy in action. "It's me," he said, the rims of his eyes reddening, "before Alex died. You found me."

Summer arrived without a word from George or Isabel. Over lunch, Cate said, "I was shopping in the Back Bay. There's a for sale sign on their building. It's not their place, is it?" Natalie shook her head, not willing to admit to her friend that she had no idea. A few days later, she was studying a new book on Duchamp at the Harvard Bookstore when she caught sight of a woman with straggly gray hair, wearing a cotton, crimson scarf. She was jowly, and the flesh of her arms pinched against her short sleeves. Natalie was shocked to realize it was Ellen. She shut the Duchamp, returned it to the shelves, and strode out of the store.

Three afternoons a week, she worked on her "project"—the tricky staging—experimenting in Photoshop. Somehow, more than a year had elapsed since Isabel's accident when Natalie's imported images in Lightroom gelled. She recognized the scope and intensity of what she'd hoped to achieve. She was nearly there. Natalie mentioned her project to Jessa at the studio they shared, gathering her courage. "I'd love to talk to your friend, Susannah," a gallery owner on the South End, "when I'm ready." Studying a couple of the pictures, replicas of the crash scene, Jessa said, "I think you should."

"Not yet. I have more to do."

One late afternoon, Natalie arranged the photos on her dining room table. Hadley wandered in from her bedroom in her Ugg slippers, now flecked with Reed's yellow fur. "What are you doing?"

"I might have an opportunity to show some pieces to a gallery owner."

Hadley looked over Natalie's shoulder and pointed to the lizard perched on the roof of a car at the beach's shore. "That one. Definitely that one."

"Really?" Natalie turned toward her daughter. "You're not just humoring me?"

"No. It's great. I'd love for you to teach me how to set up a scene like that!"

Natalie felt a tingling in the notch of her neck, running down her chest, at the pleasure of her child's request. "Anytime, kid, anytime."

Nights later, the Easter moon waning in the sky, Jeremy turned to her in bed, "You seem happy. What's up?"

"You," she laughed. "And something else. I didn't want to jinx it till I knew for sure. I have a show, Baryshnikov."

~

THE EVENING OF her opening, Natalie arrived in the city early. She drove with Hadley to South Boston, nabbing a spot outside Jeremy's apartment, which was a five-minute walk to the event. It was a warm day in late June, the sky hydrangea blue, the trees flowering, and the slight breeze a caress on the back of her neck. Natalie had settled on a short-sleeve dress with a full shirt. She carried a cardigan over her shoulder in case the air conditioning was turned up inside the venue. Hadley had insisted she buy pumps because "they make you look like a grown-up."

Jeremy emerged from the building, clean-shaven with his hair trimmed for the occasion. He gave Hadley's arm a quick squeeze, and then kissed Natalie, his mouth tasting of cherries. "Ready to roll?" he asked.

Natalie laughed. "Been ready since dawn."

They hurried past the string of brick buildings towards the renovated factory. Even though there was no rush, Natalie couldn't wait. She wanted to be there before everyone else other than Susannah.

"How do women walk in heels?" Natalie asked.

Hadley said, "Mom, I'm wearing two-inch heels. Henry could run in them."

"Doubt it. He can barely lift his head."

Henry: Elizabeth and Marc's two-month-old. The last time Natalie dropped off Hadley at their place in Brookline, Marc had opened the door with the infant, slack as a sack of clothes, asleep on his chest. Marc's eyes were blood-shot and his hair, badly in need of a cut, curled on each side in George Washington-style wings. On the ride home, she thought about what it was like when Hadley was so small, the topsy-turvy sense of time, the zaps of exhaustion, the sour-sweet smell of breast milk and rancid diaper pail. "Glad that's behind me," she'd confessed to Jeremy.

"Fine with me," he smiled.

Natalie said to Hadley, "I hope you don't plan on wearing those stilettos to college interviews."

"These are so not stilettos, and they won't work in the fall," Hadley said. "Unless I apply to Pomona. We should go tour it, Mom! They have good financial aid, great weather."

"Don't even joke about that. You're not going to school in California."

"You're going to have to let go sometime."

Jeremy said, "Beautiful place, Pomona. Everyone jokes that they put Prozac in the water. Loads of mindful meditation."

"Really?" Hadley scrunched up her face. "Ugh."

"Might be too earnest for a hardened East Coaster like you."

"Totally."

Natalie squeezed Jeremy's hand. "Glad to hear you're sticking around," she said to her daughter.

Jeremy shimmied up to Natalie and whispered in her ear, "We should move in together."

A powerful sense of relief arose in Natalie, as if she'd been traveling for hours and, finally, home was in her purview. "I'd love that."

"What?" Hadley asked and waved her hand. "Enough with the secrets. Remember I'm here?"

"Always," Natalie said.

"Way to go, Mom," she imagined her daughter's response to Jeremy's invitation. She'd be reassured that Natalie wouldn't be alone, pining for her, that she could step into college, independence, and then the world, without carrying the burden of her mother's loneliness with her. But this news was a discussion for another day. This day was momentous enough.

A few minutes later they had arrived. The huge windows showcased the gallery on the first floor.

"Wow, Mom, so cool!" Hadley cried out.

Natalie paused before ascending the wide, wrought iron stairs, painted a fierce red. She zeroed in on the first section of the staging, the black and white car crash series. As Jeremy pulled open the heavy glass door, Natalie pressed her fist to her mouth: *this is happening.*

The space was well lit with polished wood floors and white walls. Her work hung in its clockwise progression: the collision sequences, the color shots of the Cayman Islands, and the de-saturated ones of Isabel. Susannah was at the front table, arranging the brochures in neat piles. Everything, more or less, was in order.

"Good to see you," Susannah said. She was streamlined and tasteful in her pencil skirt and silky blouse with diamond studs glinting in her ears. To Hadley, she said, "Ah, the passenger."

It was a reference to the title of a print: Hadley, suspended in the sky, holding a flashlight superimposed above a dark deserted street. Natalie had wanted to hire a college kid, but her daughter insisted she let her try first.

Natalie hadn't discussed the subtext of the photograph with Hadley. She'd claimed they were all surreal interpretations of what she'd lost.

Natalie said to Susannah, "And this is Jeremy Sonnenberg."

"Mr. Wreckage," the gallery owner said, the nickname she'd adopted for him.

"That's me," he said.

To capture the original image—which acted as the backdrop for the pictures of her mother—Natalie had spent weeks racing to accident scenes. This was thanks to Jeremy's information via his friend, a metro reporter at the *Globe* who covered news and local stories. Of the crashes she'd captured, the one she decided to use was of a Toyota whose front had crumpled, the fender hanging open like a lip exposing a mouth full of sores.

"Go look around," Susannah said. Her sharp, foxlike eyes peered at Natalie.

She couldn't bear further inspection of what she'd created. But Natalie glanced at her name in stark black letters on the far wall. She experienced a burst of adrenaline, a quiver of delight. This was *her* show, *her* effort—dare she think it—*her* art? This wasn't some bohemian venue in an iffy area, peeling paint outside and rickety floors underfoot. This was legitimate, grown up, Natalie's story hanging in pieces, her history and her rage exposed. But, also, there was pressure to sell.

"Come on," Jeremy urged.

The prints were hung from left to right. Jeremy stopped to examine a shot of Isabel. She appeared frozen, her face masked by a gradated shadow so that only her eyes were in focus. Natalie had blended the image into the background of the police report and blurred everything but the statements: "Driver deceased," and "Signs of another motorist at the scene." The small label under the photo read: *Crash Narrative.*

"This is great," Jeremy said.

"You're just saying that because you like me."

"I *do* have excellent taste."

Jeremy touched Natalie's wrist, then moved onto the next picture.

"Seeing them here in public makes it so real," Hadley said. "Mom, it's so weird and good."

"Thanks, kid."

Her daughter rushed to observe the photo titled *The Rebuttal.* It was a composite of Laura and Isabel's faces, side-by-side, a black mask superimposed onto Isabel's. The word happy floated above Laura, the letters piled up against each other, with the H smashed into Laura's skull.

Hadley said, "Someday you're going to have to tell me what went on between you and Aunt Isabel."

It wasn't the "what" that tripped Natalie up, but the "why," a question that would haunt her if she let it, would render her like a child trying to construct an ontological theory of the world. She had to fight against pondering that mystery.

Jeremy sidled up to them. "Jessa is here."

Natalie turned to see her friend, sleek and leggy in a black pantsuit, her russet hair slick down her back. With her was a slender man in a faded denim shirt and distressed lace-up boots.

"So good to see you."

Jessa hugged her. "Well done!" She pointed to her husband, "This is the elusive Michael."

"Just busy chasing tenure." He offered Natalie a flimsy handshake.

She could see that women would find Michael attractive, with his runner's build and cheekbones and blond stubble. Natalie guessed that he carefully curated his crumpled look. "Extra thanks then."

Jessa led her husband closer to the pieces, all of which she'd already seen. As it turned out, she was canny enough not to question Natalie about the narrative. A couple of times they'd discussed technique but nothing more. Never mind what the collection "meant." For that, Natalie was grateful.

Even Susannah hadn't pried, not really, when she witnessed the final products. She'd scratched her neck with hers painted fingernails and said, "Interesting. Some scandalous betrayal."

Natalie had nodded. "That's what I was going for."

The room was filling up. Most of the people were strangers, Susannah's colleagues in the art world, a handful of Jeremy's co-workers at the *Globe*, random students and curious folks off the street. Natalie's circle made up the smallest contingent. Cate was there with her assistant from Spice It Up, another mom from town. When her friend kissed her, Natalie could smell her woodsy shampoo.

"This is so exciting! I can't wait to look at everything," Cate said. "Your mom would be so proud of you."

Natalie's eyes stung. "Oh, thank you for saying that."

"I'll never forget how she hung up your report card." Cate's silver bell earrings chimed when she shook her head. "And, those times I went to the rink with you guys, your mom was so excited when you did a double axel. She was the best."

"I'm so lucky to have you," Natalie said.

The only person in the room who knew my mother.

Natalie hadn't relayed to Cate the details of her falling out with her stepsister, worried that Cate would respond badly to the photos. She hadn't wanted to risk disclosure about her damaged family with her friend, the bellwether of decency. Now, Natalie felt the flicker of regret, the urge to explain. But Susannah's hand was on her shoulder, directing her away. Next to her dealer stood a young-looking man with a slight paunch and a slighter beard.

"This is Marty Silverman," Susannah said. "He's a professor at MassArts, his work's shown everywhere. And a book out from Aperture last year."

"Not everywhere, Susie," Marty corrected with a little laugh. "Don't embarrass me. And it's only *assistant* professor." He stroked his goatee.

The discussion would be about Marty Silverman then. Which would be okay, Natalie thought, a diversion from the high stakes. But while they conversed, requiring little more from her than a murmur or two of recognition, Natalie's attention wandered.

She caught Hadley gesturing to a man nearby. Her daughter mouthed: "Oh my God. He's gonna buy the iguana." That was the picture of the car at the beach with the reptile atop and the woman in the driver's seat, whose only identifying feature was the black diamond on her ring finger. The title: *Simon in Love.* When her daughter had asked "Who's Simon?" Natalie said, "Just a man we met in the Caribbean, one of Aunt Belle's crazy fans."

She winked at Hadley and thought of the new pieces she was working on, her different approach: close-ups in a naturalistic, straightforward style, one after the other of the same subject. She wasn't certain yet what she hoped to capture but for now was excited by the nuances in the smallest changes of the model's expression, that microcosm of the human experience.

Through a gap in the crowd, she caught a glimpse of the frozen Isabel picture in the black frame. She couldn't look at it anymore; it was just a photograph. And a good one. But she would do other fine ones that didn't demand such a steep price from her. She moved deeper into the crowd, toward the window to get a breather. And that's when she saw her.

Just beyond, standing on the street outside the gallery, as if she'd been summoned, was her stepsister: those fine bones, and delicate features, the nearly translucent skin, and bluish green vein in her forehead, the flash of yellow hair. The corner of her mouth drooped as if pulled down by a fishhook. It was a Dalí reinterpretation, a grim transformation that caused Natalie to recoil. A look of bemusement quickly passed over Isabel's eyes. Her weight rested on an ebony cane with a silver knob.

How was that possible? Natalie tilted her head to gauge the light. Had it dimmed?

She said, "Excuse me one second."

"What inspired the first series?" a young man asked, tapping her on the elbow. "It's so intriguing."

"Thanks. That means so much to me. I'll be right back."

Natalie raced towards the windows, now blocked by a couple of college-age kids holding plastic flutes of champagne. When she reached the front, all she saw was a red Volkswagen Beetle. It was polished, nearly gleaming with perfection, other than the grayish-white bird poop splattered on the glass. There was no sign of her stepsister.

Natalie stared out into the stillness, trying to revive her vision. What was real? What had she imagined?

She felt the tightly threaded muscles in her neck, the pulse of her blood. But she would not allow herself to cower before danger.

Slowly, she turned around to the guests holding their drinks, some chatting with each other, some studying the photographs. She saw Jeremy holding up two glasses, one meant for her. She saw Hadley talking with Cate.

Natalie glanced back at the street, again, and saw nothing but traffic and a kid walking a French bulldog, a woman in a tangerine-colored dress. Maybe there had been nothing. Maybe there would always be nothing. Or maybe Isabel would resurface. She couldn't predict. But, for now, the reality of her life was this: her show. These were her people, here for her.

Natalie turned away from the windows and walked towards the family and friends she loved.

Acknowledgments

Thank you to:

Caroline Leavitt for her fantastic edits, encouragement, and friendship. Her support and generosity are what every writer needs—and few get.

Brooke Warner, Lauren Wise, and Shannon Green at She Writes Press for their professionalism every step of the way.

Caitlin Hamilton Summie for being such a wonderful, hardworking publicist.

Marly Rusoff for championing this book.

Kimmi Berlin, Meredith Finn, Abby Sher, Susan Shapiro, and Judy Batalion for reading this novel in various stages.

Tess Callahan for reading every single word. As always, she was big-hearted and thorough.

Sasha Troyan, Suzanne Roth, and Caprice Garvin for being such supportive fellow writers and friends.

Brenda Copeland and Shannon Jamieson Vazquez for their excellent editing advice.

Sara-Kate Astrove for her keen proofreading.

Michelle Cameron, Jessica Levine, and Anne Leigh Parrish, fellow writers, for their kindness and advice.

Everyone in the "Sue workshop" who inspired me with their perseverance, even in a pandemic.

Noah and Spencer, wonderful sons, endless sources of inspiration and knowledge. I've learned so much from them both.

Jay, who has read more drafts of this novel than anyone should ever have to—and has kept the faith.

About the Author

Credit: Jay Lindell

NICOLE BOKAT is the author of the novels *Redeeming Eve* and *What Matters Most*. *Redeeming Eve* was nominated for both the Hemingway Foundation/PEN award and the Janet Heidinger Kafka Prize for Fiction. She's also published *The Novels of Margaret Drabble: This Freudian Family Nexus*. She received her PhD from New York University and has taught at NYU, Hunter College, and The New School. Her essays and articles have appeared in *The New York Times*, *Parents* magazine, *The Forward*, and at More.com. She lives with her husband in New Jersey and has two grown sons.

SELECTED TITLES FROM SHE WRITES PRESS

She Writes Press is an independent publishing company founded to serve women writers everywhere. Visit us at www.shewritespress.com.

Water On the Moon by Jean P. Moore. $16.95, 978-1-938314-61-2. When her home is destroyed in a freak accident, Lidia Raven, a divorced mother of two, is plunged into a mystery that involves her entire family.

The Moon Always Rising by Alice C. Early. $16.95, 978-1-63152-683-1. When Eleanor "Els" Gordon's life cracks apart, she exiles herself to a derelict plantation house on the Caribbean island of Nevis—and discovers, with the help of her resident ghost, that only through love and forgiveness can she untangle years-old family secrets and set herself free to love again.

Last Seen by J. L. Doucette. $16.95, 978-1-63152-202-4. When a traumatized reporter goes missing in the Wyoming wilderness, the therapist who knows her secrets is drawn into the investigation—and she comes face-to-face with terrifying answers regarding her own difficult past.

We Never Told by Diana Altman. $16.95, 978-1631525438. In the 1950s, when Sonya was fourteen, her glamorous, beautiful mother left her two teenage daughters for months, seeking treatment for a "stomach tumor." The secrets surrounding this event haunt Sonya well into middle age, when she finally unravels the lies—which turn out to be not at all what she expected.

A Cup of Redemption by Carole Bumpus. $16.95, 978-1-938314-90-2. Three women, each with their own secrets and shames, seek to make peace with their pasts and carve out new identities for themselves.

A Drop in the Ocean: A Novel by Jenni Ogden. $16.95, 978-1-63152-026-6. When middle-aged Anna Fergusson's research lab is abruptly closed, she flees Boston to an island on Australia's Great Barrier Reef—where, amongst the seabirds, nesting turtles, and eccentric island-ers, she finds a family and learns some bittersweet lessons about love.